The Eye of th

**ff**

# THE
# EYE OF THE
# BEHOLDER

## Minette Marrin

*faber and faber*

LONDON · BOSTON

First published in 1988
by Faber and Faber Limited
3 Queen Square London WC1N 3AU
This paperback edition first published in 1989

Photoset by Parker Typesetting Service Leicester
Printed in Great Britain by
Cox and Wyman Ltd Reading Berkshire
All rights reserved

*British Library Cataloguing in Publication Data*

Marrin, Minette
The eye of the beholder.
I. Title
823'.914[F]     PR6063.A656/

ISBN 0-571-15481-6

AUTHOR'S NOTE

There are many people I should like to thank for their
kindness and help, though in doing so I should not like
to associate them with any shortcomings in this book.
I am especially grateful to Dennis Marks,
Michael Sissons, Ian Hislop, Melanie Saville,
Blair Worden, Helen Bergen, Roger Stott,
Christopher Wright, Thomas Gibson
and Stuart Fleming.

Life is not neutral; it consists in taking sides boldly. No neutrality is possible between truth and falsehood, between good and evil, between health and sickness, between order and disorder.

Marshal Philippe Pétain,
Words to the French People

The sky had been heavy with rain and thunder all afternoon and finally the storm broke. 'Well, Dan', shouted the cameraman above the wind, with the murderous *bonhomie* that comes naturally to film crews at moments of strain, 'you wanted a bit of moody and you've got it. Any idea what it's for?'

He grinned broadly as he dismantled his camera in the driving rain.

Dan Cohen had a short temper, and his attempts to control it were famous among the Corporation's film crews.

'Don't wind me up, Rick,' he shouted back, struggling for charm. 'Not in this weather, and not in the middle of bloody nowhere!'

Even I smiled, despite the rain. It was true that Dan had little idea of how he was going to use the shots. He'd had a full crew in Lorraine, near the German border, for five days, with very little to film. Several of our interviews had mysteriously fallen through at the last minute. Cooperation from the university at Nancy had suddenly gone cold, and now the departmental archives were on strike.

Dan had hoped that the shots outside the chemicals factory would somehow suggest the ugliness and fear bound up in his subject, but there was no particular reason for filming there. It was true that the chemicals plant had been run by Germans during the war, and had always had a lot of German capital; there were certainly interesting stories among the employees. But research had produced nothing. There weren't very many people who would talk.

That, strictly speaking, was my problem. I had been brought in, reluctantly, to help salvage a film started by someone else. So had Dan. It had never seemed like a starter to me, but then my alternative had been short film inserts on *Pop Goes the Weasel*. I couldn't imagine how they had persuaded Dan. He was already a well-established director. And I couldn't understand why the whole thing hadn't been dropped.

'Cohen's second law of programme-making,' Dan had said to me in London. 'If someone's initialled it, it must be true; if there's a budget, it must be happening; if it's not happening, someone must lose face.' That was something neither of us intended to lose – aspirations, hope, time and illusions perhaps, but not that.

So we were stuck, making someone else's programme about wartime collaboration in Lorraine, constructing it out of thin air, out of bad temper and rain. Running towards the hired van, with the thunder getting louder beyond the factory chimneys, I began to wonder whether there ever had been a German occupation of Lorraine at all, or whether someone hadn't made the whole thing up. Most of all, I wondered whether my luck wasn't beginning to run out.

The rest of the crew were already in the van, cramped between the battered cases of equipment. Dan got heavily into the driver's seat, crashed the gears, drove jerkily out of the car park, and south towards Nancy. Everyone was wet and irritable, particularly the sound man Eric, who had been soaked through to even less purpose than anyone else. He'd spent the whole afternoon standing about in the shadow of the factory complex, recording a mass of noise which might just as well have come off Corporation sound-effects records.

'I suppose messieurs les so-called workers of the Archives Départmentales de la Meurthe-et-Moselle will still be on strike tomorrow?' he asked.

I said that I was afraid so.

'Don't be afraid,' said Rick. 'Give us a cuddle and cheer up.'

'No goosing the staff,' said Dan, a little too sharply.

'Director's privilege, is it?' asked Rick.

We drove uneasily into the suburbs of Nancy; the traffic was bad in the rain and Dan was an erratic driver. Finally he stopped the van outside the Hôtel Choucroute, and we all got out and started unloading.

Most of the crew were in a better temper when after

showers and telephone calls we met in the hotel bar. Dan bought drinks all round.

'It may have become apparent to you,' he said, in the jocose, placatory way he thought best for dealing with difficult crews, 'that we have no story, or very nearly no story. Most of the interviews have fallen through, we still can't get into the archives, because of the strike, and one-take-Rick himself was rained off this afternoon. You're booked here for three more days, before we go to Rome. I want you to take tomorrow morning off – we meet at 2.30 at the Café Saint-Roch.'

'If it weren't for this I could be in Ethiopia,' said Rick, quite clearly. 'I think we'll just drift out and get our trotters stuck in the trough somewhere – somewhere cheap and cheerful. I feel like a large steak with added cholesterol. Personally I've had enough of plaited pig's gut and strangulated geese, but we won't hold it against you, Dan old dear, if that's what you're after. Coming, Eric?'

That was a dismissal. Dan and I accepted it with relief and relaxed for the first time that day. Dan ordered a dry Martini for me and a double Scotch for himself. The barman brought olives and miniature quiches lorraine: the place was dark and extremely comfortable.

'Not quite what we're used to,' said Dan.

'No,' I said.

I was glad to be away from the uneasy jargon of the film crew. It varied slightly every trip, but it always accentuated the differences and resentments it was meant to hide. The mannered endearments, the faded humour, the wearisome *cameraderie* in which everyone unwillingly conspired – these were all most pronounced when things were going badly. They were stratagems everyone used, more or less, to deal with the embarrassing fact that there were still officers and men, gentlemen and players.

'What a load of shits,' said Dan. 'And have you ever come across a more manipulative prima donna than bloody Rick? They should never give prizes, it spoils people. Especially cameramen.'

'So you'll be giving yours back?'

'I'm no worse than I was before,' said Dan. 'What I really

can't stand is the way they're always complaining – if it's not that the Corporation is crushing their talent and squandering public money, it's that the bloody producer is incompetent. When they haven't got two neurones between them, let alone an idea.'

'Come on, Dan, you don't mean it. Not as a good socialist. Let's forget it. What about some more Alsatian wine, and some plaited pig's gut, as Rick suggested? We haven't tried that two-star place in the rue de la Madeleine.'

'I think I'll just have a sandwich and make some calls,' Dan said morosely.

'Oh,' I said, looking at him, 'now you really are demoralized. Don't worry: there will be a story here. We will get it, even if I have to make it up myself.'

I reached my hand across the olives and ruffled his hair, slightly sadly. To the other people in the bar, to those who noticed, it might, I suppose, have looked like an invitation. But that was all there was to it, at that time.

One of the consolations on location filming, between an anxious night and a frustrating day, is breakfast. But, inexplicably, the next morning the Hôtel Choucroute had abandoned all Gallic standards and was serving instant coffee, prepackaged brioches and little plastic containers of jam, butter, milk and juice. In the middle of the room, impervious to the atmosphere, sat the Corporation crew at two tables, arguing fitfully, and looking conspicuous in their jeans, running shoes and padded jackets.

I told Dan that I had at last succeeded in contacting Claude Mesnil and had fixed a meeting for that morning at his house outside Nancy.

'Claude Mesnil? Do I know him? I do, don't I?' asked Dan.

I felt a sudden pain in my neck and shoulders.

'Don't you read your bloody research notes? What's the point of my doing them?'

Then I saw the tired expression on his face.

'Yes, we do,' I said. 'You do, and I do. Both of us. We came here a few years ago, to do a piece on some Lorraine painters – Claude Gellée, people like that. My first glorious year in television.'

'No, I didn't.'

'Yes, you did. It was for a ten-minute insert in something; we were really on the way to Strasbourg for a political story.'

'I wasn't,' said Dan, 'I can't have been. I never touch EEC stories.'

'Good for you. Terrif. Anyway, you did come here, we did meet Claude Mesnil and I've spoken to you about him since. Last time he was very helpful. Anglophile, which is unusual in a Frenchman. But he's been away. I've only just managed to speak to him.'

'Who introduced us in the first place?'

'I've no idea – he's probably on some Corporation card index – history, good food, art, Lorraine – Mesnil is the man.'

'Professor of fifteenth-century history at the University of Nancy,' said Dan suddenly.

'Is this a sudden recovery of your faculties, such as they are, or were you leading me on?' I asked.

'Temper, temper,' sang out Rick from the next table.

The little village where Mesnil lived was twenty miles out of Nancy. Even the bright cold light could not make the country attractive. We drove beside a winding river bordered with rushes, missed the turning to Saint-Symphorien and had to turn back.

'I'm sorry about breakfast. Really, I had forgotten, until it came back to me. You know how it is – the system gets overloaded. I promise I wasn't having you on,' Dan said.

'His wife's called Geneviève,' I said, and we arrived.

Mesnil's house was on a slight incline, looking down towards the river. It was a post-war bungalow without character, like every other house in the village. Both Claude and Geneviève Mesnil were standing outside to meet us, smiling. I hardly recognized them and for a moment I was embarrassed. But the feeling passed quickly. Forgetfulness is part of the job. We both smiled warmly at the Mesnils.

'My dear friends,' said Claude. 'Welcome to Lorraine. Welcome to Saint-Symphorien. Our dull landscape is always brightened by your presence, my dear young lady,' he said, turning to me.

'Oh listen, Claude, talk normally,' said his wife, laughing. 'We are really very glad to see you.'

The Mesnils were in their mid-fifties but both seemed younger. Geneviève was dark-skinned and still pretty. She had an air of being anxious to please that seemed to have more to do with her husband than with her visitors. Claude Mesnil looked like a northerner, not a southerner, pale and thin-featured, with blue eyes. His manners were precise and formal, his lips unusually thin, but he had a smile of surprising charm. Dan and I followed him into the little house.

'First things first,' said Geneviève. 'I hope you like

*choucroute garnie* and have large appetites, because I insist on your staying to lunch.'

'Yes, do please stay. If we have an early lunch you can be back with your team by 2 or 2.30,' said Claude. 'So don't disappoint Geneviève. And don't disappoint me either, because in the frigo I've put a bottle of something special. Local but special. I remember you are real connoisseurs. For English.'

'My well-brought-up colleague is the connoisseur. I'm just an East End boy.'

'Listen, my dear Daniel, you will have to explain to me. What is an East End boy?' asked Geneviève.

'It would take a long time,' I said, 'and anyway it isn't true. He just means he's more deserving than I am.'

'Well, whatever you deserve, I am entirely at your disposal,' said Claude. 'Tell me how I can help.'

It still occasionally seemed strange when people offer help so unconditionally. They were always the people who had least to gain from having anything to do with television. Even though I was making a living out of exploiting this generosity, I couldn't really understand it, any more than I could comprehend the power of television to make people say more than they mean. Claude Mesnil, though buried in the depths of Alsace–Lorraine, surely understood enough of television to know better. Perhaps it was friendship, a genuine inclination.

Claude led us into his study, and Geneviève brought coffee in pretty cups made of the local pink and white china. We wasted a little of our time and his, and then Dan began to explain what had been happening, with surprising truthfulness. Claude Mesnil listened without reacting, though his expression tightened a little.

'My dear Daniel,' he said finally, 'forgive me, but is it surprising that you have difficulties with such a subject? Can you imagine, my friend, that people are really going to tell you anything very much about the most painful, the most intense experiences of their lives, the most humiliating?'

'Well,' said Dan, 'they often do.'

Claude Mesnil paused and then spoke more drily.

'Often, maybe, but not always. After all, you have lost your two most important interviewees. I very much doubt if those can be resurrected but of course there are many such stories here; so close to Germany, such old ties, blood ties, business connections. Things happened here that were unimaginable anywhere else in France. Whole villages, whole families torn apart. Like your Northern Ireland.'

I had never worked on a foreign programme of this kind without someone mentioning Northern Ireland.

'Apart from everything else,' I said, 'we've also got some practical problems. For instance, we need to get into the archives and we're having trouble.'

'Into the archives?' asked Claude with surprise. 'You mean the archives in the rue de la Monnaie? What on earth for?'

'It's not hugely important, but it would be nice. It would enable us to make certain points about the interrelationship of a couple of French and German families. There's supposed to be a long correspondence between an engaged couple dated 1943. I haven't seen that yet, and I haven't actually got permission to film it. Not that it makes much difference – the archives have been closed for several days because of a strike.'

'Yes, I know,' he replied. After a pause, during which he appeared to be thinking, he smiled apologetically.

'I'm afraid I don't have as much sympathy as perhaps an historian should for these investigations. I think there has been enough. Enough misery and enough journalism. But,' he said, 'I will do what I can for you. As for your interviews, the ones that you've lost – bad luck.' He shrugged. 'However, I know the people at the archives. Not well, but I know them. I'll see what I can do there. At least I can find out for you when the strike is likely to end. But, if an old pedant may presume to ask,' and he smiled forcefully, 'is there really any point in pursuing all this documentation, especially, if I may say so, without being experts in the field?'

'Oh, we're not as ignorant as we seem,' said Dan. He smiled at Claude and held out his coffee cup for more.

We talked of other things until Geneviève summoned us for an aperitif before lunch. She led us into a small modern sitting room, filled with breakable objects. Dan walked across the room as if it were an obstacle course. Mesnil, though

8

much older, was more graceful. He negotiated the bric-à-brac with skill and reached a fragile wicker table holding bottles and coloured glasses.

'I forbid you to drink spirits,' he said. 'If you do I shall give you a completely different wine at lunch.'

'Oh, Claude,' said his wife. 'Really!'

He looked at her with an expression I recognized. It was the look of a man whose future is accounted for. 'No, my dear Geneviève, I insist. Pleasure must be deserved, it must be worked for, planned.'

Bright winter light shone through the picture window. Illuminated as he stood in his tiny living room, holding a bottle of Punt e Mes, Claude Mesnil avoided seeming ridiculous. On the contrary, he had a kind of presence.

'Why don't we start lunch now?' said Geneviève. 'That way nobody will have a chance to brutalize his palate, and Claude can open his Gewürztraminer straightaway.'

Lunch was remarkable. It made me wonder again why the English had so little idea of domestic pleasure. Geneviève produced an elegant tureen of vegetable soup and made us spread our lace napkins and help ourselves to bread. Distancing himself from these lesser rituals, Claude carefully uncorked the bottle of Clos Saint-Landelin and poured it into dark green glasses with fluted stems. It was surprisingly strongly scented. The taste came as a pleasant shock.

'I can see that you like the wine,' said Claude Mesnil, who had been watching me.

'Yes, I do, very much. You're very generous.'

He looked at me rather intently, as though he expected me to say something more. I began to feel embarrassed. Rhapsodizing on wine is not one of my party tricks.

'It makes sense of that Victorian hymn-writers' phrase, "transports of delight",' I said, without conviction.

Dan laughed.

'Ah,' said Claude, 'transported from our bleak countryside on the wings of poesy.'

'It's true,' I said, looking at the wine in its fragile green glass. 'Your countryside really is a little bleak. It hardly seems possible that it should produce something as exotic as this.'

'You're very unfair,' Geneviève protested. 'You mustn't

judge everything by the industrial zones around Nancy. You must agree, Nancy itself is absolutely charming. Anyway, we like it here, don't we, Claude? It's quiet, that's true and the scenery is not dramatic, our life is perhaps a little uneventful.'

'Perfect for an ageing provincial academic and his wife,' Claude interrupted.

When we had finished the soup Geneviève removed the plates and brought in a large oval dish piled with finely shredded cabbage and all kinds of meat and sausage.

'You see, my poor native land has produced at least two things of note – not only wine but also *choucroute garnie*. It's really very light, actually, a quite delicious, delicate dish, though the pieces of goose are perhaps a little rich. And Gewürztraminer was made to drink with it,' Claude said. I helped myself from the dish of *choucroute* and wondered whether it was true that men who were seriously interested in food almost always made good lovers.

'And last time you were here, you were making a programme about some of our local painters, weren't you?' Geneviève was asking.

'Yes,' said Dan, 'but I must admit that my memory of it has become slightly blurred. It was a long time ago.'

'Was it perhaps something about Georges de La Tour?' she asked conversationally.

'No, it was about the Italian school of Lorraine landscape painters.'

'I must say, I should really love to see the La Tour pictures they've got in America. But of course it's really very expensive to go to the United States. Still, I think it's a shame so many have been snapped up by the Americans. And I think it's a shame too that we have only one really good La Tour here in Nancy, and even that isn't very typical. A half-naked woman, searching for fleas. It's really hardly decent. I always think of him as a religious painter. Now there is something Lorraine has to be proud of – Georges de La Tour.'

'Geneviève, our guests are a little pressed for time – do you think they would perhaps like some more before we move on to dessert? Geneviève's desserts are yet another cultural triumph,' he said, turning to us.

After Geneviève had encouraged us all to help ourselves to

*choucroute*, she began to speak again about Georges de La Tour.

'You know, a friend of mine had the sweetest cards made to announce the birth of her first grandchild – well, of course her daughter had them made, but anyway they were quite lovely. She had the La Tour *Virgin and Child* – you know, the one where the Virgin is all in red, in candlelight, it's the one everyone knows, even if they've never heard of Georges de La Tour – she had that picture reproduced on the outside of the card and inside she had the announcement. And of course it was very appropriate, because they live very near Vic-sur-Seille, which is actually the birthplace of the painter. And by the way, if you have time you must eat at Vic. There's a wonderful restaurant there.'

Claude looked at his wife. 'I must admit, I didn't see these masterpieces of graphic design,' he said.

I said quickly, 'And I must admit I haven't seen many of the masterpieces themselves, only reproductions.'

'Nor have I,' said Dan. 'Well, I've seen the ones in the Louvre and *The Flea Catcher* here in Nancy.'

'Now we can all comfortably confess to ignorance about La Tour,' said Claude. 'It embarrasses me as a native of Lorraine that I know so little about one of her finest sons, but the fact is I don't terribly like his paintings.'

'You can't be serious,' I said.

'No, really, I find him a little unattractive. Technically, he's rather naive, and there's also something cold and introspective about him. He was a thoroughly unpleasant man, too.'

We stayed late at lunch, even though it was clear Claude could not really help us. His polite scepticism was discouraging. As we were leaving he asked us what we were going to do next.

'Well, tonight we'll try that restaurant in Vic. Next week I'll be in Rome.' said Dan. 'Something quite different. This afternoon we're going to take the crew to Metz, to get an impression of a more German atmosphere.'

'It's not pronounced Metz,' said Claude quietly. 'In these parts we say "Messe". Be careful. There's quite a lot of feeling about it.'

11

'But surely Metz is the original German pronunciation? Wasn't it originally a German town?'

'No, absolutely not. The name comes from the Romans, from the Roman name of a local tribe. It's pronounced Messe,' he insisted. 'It's not a German town, not at all.'

Metz would not give up any secrets. It provided some elegant architectural shots in the strong afternoon light, and had obviously been a place of importance and wealth. The old squares beside the river and the great cathedral made pretty pictures but the town seemed to have no more atmosphere than a stage set. It was partly because so many places were closed. The municipal workers' strike had shut down the town hall and the archives in Metz as well as in Nancy. The crew had not realized that, and when they found out, they were so angry that Dan was forced, yet again, to call it a wrap.

He was very angry too. We'd achieved very little, it was uncertain whether Claude Mesnil would be able to do anything, and now he had lost face in front of the crew. When we got back to the Hôtel Choucroute I was glad to escape to my room. Reading a thriller in a hot bath is the best tranquillizer I know. It's curious how consoling it can be. There's something very reassuring about all that violence and sudden death; there's an orderliness in it, a cosiness that the real world lacks. After half an hour of it, I felt less discouraged.

There seemed to be a small fleet of production hire cars in the Hôtel Choucroute car park. I took one and drove by myself to Vic-sur-Seille, to the restaurant that Geneviève Mesnil had recommended. Dan was sitting on his own when I arrived.

'That's it,' he said. 'I'm through. I've had enough of this crew and enough of this story. I'm sending them all on to Rome, and so long as they turn up for the first day's shooting, the less I see of them between then and now the better.'

The crew also seemed to be in a combative mood when they arrived, but their expressions relaxed when they heard that they were now free to go to Rome.

'This calls for a little celebration,' said Rick. He called a waitress and ordered champagne. We all drank a lot, but I didn't feel like celebrating. The others, even Dan, were fairly indifferent to the collapse of the film. It wasn't likely to affect any of them personally. But for me, it was one unsuccessful project too many. Failure in the Corporation takes so many forms that it's sometimes hard to identify. But I felt I was beginning to seem unlucky.

We had only just ordered when Dan was called to the telephone. When he came back he was smiling.

'Good news,' he said, 'but you're not going to like it. That was Claude Mesnil. He says the municipal archives are opening tomorrow. The employees will be lining up outside the gates at 8.15. And so will we.'

We arrived at 8. I left the crew with Dan in the courtyard, unloading, and went ahead to get someone to open the vault for us. There were a lot of people standing around, probably in the aftermath of the strike, and it was difficult to get any attention. Finally someone I didn't recognize from my previous trips produced the ancient key and came with me to the heavy wooden door of the vault. It was a very cold morning, and as I waited for him to work the lock, I began to wish we didn't have to spend several hours down there. We could have filmed the documents we wanted almost anywhere. But the vault had atmosphere. It was constructed like the crypt of a church, with stone arches, and could be lit with picturesque shafts of light. A bit of moody, as Rick would say.

At last the man turned the key, swung open the big door and stood back politely for me to go in before him. The first thing that struck me was the smell. I reached in the dark towards the switch on the wall and turned on the light. I don't know why the smell didn't warn me, but I was anxious about the day's shooting and looking for a first camera position. I walked into a side aisle and saw a trolley with something on it that immediately made me vomit. It was the body of a man in a uniform. Where his head should have been there was a slightly shining mess of pulp and bone and hair. The colours were brilliant, even in the dim light. It was only several hours later that I realized this was, for me, a lucky break at last.

3

That wasn't my first thought. Between moments of nausea and faintness I was also aware that we wouldn't get much filming done now. Everything had suddenly slowed down; it was very cold but I felt unable to move, and the man who had been with me had left. After what seemed like a long time a lot of people arrived at once, all talking at the same time, arguing excitedly and knocking into each other in the cramped passages between the stacks of cases and papers. At first they ignored me, but after a while someone led me into the bright modern reading room, and found a chair for me. In the reading room more people joined in; the fuss and agitation seemed to increase, and I had difficulty in understanding what they were saying. One or two people were crying, from excitement more than anything else, I assumed. I don't know how long this continued, but after a while I noticed Claude Mesnil. It was a great relief to see him.

He came over to me at once, with combination of gallantry and concern.

'What a dreadful thing,' he said. 'I am so sorry.'

'Who was it?' I asked him.

'Well,' he said, 'no one can be absolutely sure,' and he put his hand on my arm, 'but it seems he was the caretaker here.'

He sat down next to me.

'The police have arrived,' he said, 'and soon they will want to talk to you. I am sure you can manage on your own, but if you would like any moral support I'd be most willing to stay.' His calm and restraint immediately made me feel less disorientated. There's something irresistible about disinterested male kindness of that sort.

'But your work – ' I said.

'I have a seminar in about forty minutes at the university,

but I'm sure they'll understand if I'm a little late.'

'It would be very nice if you could stay,' I said.

Soon afterwards two detectives came in, and shook hands rather formally with various people, including Claude Mesnil, but not with me. I seemed to have a curious status – foreign and touched somehow with the glamour of mortality. They spoke across me to other people, asking who I was and why I had been there. Claude Mesnil tactfully suggested that if they took me to a quiet and empty room they might get clearer answers directly from me.

Someone at last had the idea of sending for the director of the archives. He arrived and led us upstairs to his office. He was very kind to me and offered me brandy.

'Better not, with possible shock,' said one of the detectives, also kindly. He introduced himself and his colleague and asked me to sit down. They began by talking to Claude Mesnil, asking him in very rapid French whether I was in a fit state to answer questions, and how he knew me. The director was asked to stay and they all spoke together very fast and quietly, only occasionally asking me a question. Once or twice I had to lean forward to avoid fainting and Claude Mesnil answered for me. There was very little to tell.

I could not follow everything they said among themselves, but it seemed that the body had been definitely identified as that of Bertrand Joly, the caretaker. He had been a bachelor, a man of about sixty-five, rather solitary, but well known to everybody at the archives. From the account the director gave of him it seemed that he had virtually no family and no friends. The police and the director and Claude Mesnil all seemed familiar with each other; perhaps they actually all knew each other. I supposed that they were, after all, the professional establishment of Nancy.

'Was he a local? Where was he from?' asked the younger detective.

'Well,' said the director, 'he wasn't a very talkative type, so I never knew very much about him, but I think he was originally from Metz.'

'Any idea when he came here, how long he's been here?'

'Well, again, I couldn't swear to it, but I think it was probably soon after the war.'

'Came to Nancy or came to work here?' said the detective.

'Oh, I mean came to Nancy. He was sixty when he came to the archives. It's really a retirement job. In between I think he had a clerical job, nothing out of the ordinary.'

'Sounds like a lot of legwork, this one,' said the elder detective, unenthusiastically.

'And you say he had precious few friends, no relations?' the other one persisted.

'Apart from a sister, that is, living here in Nancy.'

The director had been looking for a file in a cabinet as he talked, and at last he pulled one out.

'Here, this is his file. Next of kin, Adelaide Joly, 6 rue de l'Echelle, sister.'

'I'll deal with that,' said the older man, taking the file. 'Nasty, explaining cases like this to the relatives.'

The caretaker began at last to seem human to me, and the image of pulp and gore in the vaults started to fade. A very powerful motive would be needed to obliterate someone like that – a poor and elderly man, with few friends and almost no family.

'You say that he came from Metz?' I asked. 'And that he was a young man in the 1940s?'

There was a brief silence. The elder detective turned to me again.

'What is the subject of your documentary, mademoiselle?'

For some reason I felt embarrassed.

'Collaboration during the war,' I replied.

For a moment his expression was contemptuous, and then quickly became formal again. This must have been a studied effect, because the police department certainly knew about our film. For one thing, we had informed them of it.

'I don't suppose you will find it easy to get much cooperation,' he said. 'However, thank you for yours. I am afraid I must ask you to stay here until further notice, but I am sure we will not have to inconvenience you very much. M. Mesnil, if you would be kind enough to arrange for the young lady to return to her hotel –' he said, getting up, shaking hands and opening the door for us.

On the way out Claude Mesnil told me politely that I was still very pale, and offered to drive me back to the Hôtel

Choucroute. It annoyed me that I was so impressionable, and that he should see it. I replied abruptly that all I wanted was a drink, and he could drive me to the Café Saint-Roch. He seemed surprised at my rudeness, but he took me anyway.

The Café Saint-Roch is a big, completely unspoilt Art Nouveau brasserie with a surprising, metropolitan glamour, perhaps because it was built at a time when Nancy was still rich and important. We sat down at one of the little metal tables, and Mesnil asked the waiter to bring me some brandy quickly. He himself had pastis.

'I wouldn't want to interfere with your stereotype of a Frenchman,' he said, smiling at me. 'How are you feeling?'

'Much, much better,' I said. Suddenly I realized that I hadn't seen the crew since 8 o'clock.

'What happened to the crew?'

'I've no idea,' said Mesnil. 'Did they come in with you?'

'No, they were outside unloading.'

'Well, I imagine that after the discovery was made, everyone was kept out of the building until the police came.'

'Yes, of course. Very tactful, your use of the passive – "when the discovery was made". What delicacy. How come you were there?' I asked, wiping away some brandy I had spilt on my skirt.

'Like you,' he said, 'I've found this strike very inconvenient. There are quite a few things I've needed and have not been able to get for my lectures. So I took the first opportunity to nip in and pick some of them up.'

'That was very lucky for me,' I said. 'Thank you very much for all your help and kindness.'

He smiled rather sadly.

'But you must agree,' I said, 'that the police were trying to head me off when I asked about Metz and the man's age during the war. And, of course, that convinces me there could be something in it.'

Claude Mesnil paused.

'Possibly,' he said.

'It was obviously a crime of passion. To beat someone about the head like that, that is not done in cold blood. And what passions would surround an elderly, lonely man? Not lust, not greed – but how about revenge?'

'There may be something in what you say. But if you will excuse me, I think you are becoming obsessed with this subject. Obsession is the mother of invention,' he said in English.

'And necessity too,' I replied, but I could hardly explain to him about *Pop Goes the Weasel*.

'In any case,' he said, 'the police will not let you interfere in this. It would be quite improper. Anyway, what is the point of pursuing such a painful subject to these extreme lengths? Even if it were true, that this man had some miserable little guilty secret from forty-five years ago, and that someone else had never forgotten, what has it got to do with the British, in their front rooms with their TV sets and their TV dinners? With their stupid talk of frogs and garlic and butter mountains? I can't believe that's what you really want to do – make a sort of mini-version of *The Sorrow and the Pity*.'

'So you do think there's something in it,' I said.

'What if I did? What really concerns me is the occupational hazard of journalists – heartlessness. I appeal to you, out of pity, let it go.'

He could not have got me more agitated had he been trying.

'It's not heartlessness,' I said. 'It's a way of seeing the world, of not letting it steal a march on you. At least it's not for the money.'

'Ah, you English,' said Claude Mesnil. 'You have been poor for too long to keep up this affectation of disinterestedness.'

'It's not disinterestedness, it's a different interest, a different point of view.'

Of course the opposition of Claude Mesnil only convinced me that my instinct could indeed be right. It was then, in the Café Saint-Roch, that I realized that my luck was perhaps beginning to turn.

Dan agreed with me, when I caught up with him at the Hôtel Choucroute. The police had rather brusquely told him and the crew to leave and he was high on a combination of frustration and drama. He'd been making a lot of calls to deal with the practical problems involved – it seemed the

Corporation, which envisages almost all possible circumstances, had a policy for just such an occasion. The form was to send the crew away, or hand them over to another producer, and for not one but two people to wait for instructions from the police (in the case of friendly or stable countries). So Dan and I were to remain at the Choucroute until further notice.

'And then,' he said 'either we'll have developed some good leads on this, or else we can have a spot of compassionate leave.'

It turned out to be compassionate leave. I had barely had a chance to tell Dan about the caretaker's sister when we received a visit from a different policeman. Very urbanely he made it plain that we would not be welcome interfering in this case until it had been solved. So we decided, yet again, to cut our losses and go.

Before we left, we had a very good lunch and decided to take my compassionate leave in the form of a pig's eating holiday in the Loire valley.

'Does the Corporation's compassion really extend to you as well?' I asked, not entirely sure whether it was a good idea for us to go together. 'Do I really need several days of a senior producer's time to get over all this? I mean, what about these people who are always discovering bodies – reporters in Africa? I bet they don't get their hands held like this all the time.'

'Of course not. But then they rarely sustain such a severe shock as the one you've just had – you know, the old newsvalue rule applies. One frog equals ten wogs. Anyway, I've dismissed the crew and I have nothing else to do.'

What we actually did was to go for a walk around some of the old parts of the town. Wandering through the Place Stanislas, I realized we had underestimated Lorraine, or Nancy at least. It is a strange town of dislocated elegance, with a feeling of being out of date, even though it is full of traffic and busy, purposeful people.

We agreed to visit the Musée Lorrain, to look again at the paintings, and after getting lost in some pretty side streets, we arrived at the massive, sixteenth-century gateway. We walked through several uninteresting galleries until we got to a smaller, darkened room containing some pictures which seemed quite different from all the rest. Like the room itself, they were dark, except for patches of intense candlelight. Immediately the most striking was one of a half-naked, ungainly woman. She was sitting in a bare room at night, unmistakably alone, clenching her fists together over her big belly and staring calmly downwards.

'There, that is the one that Geneviève Mesnil was talking about, the Georges de La Tour,' said Dan. '*The Flea Catcher, La Femme à la Puce.*'

We walked closer.

'Excuse me,' said a voice from the obscurity behind us. 'If you will permit me, I should point out that the title of this picture is a matter of some debate.'

We looked round and saw that it was a museum official who was speaking to us. He was a tall man in a blue uniform rather like the murdered caretaker's. He addressed us with great solemnity. 'It's true the picture is widely known as *Woman with Flea*, or sometimes as *Lady*, or *Servant with Flea*. But we are indebted to one of our colleagues for pointing out that there is not one flea, but two. This can be clearly seen here.'

The official pointed reverently at a point on the canvas and then at the woman's knuckles.

'I can't even see one flea,' said Dan, peering at the picture. 'There's absolutely nothing there,' he said to me. 'Where are these fleas?' he asked belligerently.

'There, and there!' cried the official, but he was unable to make us see anything at all. Still, our attention was caught. There was something hypnotic about the heavy woman, with her intense pale face, alone in the candlelight.

'What the hell is she doing anyway?' asked Dan.

The official stepped forward again, with a triumphant look on his face.

'What would you say if I told you she was saying a rosary?'

'Well, now, what would we say?' Dan said to me, jocular again.

'You see, some scholars say that the peasant women of this region used to hold their rosaries like that, with their knuckles pressed together,' said the official. He smiled seriously at us and moved away.

'I suppose it's possible,' I said, looking closely at a little painted-out shadow.

'It's probably not a La Tour anyway,' said Dan. 'Probably none of the rest are either. The galleries of the world are littered with misattributions and school-ofs'.

'Still, I quite like *The Flea Catcher* or whatever she is. There's a solemnity about her.'

'There's also something very erotic about her, about her mysterious inaccessibility,' said Dan, moving towards me. 'Shall I pluck out the heart of your mystery?'

'Certainly not,' I said, looking back at him and smiling. He didn't always have to struggle for charm. 'What's more, I shall report you to my shop steward for sexual harassment.'

'Don't bother,' said Dan, laughing. 'I *am* the shop steward – anyway, since when were you a good trade unionist? You're the most revisionist hackette in the entire Corporation empire.'

'We must have balance in broadcasting,' I said, putting my arm through his. 'And you're the most decadent shop steward I know. How much *foie gras* have you consumed since we've been here? And what about your Armani suits and Paul Smith boxer shorts?'

'Nothing is too good for the workers,' he said. 'Besides, what do you know about my underwear? Not nearly enough. I can give you a full briefing on our compassionate leave.'

'That is going to be gastronomic only,' I said. 'A pig's holiday, not a satyr's.'

4

I should have remembered that driving long distances is not something to do with Dan for pleasure. It rained nearly all the time, and the Loire valley is not much fun in February, in the rain. We saw more of the windscreen wipers than of the *route touristique*. From time to time we stopped at expensive restaurants listed in the Gault Millau guide, and we never ran out of things to say to each other, but we weren't at ease, and I think we both wanted to go back. Though I had known Dan for a long time, it had only been through work, and that's a deceptive kind of intimacy. I really didn't know him well enough to be alone with him without going to bed with him. At last we started back towards Paris.

We drove with the river on our left, shining silver in the rain. On our right were deep woods, the bare trees lining the road closely and dripping heavily. The main road began to wind away from the swollen brightness of the river, and soon we lost sight of it.

'Let's get back to the river,' said Dan and suddenly swerved down a tiny side road into the woods. At first it seemed to lead in the right direction but in fact it wound aimlessly among the trees and I began to think we were getting lost. The road narrowed and I felt sorry that I'd left all the Michelin guidebooks and maps locked in the boot of our hire car.

I could see that Dan was close to losing his temper. Suddenly, rounding a sharp corner, I saw a small, almost hidden sign.

'Château de Villancourt-le-Chapitre, seventeenth century.'

'Oh, let's stop here,' I said. 'Please slow down.'

Almost obscured by the trees was a small, run-down looking country house, hardly a château, but of great elegance.

'Let's stop here,' I repeated. 'I'm sure this is one of the ones that are supposed to be worth seeing.'

'What's so special about this one?' said Dan. 'I've never heard of it.'

'That doesn't mean a thing,' I said.

'Well, what's it got, how many stars? Is it worth a detour?'

'We've done the detour anyway. It doesn't have to be so good if you're there already.' In fact I now couldn't remember why the name was familiar.

'Stop being so Irish, Jane. It's cold, it's bloody wet, and we've already seen more than enough châteaux.'

'I've read something about it, I can't remember what, but I'm sure it's supposed to be interesting. I could get the Michelin out of the boot and look it up, but I want to see it anyway. Please. We've just happened on it. It appeals to me. We don't have to stay long.'

'I don't suppose it's even open to the public,' said Dan.

Grumbling, he turned towards the wrought-iron gates and I got out to open them. It was raining even harder now and I got very wet. We drove slowly up the poorly kept drive. The house looked completely deserted and Dan gave me a very hard look as we stood outside the front door, wondering whether the heavy bell-pull worked.

We'd almost decided to go away when the door was opened by an old woman.

'We've come to see the house,' I said brightly.

'Oh yes,' she said without enthusiasm. 'You haven't got a very nice day for it. You won't see much of the grounds.'

'But you are open, aren't you?' I said.

'Yes, certainly, we're open nearly all year, twice a week. We don't get many visitors in winter. I don't know why they bother to keep it open. It's nothing but a nuisance. It must be something to do with the taxes, it's always taxes these days, isn't it? Come in,' she said impatiently. 'Taxes and the cost of living. You can tell from the drive, can't you? You won't be wanting the full tour, will you?'

'Whatever you suggest,' said Dan.

'Well, the full tour's for groups really. In any case the guide's not here. I'm not the guide myself, though if you were to ask me who knows more about the house, me or the guide, well, that's another matter. If you'll come this way.'

Despite her claims, she did not appear to know much about the house or its contents. She told us very little, and waited impatiently at the door of several rooms while we inspected the contents of glass showcases and the faded hangings at the windows and on the fourposter beds. I suspect she only let us see a few of the rooms that were normally open. It was a gloomy, unmemorable place, except for some obviously valuable furniture.

'This is the salon, and the end of the tour,' she said at last, pushing open double doors to reveal yet another large, gloomy room. It was heavily overfurnished and most of the tables were covered with photographs. It must be a hack's instinct, but given a choice in a great house between looking at priceless pictures and furniture or the family photographs, I always look at the photos. Marie-Blanche de Grigny, the mainstay of the Corporation's Paris office, calls it a *goût de concierge* – tabloid taste.

All the same, the rich themselves are usually disappointing, rarely as splendid as their houses or their painted portraits or their scandals. These family photographs were typically dull: the heavy silver frames in the styles of different periods were far more remarkable. There were a few awkward débutantes, a couple of hesitant safari shots showing the emaciated legs of European upper-class women of the twenties and thirties and some stiff-backed hand-shakings between unsmiling old men and women. Their clothes had an amateurish, poorly fitting look, as though these were records of country house theatricals. There were one or two faces which stood out, and a couple of beautiful women, but with something so safe and solid about them that they invited little speculation.

The old woman noticed my interest in the photographs and told me that one of them was a picture of a German princess, who was a grand-daughter of Queen Victoria and who used to stay at the château.

'Of course royalty have always visited here, at least until the war,' she said. 'After that – well, most of them have been deposed, haven't they? And of course here it's been nothing but expenses, taxes and inflation. Things aren't what they were once, you know, not at all. There was a time when the head gardener wore white gloves when he went out, not so long ago. Things aren't what they were at all.'

What she said was obviously true. Everything, everywhere, was faded. There was a smell of age about the house, not quite a smell of damp but of old material, old dust, old flesh. The salon probably hadn't been decorated since before the war.

'And now,' she went on, slightly repositioning the pictures, 'who knows what will happen? If anybody does know they haven't bothered to tell me. But what do you expect?'

'What do you mean?' I asked.

'Well,' she said, 'who's going to be taking over? Who's going to be saying who stays and who doesn't? Will the château be shut up? Or sold?'

'Why should it be?' I asked.

'Of course,' she said, turning to me, 'you wouldn't know. Monsieur le Comte has just passed on. Only three weeks ago, three weeks last Monday. Very sudden, it was.'

The sun must have come out: strong light filtered through the window and illuminated the heavy dust in the room. It lit up the old woman's fragile, wrinkled face.

'Very suddenly?' I asked, trying to appear only mildly interested.

'Oh, yes. It was quite a shock.'

'I'm very sorry to hear that,' said Dan urbanely, despite his bad French. 'May I ask how old the Comte was?'

'Well over eighty,' she said. 'Nearly eighty-six. He'd been taken out to the terrace to get a little sun in the morning. It was cold, but he was well wrapped up in his wheelchair – he always used to sit there for an hour or so when it was nice out, for the fresh air, but of course he must have forgotten to leave the brake on, or he must have dozed off, because the chair rolled forward and off the parapet, right down on to the terrace below. A silly sort of accident. Broke his neck. Of course he shouldn't have been left alone really. He wouldn't be told; he was a very obstinate old gentleman but his mind used to wander. He hadn't been himself for years, not really. I never knew him, not in what you might call his right mind. Of course that's why it's like this here, all so disorganized, nothing kept up, nothing put to rights. The guide used to grumble about it.

Never knew where anything was or what anything was.'

'Well,' I said, 'I expect his heirs will put it right.'

'No, that's the pity of it. There aren't any heirs. The Comte was the last, the last of the direct line. I suppose it will go to some cousin from somewhere or other, or some trust or to the lawyers or something. Not that anyone's troubled to tell me.'

'Did he never marry?' I asked, even though I could sense that Dan was getting more and more bored and irritated.

'Oh yes, and he had a son and heir. Just the one child, Monsieur Charles. But he died years and years ago, in a shooting accident. This family is a great one for accidents. He got himself shot out hunting.'

The more old foreign films you see, the more reality begins to resemble them. Perhaps it's something about the subtitles. I was beginning to have fun, to enjoy the sensation that we had stepped into a Renoir film. But Dan almost dragged me out of the house, assiduously thanking the old woman in his bad French, and holding my arm so tightly that it hurt.

He pulled me on to the terrace and led me out of earshot.

'You're supposed to be an intelligent woman but you think like a B movie. You needn't tell me what's on your mind. I know. It's perfect for you, isn't it – ancient retainer, dust in shafts of sunlight, crumbling château, sudden death. One body and you're suddenly Miss Jane Marple – one body's not enough for you.'

'Just because I wouldn't have anything to do with yours,' I said, regretting it.

Rather surprisingly, Dan put his arm around me.

'I'm sorry,' he said. 'You really did have quite a shock. But I'm beginning to think you have a little weakness this way – too much detective fiction, too many fantasies.'

'Too many clichés. The world is far stranger than fiction, for instance.'

It was still raining, but the sun was out, making a curious effect, a little like spring. Beyond the terrace and the formal gardens a sodden *parc anglais* stretched towards the dripping woods.

'Your world is not as strange as you would like to think,' said Dan.

'But stranger than you imagine,' I said.

Dan laughed. 'Seriously,' he said, 'a nice girl like you should not have murder on the brain. You should concentrate on a nice boy like me, instead.'

'Whatever you say,' I said, as we walked more amicably around the outside of the house towards the car, 'some instinct tells me there's something odd here.'

'It's not an instinct. It's weeks of this bloody, incessant rain. It depresses everyone. It makes you morbid.'

I didn't answer him.

'Just because an old boy, a man of nearly ninety, falls off his perch,' Dan said.

'He didn't fall. He had a slightly curious accident in his wheelchair.'

'He was gaga. He probably mistook the brake for the gear of some ancient jalopy and was driving himself around the Jazz Age. Or maybe his minders got careless and won't admit it.'

'I don't care what you say,' I said, turning to him and staring at his irritable frown. 'There's something about this place, something about the atmosphere, something knocking at my memory, some connection I can't quite make.'

'It would be quite a coincidence if you were to discover not one, but two murders.'

'Beginner's luck,' I said and we got into the car and drove to Paris.

5

Since the invention of steam radio the Corporation has always – except during the German occupation – had an elegant Paris headquarters on the first floor of an hôtel in the rue du Faubourg Saint-Honoré; it was once a set of apartments belonging to a noble family. The Paris office is the envy of every other overseas Corporation outpost. It is a reminder to visiting hacks that Corporation life was once a thing of dignity and leisure.

I accompanied Dan through the anonymous wooden gates, past a concierge behind net curtains, through a bright and serene courtyard up to the sort of apartment where you might go for tea with a slightly down-at-heel duchess. Marie-Blanche de Grigny, who was waiting for us, fitted into this environment very well. Gently, even nobly born, she made very few concessions to the second half of the twentieth century: she'd been wearing short Shetland pullovers and knee-length tartan skirts since the mid-sixties.

I had never understood why she worked for the Corporation. It wasn't even a very elevated job; underneath all the charm and the rather patronizing manner, she was really just an all-purpose researcher for itinerant Corporation journalists. Perhaps it was the residue of an anglophilia which her long association with the real world of English television had not yet subdued. It was certainly a mixture of anglophilia and snobbery that had made her, from the beginning, and to my embarrassment, exceptionally nice to me. The French aristocrats' sense of pedigree is the most highly developed in Europe; it must have something to do with the annihilation of most of their own. They can detect a person with a title or two behind them almost in the dark. I sometimes wondered whether, having detected the titles behind me, she knew that they were on the wrong side of the blanket. If so, it didn't seem to matter to her. Despite all that, out of all the Corporation's foreign representatives – researchers, gophers and gladhanders – she was one of the best, when she felt like it.

'I've arranged for your hire car to be collected tomorrow,' she told us. 'And your hotel booking for tonight was arranged from London, wasn't it? All the archive film material you asked for is here: I've also got a 35 mill. print of the Ophuls film, and I've done a typed breakdown of anything I thought would be useful. I've got a viewing arranged for all of tomorrow – when do you want to go?'

'Today,' said Dan.

Marie-Blanche gave him a nasty look. 'I'll try for you,' she said, reaching for the telephone.

She came with us to the viewing theatre nearby.

'It's been rather difficult,' she said to me, while we were waiting in the dark for the technicians to begin. 'I really didn't know what you're trying to achieve.'

'You're not alone,' I whispered. I started to tell her about the background to the film, but *The Sorrow and the Pity* began and Dan asked us to be quiet. There can't be anyone who has seen that film who doesn't bring away some lifelong painful images; mine are a series of expressions on the faces of the young women whose heads were being shaved in public because they had had German lovers. I wasn't sure that I wanted to see it again, but either Dan or I would have to look through it, if only for the clips of archive film.

'Listen,' said Marie-Blanche, 'I've seen this at least once too often – do you have to stay?'

In a café just behind the rue du Faubourg Saint-Honoré we ordered two large *café crèmes*.

'So,' she said. 'I want to know all about this body.'

Of course she'd already heard. She had the kind of discreet bossiness that made me feel that she knew more about it than me, and I said so.

'No, don't be absurd, I want all the details.'

I told her everything I thought she'd find entertaining and she didn't seem to be squeamish. I also told her my guess that the murder might, perhaps, have to do with revenge for some wartime crime.

'Wishful thinking, wouldn't you say?' asked Marie-Blanche. 'All the same, anything is possible.'

She sensed, without my having to explain, that our film was one of those Corporation muddles, which take extra time and effort for a poor result. None the less it interested her. There is a kind of challenge in turning a bad programme round, and researchers are addictive problem solvers: she looked at me with a heartless kind of interest.

'So,' she said, 'as someone said to the editor of the *Washington Post* when the Watergate stories were breaking, and she was staking her reputation on them: "Your tit is on the table".' Marie-Blanche de Grigny conceitedly talking Yanqui in a smart Parisian café made a memorable picture.

'I wouldn't put it quite like that,' I said. 'I've just got to make it work, if it's humanly possible, or I'll have to move over into the slow lane.'

'Perhaps your luck is turning. Normally I'd say that all this has been done before. For a start there's *The Sorrow and the Pity*. You couldn't possibly hope to do anything in that league, Marcel Ophuls' league, of course. I mean, he was a refugee from Germany to France, French by adoption, a Jew, a refugee from anti-Semitism here – excuse me, but I think that his is really the last word on this kind of retrospective. And yet, and yet. Perhaps there really is a story in Lorraine. There are still things to do – look at the Klaus Barbie story. Anyway,' she said, laughing at me, 'there's something very romantic about the sight of a journalist's nose twitching.'

'You may laugh,' I said to her, 'but the odd thing is that I've just found another body.'

'Heavens alive,' she said, sitting back and smiling.

'I don't mean I actually saw the body, but I think that the man died in suspicious circumstances.'

I was expecting another of those sixteenth-arrondissement smiles. But Marie-Blanche surprised and encouraged me by getting out her standard red Corporation notebook.

'What do you want me to do?' she asked.

'I want you to find out everything you can about the Comte de Villancourt-le-Chapitre – especially about his politics, his social life, about his relationships with Germans, gossip, anything. What he did in the war, of course. He would have been about forty-five when the Germans arrived. But I don't want anyone to know that I'm interested. It shouldn't be too difficult for you, considering.'

'Considering that I'm really very well placed for this,' she interrupted, smiling.

And she was. I told her everything relevant that I could think of, then I went back to Dan and the film archives.

6

Wireless House dominates a flat industrial wasteland as though it were broadcasting a blight in all directions. Someone who did not know could not possibly guess that it stands close to the centre of London. On one side lie bare parking lots awaiting development, leading down to the railway line. To the north a tangle of motorways rises, cutting through several layers of skyline, and beyond the ceaseless traffic a Victorian prison stands in the middle distance. To the west is a half demolished stadium and one or two isolated terraced houses without a terrace. Wireless House itself, now used only for television, has an imposing façade, built for the time when Britannia ruled the air waves. *E Pluribus Unum* is the motto, carved in Art Deco stonework and supported by well-developed stone maidens.

Behind this reassuring frontage is a vast kingdom of sprawling buildings, of tacked-together sheds, converted terraced houses, lavish office blocks, Nissen huts, interconnecting bridges, tunnels and walkways, warehouses, studios and ventilators. It is a place where someone could be lost for days; many people spend a whole lifetime there without really emerging, except to board a Corporation minibus.

Such is the loyalty this strange institution inspires that many people work there for half or a quarter of what they could earn somewhere else. They become willingly institutionalized: to work there is to become part of something magical, to be touched officially by the idea of Science, of Technology, of Stardom, of Entertainment or Tragedy or News. It is to belong to an immense internal network of specialists, engineers, technicians, telephones, rules and conventions, an international information retrieval system, a view of the world, an entire way of life from canteen breakfast to pension scheme. It's to become a chip in a vast multi-national computer, and all the while to have a very English illusion of individuality. I loved it.

There is activity in this labyrinth nearly twenty-four hours a day: it is never too late to ask someone a question. And so when I finally got back from Paris, although it was after 9 in the evening, I went straight to one of the main reference libraries. Straight is of course a figure of speech in Wireless House. I followed several passages, one of them apparently circular, went down a service lift and back on my tracks, and reached the library by a connoisseur's route.

As it happened, one of the librarians on duty that night was Peter, the man who had originally helped me with Lorraine. I knew him well and trusted his judgement. I would almost have called him a friend. He didn't ask how things had gone in Lorraine; librarians never do. I've often wondered why not. Having spent a lot of skill and energy bringing together people, facts, theories, addresses and train timetables, having drawn on many years of accumulated intelligence, they are almost all incurious about what actually happens. Perhaps it is to avoid the knowledge that their efforts have very often been wasted. Perhaps it is because so few people think of thanking them after the event for producing just the right landscape or obscure fact. Perhaps the results of all their burrowing and ferreting was of no interest to them, as if the activity justified itself. Peter, I knew, did not even own a television set. But then they didn't get credits.

'Loire valley,' I said to him. 'Minor aristrocracy of.'

He started writing in one of the big red books.

'Room and project number?' he asked.

Mentioning a project number in the Corporation is like saying Open Sesame. It is the computer identification code for all a programme's expenses. If you mention a project number almost anything becomes available, short of hookers or fake passports. Video editing suites, focus pullers, Corporation Sellotape, wigs, sandwiches, lenses, lights, books, old film, computer time and even large handfuls of foreign currency appear almost magically. A project number is even more powerful than the name of the Corporation itself in the world outside.

I gave Peter our project number and he sat silently waiting for me to be more specific. He knew and I knew that he could probably make the programme better than I could. But he had the kind of temperament which prefers resignation to indignation.

'What I want to know,' I said, 'is anything and everything about an obscure French comte who lived until three weeks ago at the Château de Villancourt-le-Chapitre. I want to know about his ancestry, his career, his hobbies, his social circle. What happened to him during the war.'

'Any particular angle?' Peter asked politely.

'Not exactly, just a guess. He fell off his wheelchair recently, aged eighty-five or -six and I want to know why.'

Peter smiled openly for once.

'Foul play, you mean?'

I think this was probably more entertaining to him than the shape of farthingales in the 1590s or the number of canals commissioned by nineteenth-century Anglo-Irish philanthropists, or Neil Kinnock's dentistry.

'There's probably nothing in it,' I said, suddenly depressed by the implausibility of the whole thing, of the entire programme, of my ineffectual strugglings with the Corporation.

'Give me forty-five minutes or so and I'll get you a few basics – if you want to pursue it further I'll have to do the rest tomorrow: I'm on Middle East priority standby tonight.'

I had nothing better to do than to wait. Besides, idling in a good library is one of the best of life's less glamorous pleasures. The library in which Peter worked was one of the Corporation's oldest and biggest. There was still an old-fashioned, open-shelved books and news clippings section, which relied on inspiration and muddle. There were even some limp yellow index cards left, but most of the indexes had been gradually and inefficiently transferred to microfiches – this process had taken several years and there was an inconvenient selection of different-sized bits of celluloid and different kinds of battered machine.

To use what books happen to be visible on the shelves, or to struggle with a damaged bit of blue plastic in a machine with a blurred screen and broken controls was not my idea of accuracy. But some hacks and librarians prefer this intuitive, chancy way of working: it does, I admit, exploit the possibility of stray connections. The important part of the library was the new, highly computerized section, which could use all the best information services and libraries in the world. But for this there was always a queue.

I was absorbed in a 1950s train-spotters' annual when Peter came up to me in the readers' section. He held a large pile of old books which he'd summoned up from the basement and a lot of photocopied sheets.

'There's not much, I'm afraid,' he said.

Librarians always say that, but this time he seemed to mean it. None of the material looked very promising. I started with the photocopied entry from the *Almanach de Gotha* of 1984. Hubert Guillaume de Villancourt. It's one thing to understand French, another to decipher the significance of an entry like that. As far as I could tell the Comte was rather unremarkable, not very aristocratic, not very interesting, not very rich. He wasn't even very fruitful; he had produced one son, Charles Henri Taillis de Villancourt, born in 1922. His wife Ghislaine Françoise de Saint-Paer had died not long afterwards, in 1925. He hadn't remarried. As the old woman at the château had said, the son had died young, when he was only twenty-one. A hunting accident, she had said. It had happened in 1942.

I wished I had Marie-Blanche de Grigny's instinctive understanding of aristocratic habits. It seemed to me that the Comte's clubs and few interests were of the old-guard conservative aristrocracy, of the true blue French upper-class right that had produced so many supporters of the Vichy regime, but it would have been wrong just from that impression to assume anything about his political views. I wondered whether there was anything of interest in earlier entries. The old Comte had probably not changed his entry for years, but I thought it might be worth looking up a much earlier edition of the *Almanach*. I went through the library to Peter's desk, where he was taking a telephone call.

General knowledge was to Peter what women were to Don Juan. He was genuinely promiscuous about facts and ideas: everything for him was of equal significance, or insignificance. I suppose it's an occupational hazard. Although I was impatient for him to get off the line I couldn't help being interested in what he was saying.

'Yes, I think you'll find quite a few women's groups are or were interested in this – I could give you some addresses but off the top of my head I think there was some organized protest in Vermont or Connecticut in the early eighties. I'll get a print-out for you, but I'm fairly sure the issue is dead. No, the vimule cap is something different. It was the other one that was being smuggled into the States. The Food and Drugs Administration wouldn't license it. Yes, odd, isn't it, even though it was pioneered in the forties. Yes, days, even weeks at a time. Obviously not a good idea. Yes, I'll let you have everything that seems relevant. No, no trouble.'

Waiting for this arcane conversation to end, and looking round at all the new computers, it occurred to me that the human brain was still ahead. I asked Peter to order up an earlier *Almanach de Gotha*, if there was one in stock, and went back to the piles of books he'd given me. At first I was annoyed: several of them were ones he'd produced for me before – a few standard modern histories of Vichy France, and several contemporary ones with dated titles: *France: the Shameful Struggle; The Shame of Vichy; Vichy Today; De Profundis*. Then there was a selection from the intervening years. Peter must have known I'd seen these before.

I started looking at random in the indexes and before very long I realized I'd been doing Peter an injustice. In the index of one of the bigger, duller books, a tedious account of Franco-German relations since 1870, the Comte's name was listed. There was one page reference.

In my excitement I fumbled with the soft pages, but finally I found the place. The page was part of a complex argument about political and social divisions among French conservatives after the Nazi victory: there were corresponding distinctions between different kinds of collaboration in the different zones. The argument was extremely convoluted and I was too impatient to follow it. All that interested me was the Comte's name. Hubert Guillaume de Villancourt was listed with ten or twelve others from different parts of France, as aristocrats and landowners who, uncharacteristically of their class, had moved into active collaboration, active fascism, active persecution of their fellow Frenchmen.

I had to read the section twice. There was nothing specific, no detail, just a sociological argument. But I hadn't been wrong. There had been something about the atmosphere at the Château de Villancourt-le-Chapitre. Perhaps I'd read the paragraph before. Perhaps at some level I'd remembered the name. At any rate I had been right. There was a bad smell attached to the Comte's name and it had to do with collaboration. I sat for quite a long time in that ugly empty room, wondering whether any of it amounted to anything. His death could so easily have been just an accident: I couldn't understand why I was so dissatisfied with the obvious explanation. Forty-five years is a long time to wait for retribution, if retribution had anything to do with it. Perhaps instead it had something to do with hidden secrets: so many hacks like us were nosing around the rotten places of recent history that people were beginning to be afraid again that their secrets were at risk. At risk from the indiscretions, perhaps, of an old boy who was gaga?

Peter interrupted my thoughts. 'I'm afraid we haven't got the old edition of the French Debrett thing here in stock, but we can have it here for you some time tomorrow. I've found a couple of other things, nothing very important, I don't suppose.'

He had a photocopy of some news clippings of about ten years ago. They were more about the house than about the Comte. An English academic had found some interesting old documents in the Comte's collection, a few letters to the monks of a monastery on the property, of considerable historical interest, to those who are interested. I glanced at the photocopies quite quickly. They weren't of much interest to me. It had been a good idea of Peter's to look in the index under the name of the château, but like so many good ideas, it hadn't come to anything.

It was late and I should have gone home, but I was restless. I wanted to talk to Marie-Blanche but I didn't have her home number. Besides it was probably too late to call. Instead I stayed in the reference library, wasting time, wrestling with the coffee machine, taking a few notes and reading bits in irrelevant magazines. Wasting time is probably the wrong expression, but that's what it usually feels like. In fact, I suppose I was ruminating, but without much to chew on. And there was no one to go home to.

Tomorrow I would have to compose a lot of letters of thanks and persuasion. Dan was one of those producers who like to write their own letters; that is to say, he would expect me to write them for him in his own style. I've often thought this to be a journalistic knack above and beyond the call of duty. But I was determined to be cooperative, mainly, I suppose, to still the faint disturbances between us. I thought of the afternoon in the museum at Nancy when we looked at the painting of *The Flea Catcher* together. La Tour, G., I thought automatically, as I was in a library. Perhaps it would be under D, De La Tour, G. or T, Tour De La, G. Libraries promote obsession.

Almost without thinking, I looked among the microfiche book index somewhere near DE, took out a blue rectangle of plastic and tried to put it into one of the viewing machines. It did not fit the suitable-looking slot. I moved to a slightly different machine and this time the flimsy plastic, by now much fingered, slid neatly into the tray. But the tray itself would not engage with the machine. At last I got the better of it and found Georges de La Tour. There appeared to be only two books in English on the painter. Not much of a La Tour industry, I thought. The most recent sounded like a pretty picture book, and I wrote out a requisition form for it.

I remembered vaguely that La Tour had been in the news a lot at one time, and since I was there, I thought I'd look up the news clippings. The stacks of microfilm casettes were right next to the microfiche, and I took the relevant one to a viewing machine. This time everything worked except the fast forward control. But I was determined not to be defeated by the machine.

I hit the Georges de La Tour section in the middle – I could only move through the files much too slowly or much too fast. For a seventeenth-century painter he had a lot of inches in the twentieth-century press. Some of it went back to the mid-1940s, which was where the microfilm started. It was mostly sale-room pieces. As I skimmed through, whole years rushing past when I touched the fast forward button, it emerged that quite a lot of La Tours had been rediscovered, or reattributed to him. Two had been discovered in England – one had been found lying neglected in the basement of a museum in Stockton-on-Tees in the early 1970s. The Queen had a La Tour at Hampton Court.

It didn't mean a lot to me. Until I had seen *The Flea Catcher* I hadn't though much about La Tour one way or another. I was just about to give up playing with the uncooperative machine when suddenly and by chance, as it often happens, I saw what it was that I'd unconsciously been looking for, the connection that had been troubling me. Somewhere among the short pieces about exhibitions and sales there was a large, attractive-looking feature piece in *The Times*. What had caught my attention was a big photograph of a house. Although it was very blurred on the microfilm, it looked familiar. The caption underneath named it: the Château de Villancourt-le-Chapitre.

I read very hurriedly. The story was about the sale of a La Tour painting to the Rensellaer Collection in Washington in 1981. There was a long account of who had bid against the curators, where the picture had been found and so on. The price struck me as high, reportedly well over $7 million, but then the Rensellaer was famous for paying crazy prices. In fact the château played only a very small part in the story: it was there, years before, that some seventeenth-century letters had been found – they must have been the ones mentioned in the photocopy Peter had produced for me. One of these letters had supported the attribution of the Rensellaer La Tour.

So that was all there was to it. The unremembered connection in my mind that had troubled me so much, that had coloured our day at the château with significance, the powerful journalistic instinct which had convinced me that the two bodies – one of which I had not even seen – were connected, that Lorraine and the Loire valley were connected, all this was just garbled around an irrelevant historical fact – a half-memory from a newspaper. It was, in fact, quite trivial. Memory, which can perform such wonderful stunts, can also play foolish tricks. I was just getting my wires crossed. I rang the main reception, ordered a taxi and, at last, went home.

7

It was nearly midnight on a bright night. All I had to show for my efforts was a caseful of dirty clothes and a feeling of anxiety and sadness. But there isn't very much that can obscure the charm of London on such a night. We drove quickly through Hyde Park, very bare in the moonlight, to Apsley House, past the Buckingham Palace Statue of Victory standing out boldly against the light sky, down the Mall, out through Trafalgar Square and across the Thames. At that time of night it doesn't take very long to reach the East End and I was soon standing alone at the bottom of the warehouse by the river where I lived. There was a smell of cinnamon in the air, from a factory close by.

Upstairs in my flat there was a large pile of mail, which I looked through for personal letters. There weren't any. I turned on the answerphone tape and went to the refrigerator. There were a lot of bottles, some lumpfish roe, some tomato paste and some yoghurt. I threw the yoghurt away and mixed some whisky and soda. I found some chocolate in the cupboard and a vitamin pill to go with it. The messages on the answerphone made me wish, yet again, that I didn't have one. I wrote down a few notes about the calls I couldn't avoid and sat looking out at the lights on the river. Towards the end of the messages I heard Marie-Blanche de Grigny's voice, telling me to call her. I turned off the tape and picked up the telephone immediately. But then I hesitated. I couldn't quite imagine what hours she kept, whether she lived at home, or even with her parents. She was probably too respectable to be rung late at night, but on the other hand she was used to journalists and she had left me her home number. I dialled it.

'Ah, hello,' she said loudly. 'You called. You are home now – is everything all right?'

'Yes, fine,' I said.

'Listen, I've found out rather a lot about this Hubert de Villancourt. Yes, very quick, wasn't it? I'm glad you appreciate it. First of all, nobody thinks there was anything interesting about his death. No. He was completely gaga and very difficult, very obstinate. Besides, there's no one to benefit from his death. I don't know what's in his will, but there are only extremely distant cousins. Anyway there's not much money, only some furniture, and without money a house like that is no use to anybody – besides which the death duty will be quite incredible.'

'But,' I said without any confidence, 'I wasn't thinking of a mercenary murder.'

'Exactly,' she said. 'That's what might, just possibly, be interesting. Your little fantasy of an investigative coup. Maybe that Anglo-Saxon nose has not been twitching in vain. There are quite a few bad smells about the Comte's name, as you would say. He's never been liked, I don't know why, but the real issue is what he did during the German occupation. It seems that he wasn't just a certain kind of upper-class pro-German conservative type. This isn't at all widely known, it's been more or less buried, but he was implicated in the selection of Jews to be deported. French Jews, to be sent to a collection centre and then to the camps. I think this is just beginning to excite quite a bit of interest.'

'Who've you been talking to?' I said, immediately jealous that she might have been speaking to other journalists.

She understood me, of course.

'That, *chère amie*, is my business. They're friends of mine, and just remember that so far from giving them your story, I'm really giving you theirs.'

'All right, I'm sorry. Go on.'

'I can't give you any details about it. But it's just what you want to hear, isn't it?'

'Marie-Blanche, you are wonderful. But is this really any different from the cases we already know, the things you can read in the history books about Frenchmen deciding that they could save many Jews by sacrificing some – the least worst principle?'

41

'Well, I don't know. Anyway, the thing that's interesting in this case is that his wife was Jewish.'

'Oh my God,' I said. I was still staring out at the river, sitting in my peaceful room, and just for a moment, the subject took on a little reality.

Marie-Blanche was enjoying her dramatic pause.

'What do you mean, Jewish?' I said. 'Her name was Ghislaine Françoise de Saint-Paer, deceased 1925.'

'I'm glad to hear that you too have been doing a little homework,' said Marie-Blanche. 'Of course that's an aristocratic name, but it was her father's name. Her mother was a very beautiful singer and dancer called Rosario Martinez. We're talking about the Naughty Nineties – you know, monocled boulevardiers, Toulouse Lautrec. I think she had some sort of gipsy flamenco act. Black hair, flashing eyes. But she wasn't Spanish at all, she was Jewish. And, as you know, Jewish descent is through the mother. So the Comtesse de Villancourt was Jewish.'

I was really astonished.

'Who knew about it?'

'That's the interesting question, isn't it? It certainly wasn't generally known – I've spoken to a couple of people in that world who had no idea. They knew that her mother had been a chorus girl, of course, but no more than that. Besides it was all so long ago: Ghislaine herself died years and years ago.'

'1925,' I repeated. 'Nearly twenty years before the Jewish deportations. Which year were they?'

'1942, probably. That was the worst time,' said Marie-Blanche.

'That', I said, waking up at last to the nastiness of it all, 'is the year in which Ghislaine's son died, in a shooting accident. And Jewish descent is through the female line.'

'Curious, isn't it?' said Marie-Blanche.

'It's more than curious,' I said. 'It's a programme.'

'Oddly enough,' said Marie-Blanche, 'I think your instinct was right. You may be on to something. I ought to tell you that my friends here will soon start wondering about the son too, if they haven't already.'

'I want to know all about that accident,' I said, 'and

whether there was anything about it, anything at all that was suspicious.'

'It's always faintly suspicious when someone shoots himself.'

'He shot himself?' I asked.

'Yes, that's what I was told. But people's memories get garbled. One old woman said he shot himself climbing over a gate, someone else said that it happened when he was cleaning his guns.'

'I was just told it was a hunting accident.'

'So it was,' said Marie-Blanche.

'He must have known that he was Jewish,' I said, not quite sure what I thought.

'If you knew a little more history,' Marie-Blanche said, 'you'd realize that in France at that time it wasn't quite so simple. He was and he wasn't. At that time, under Vichy law, you had to have two Jewish grandparents to be officially Jewish, from the point of view of the authorities. He only had one, assuming anyone knew it.'

'But by Jewish standards he was Jewish.'

'Yes, presumably.'

'Through his mother, and he shot himself. Do you think his father knew?'

'Of course, that's the important question. But there's a limit to what even I can achieve in two or three days.'

'Yes, of course – I'm sorry, Marie-Blanche. I'm really very grateful and very impressed.'

I didn't think she had any more to tell me, but I was tired and excited and I kept her on the line, speculating and thinking aloud. I was puzzled by the way the story kept collapsing, and then rising again in a different form. And I still had an almost superstitious sense, based on ignorance no doubt, of the interconnectedness of my experiences in France. In this weakminded mood, I asked Marie-Blanche whether she could imagine any possible connection between the château and the murder at Nancy.

'Why on earth should there be?' she asked irritably.

I drifted into a muddled account of the way things had, so far, been oddly linked, how things tended to be interrelated, how France at that time was somehow very small, that everybody involved with the Vichy Government or the Germans was somehow or other connected with everybody else.

I expressed myself badly and before long she interrupted.

'The people who are *not* connected – the only people, actually, who have nothing to do with it,' she said angrily, 'are the foreign journalists who simply try to rise on the back of other people's disgrace and tragedy.'

I tried to protest, but Marie-Blanche had already rung off. It occurred to me that being so very correct and Faubourg Saint-Honoré herself, Marie-Blanche was just the type to have parents with a distressing past. It's easy to forget that, though it started nearly fifty years ago, the Second World War is still very close.

I put down my notepad, picked up my drink and sat back in my chair. By now I was beginning to feel confused. Almost at once I got up again and put on some music, and tried to listen to it for a while. But my thoughts were too restless and disordered. I felt I was being pulled around meaninglessly by the story. At least there did seem to be a story.

I was too tired to start thinking about reshaping the film, about whether to drop Nancy altogether and concentrate on the Comte. The Jewish aspect of it was likely to recapture Dan's interest. And I needed to have Dan between me and the prospect of *Pop Goes the Weasel*. I sat for a long time by the big windows overlooking the river, worrying at random details in my mind, hurrying from a few words spoken at one time to a page in a book, to something quite different, until they all turned into the confusion of an anxious dream and I was asleep.

8

Wireless House is open day and night, so there's nothing to stop anyone turning up for work at 9 in the morning. In practice very few people in production teams arrive before 10, which is why I was able, very often, to swim in the morning at the RAC club pool in Pall Mall. It is the nearest I will get to belonging to a gentlemen's club, and probably near enough. I quite enjoyed seeing a few old buffers stoutly forcing themselves up and down the marble pool. I even got to know some of them.

I went there the day after I got back from Paris and swam twenty lengths with my usual reluctance. As I was getting out, I saw one of my acquaintances getting out at the other end and looking for his towel. I found mine and went up to him.

'Hello,' he said. 'Haven't seen much of you recently.'

He was in good shape and still had the posture of a career soldier, but even swimming in a marble pool cannot hold back the force of time: he must have been about sixty-five.

'I've been on a filming trip,' I said. 'To France.'

'All right for some,' he replied, without a trace of resentment. 'Gay Paree. 'Course we're not allowed to say gay now.'

'I'd like to ask your advice about it, about something that came up.'

'My dear girl, I would be delighted. Like to get out of my trunks first, though. Why don't you come and have some coffee with me upstairs in fifteen minutes.'

I didn't really know what he had done in the army – ours was only, as they say, a poolside friendship. But it had occurred to me, as I saw his pale form emerging from the water, that he might be able to send me to someone who'd have expert knowledge of that time in Vichy France. It's difficult to tell with some of these ancient warriors. They make such an art of concealing their intelligence, particularly from women. I've always found that very reassuring, though not always very helpful for journalistic purposes. It was worth a try, anyway.

He took his time, assuming no doubt that a woman would not be punctual. I hurried, assuming that he would be. When we had finally finished apologizing to each other and had ordered some coffee, I told him briefly about the death of the Comte de Villancourt, making my suspicions sound far more solid than they were. I mentioned the Jewish mother and the son's accident. It occurred to me as I talked that if he had lived, Monsieur Charles would have been about the same age as my retired colonel, a little overweight too, with broken blood vessels on his face, perhaps, and a kind of sagging about him, as if the surprise of being old had taken the wind out of him.

My companion paid me the compliment of taking me seriously.

'I'll do what I can for you, my dear. It wasn't my part of the world, but I'll ask around.'

I couldn't tell, from his manner, whether there was the slightest chance of anything coming of it. We talked for a little and rattled our coffee cups around in our saucers for a while, and I stood up to leave as soon as I reasonably could. He had been kind and I would have liked to have spoken more freely to him, to have known what had happened to him, but too much convention and too much time stood between us. He walked with me to the street door.

It's a surprisingly short distance from Pall Mall to the barren wastes of Corporation territory and its high rise car park. I got to my office by 10.30, and noticed that quite a lot of surrounding rooms were still empty. I liked my office. It was on the sixteenth floor of a tower block, the highest building in the complex, and my room faced west. It was a good-sized room but a poor location, as far as office politics went. The furnishing also reflected my ambiguous position: I had a high-grade desk and superior carpeting but the blinds were plastic and I did not have an executive swivel chair. I remedied this by having a tweed secretarial swivel chair, which was technically beneath my station, as opposed to an immovable executive chair, which would have been mine by right.

I was supposed to share this room with an unpleasant man who was writing a play. Fortunately he preferred to do it at home and I ignored all his calls. When people asked me his whereabouts I always said he was in the lavatory; I think people thought that he preferred to write there. So I had the room to myself, and all his filing cabinets, which were innocent of Corporation business.

There was a very large pile of letters for us both. I sorted out his and began looking through mine. I knew that somewhere there would be a memo from my Staff Mobility Officer. She is the woman who has the job of giving you bad news about your Corporation life. The good news you always know before she does. Sure enough, there was a pleasant, optimistic note, advising me yet again of the many advantages of working for *Pop Goes the Weasel*; there was no mention of the absence of other prospects.

'The team on *Pop*', she wrote, 'feel you will make a very valuable contribution to the programme, and appreciate the relevance of the experience you will bring to it.'

They clearly knew something about my experience that I didn't. *Pop Goes the Weasel* was a famous children's show. I could not have been more unsuitable. Perhaps they felt, somehow, that it would be relevant to have someone who knew nothing about children.

'You will, of course, continue to be paid at the RQR 411 rate, with an IRA as and when appropriate.' An IRA was an increased responsibility award, but a diminished responsibility reduction would have been more appropriate. However, I could not be seconded to *Pop* while I was officially working on another programme, especially a programme funded by a more prestigious section than the Young Persons Department.

I was not defeated yet. I walked into our Assistant Manager's Office. The sign on his door said AM.CA.TV, meaning Assistant Manager, Current Affairs, Television. The apparatchiks actually called each other by these acronyms.

'Which cutting room is Dan Cohen in?' I said.

'He's in 7011, with Hank. How was France?'

'Marvellous, absolutely marvellous,' I said. 'Apart from the corpse. Dan's very pleased. When can I see the rushes?'

'Anytime,' said the Assistant Manager. 'Fix it with Hank. Glad it all went well.'

'We'll have to go back, unfortunately,' I said. 'I'll call you when Dan's made a decision about it. Meanwhile we've got a lot to do.'

'Keep up the good work,' he replied brightly. He seemed relieved by my enthusiasm: he knew very well that Dan and I had both tried hard to avoid having anything to do with the film.

Hank was an old friend of mine. He'd been the film editor on many of the programmes I'd worked on. His cutting room was a disorderly tip on the seventh floor, a place where I felt completely at home, among filthy ashtrays, misplaced messages and spools of lost film.

'A sweet disorder in the mess,' he would say, waving his hands and shifting his weight on to the Cuban heels of his cowboy boots. He often brought in brownies or cold bread and butter pudding, which he would offer round, chain-smoking Gauloises himself. Above one of the work-benches he had a white chinagraph board on which he used to write comments that were made in his cutting room, during the endless arguments that go into making a film. It was his form of protest at some of the pretentiousness he had to listen to, day after day, in his smoky room.

When I went in that morning, Hank was holding up some film trims against the light, flicking the trailing ends round his wrist in the way film editors have, and staring at the narrow strip of pictures. Dan was sitting with his back to me at a Steenbeck editing machine. The nudes on the wall were the same, but there were some new remarks on the chinagraph board.

'Help yourself to some coffee,' said Hank, as if I hadn't been away.

'*If you want it, it works,*' I read out from the board. '*Until you make a film, you don't know how you don't want to it to be.*'

'How true,' said Hank. 'That was a trainee.'

'*We're not here to tell the truth. We're here to make a film,*' I read out again.

'Said in all earnestness. I kid you not,' said Hank.

'Probably one of Dan's,' I said. '*When in doubt, think vulgar.* Who was that?' I asked, but Hank had turned his back and was hanging up the trims on their numbered hooks.

'What's this?' I said, seeing some unfamiliar pictures on the Steenbeck.

Dan hardly looked up. He was clearly in a hurry.

'Just making a few changes to Dan's last film' said Hank. 'Transmission next Friday week.'

'What about the Lorraine rushes?' I asked Hank.

Hank spoke loudly to Dan, above the squeakings of the sound track running backwards and forwards.

'Do you want to see what you got in Lorraine? It's all here and ready.'

'Not really,' said Dan. 'Anyway, I must finish this first. Hello,' he said to me at last. 'Did you remember to bring in my duty-free cigarettes?'

'I can see you're very busy,' I said, 'but I've got a lot to tell you. It's very important.'

'I am busy,' Dan said. 'Can't it wait?'

'It could wait, but if you knew what it was, you wouldn't want to wait to hear.'

'A good try. What is it?'

I told him the story of the Comte's family. At first he seemed mildly impressed with it, but after a while his attention faded. I was surprised.

'Even if there is anything in it,' he said, looking not at me, but at the screen of the editing machine, 'which is highly doubtful, we're supposed to be making a film about Lorraine. That's the whole point. We can't extend the programme to the whole of bloody France.'

'Why not?' I asked. 'Plenty of programmes, as you damn well know, start with ballet in Bournemouth and end up with ice skating in Cumbria. Very often the Controller doesn't even notice.'

'Ha ha,' said Dan.

'This could be an outstanding programme.'

'Forget it,' said Dan. 'We've done our bit, tried our best to salvage a hopeless project, we've got the perfect out, and I'm going to take it.'

'Think again, Dan,' I said. 'Have I let you down before?'

'Forget it,' he repeated, and left the room to go to the coffee bar.

'You're on to a loser, pet,' said Hank. 'He wants it to fall through. It's Wagner,' he whispered dramatically. 'Slightly under the counter. Don't for heaven's sake say I mentioned it.'

Dan came back with a sandwich and a sausage roll. He looked preoccupied and pleased to be so.

'What's keeping you so busy?' I asked. 'It couldn't possibly be Wagner, could it?' I looked at Hank but his face was motionless: he was used to treachery.

'You accuse me of obsessions,' I said to Dan, 'but what about you – you've been stealing Corporation time and money for years for your pet obsession. Wagner. Does our esteemed Head of Staff Mobility know of your absorbing interest in an unbudgeted programme?'

Dan gave me one of those looks that reminded me that office politics are best left to other people.

'You're not the only person who is trying against the odds to get something done,' he said.'My Wagner film means a lot to me, it's worth putting up with all the shit that flies around this institution, just to achieve something like that. All right, so I'm cutting a few corners. You do it all the time. Listen, this could be good for both of us. Officially we're still doing the film. We have a project number. You carry on – Lorraine, Bordeaux, Club Méditerranée, for all I care, and I'll carry on. And if you get anything good, I'll drop everything.'

'You'll have to, you rat.'

'Why don't you shoot it yourself?' he said. 'If you get it. Do everyone a favour.'

'Except me,' said Hank. 'No, sorry, sweetie, I didn't mean it. I'm sure you'll bring me back some lovely footage. Very good idea.'

I thought so too.

I went back to my office and tried to deal with some of the mail that had accumulated. I sent some books back to the library and chased after some cans of archive film that had got lost somewhere. At lunchtime I bought a sandwich from one of the coffee bars in our building. It was an old-fashioned one, made of white pre-sliced bread and processed ham with some unidentifiable butter substitute. It surprised me that they were still making them like that. One or two friends drifted in and out. I received a few calls for the playwright and a few for myself. One of them was to remind me that I was supposed to go to an office party early that evening.

It was one of those occasions when some of the senior management try to mix democratically with some of the production staff. I don't know how the selection is made. It can't be random – pure chance could never throw up such an ill-assorted collection of people. I almost always enjoyed these occasions, despite their mysterious lack of direction. That evening, after a few drinks, I began to think with affection of the Corporation, and the strange opportunities and friendships it offers. If the price was often frustration and delay, it wasn't necessarily too high. I was in this elevated mood when the Head of Factual Programming came up to me.

'How's the collaboration film coming along?' he asked. I expressed the childish enthusiasm I thought appropriate.

'Extremely well,' I said, smiling at him. He was a reserved man in his late forties, both distant and tough. I imagined that he hated parties like this one. There was just a suggestion of detachment about him, unusual in television executives, which was attractive. But he was not a man to tell the truth to.

'Good, good,' he said. 'I was beginning to think you were losing your touch.' He laughed. 'Didn't you find a body or something?' he asked over his shoulder as he moved away, not waiting for an answer. 'We don't want too many of those.'

My expansive feelings disappeared. Soon afterwards I left the party. As I went out one of the secretaries told me that there was a message for me in my office. I wouldn't have gone back, except that I had to get my coat. It was a message to call a man whose name I didn't know, Andrew McAusland. Victoria, I thought, from the telephone number, and went home without doing anything about it.

When I finally got round to calling the number, it did turn

out to be in Victoria. My poolside colonel had been quick; the call from Mr McAusland was the result of our short conversation in the RAC Club. I never discovered what the connection was between them, but I suppose one wouldn't. McAusland identified himself rather vaguely and said he felt he could help me. I agreed to see him in an office in Victoria the next evening, after work.

The building where he arranged to meet me must have been designed to be unmemorable. There were no colours, no features: it made my own office block look positively rococo. He himself appeared completely unremarkable, a man without any special qualities. I felt very uncomfortable not knowing whether I was talking to the army, or the police or the secret service, or some hybrid in the quiet person of Andrew McAusland. But I didn't have any other leads.

He was polite and brief.

'I'm sorry I can't offer you a drink,' he said. 'It's all rather functional here. Now, how can I help?'

'I would love to know how you could help, and also who you are,' I replied.

'I don't want to be stuffy about this, but let's just say I might be able to offer you privileged information about the German occupation, the Vichy period and even possibly the aftermath. Depending on what you need to know, of course.'

'And depending on what I'm like, of course.'

'Oh, you're all right, according to our records. Despite those early indiscretions.'

'I thought you'd stopped security vetting us.'

'We have,' he said, giving me a look which left me in no doubt about the truth. 'But you must realize that you caused a little interest quite some time ago. Storm in a teacup of course. Unfortunate set to get into. It's very lucky for you you weren't in television at the time.'

'Well,' I said, after a pause, 'what I want is to find out as much about the Comte de Villancourt-le-Chapitre as you seem to know about me.'

Starting from the beginning, I explained my interest and my half-formed theories. For some reason I didn't include my thoughts about the body in the vaults at Nancy. Even to me the connection was beginning to seem implausible, and I didn't want to lose whatever credibility I had. Besides, I thought there was a lot I could find out for myself.

I couldn't tell what he thought of it all, but he promised to try to help and to get in touch later. It occurred to me to wonder why he was prepared to help, if he really was. He got up to show me out of the building.

'Isn't Henry Etherington your godfather?' he asked me over his shoulder as we walked down the passage to the lift. 'I should have thought he could have given you a few leads if you'd asked him. Wrong generation, of course.'

'I never see him,' I said. 'I don't think I've done him much credit.'

McAusland smiled as we stopped by the lift and pressed the button. He gave me one of those all-purpose rueful looks, which are so usefully ambiguous and which give an impression of comprehensive understanding. People like that make the world seem very small.

9

The next morning I woke up late in my flat. At first I was glad that it was the weekend. I wanted to be alone and to be left alone. There was nothing very high-minded about it. I wanted to wash my clothes and my hair, to feed hormones to my plants and light machine oil to my microdot printer. I wanted to empty the refrigerator and fill it again, and to read some of the papers and magazines that had piled up.

As I lay in bed I could just see London Bridge. It was not a morning to be cheerful; it looked damp and cold outside, the kind of weather that makes people wonder why they live in England. But I was very glad to be home again; my flat always surprised me with its space and calm, whenever I came back to it. I had bought it after my divorce, astonished by the settlement my solicitor negotiated. It must have been almost the end of the time when you could asset-strip rich husbands. Today I don't think I would have got anything. As it was, I hadn't expected anything. I hadn't really meant to get married in the first place and I certainly hadn't known that he was rich. But then I hadn't expected any of the rest of it either.

My solicitor had been very kind. 'Put it behind you – you're young enough. Think of yourself as twenty-one not twenty-three. Pretend it never happened,' he had said. Already it was a long time ago. But nothing that happens is ever forgotten; sooner or later everything will be remembered, or reconstructed or reinvented. Every sound we make is supposed to be squeaking homelessly in space, waiting for some past or future audience, and here on earth there seem to be more entries on computers than on our memories. My own meeting with McAusland, for instance.

'D for drugs,' I thought, as I lay on my once matrimonial

sheets. 'P for political activism, L for lies, G for guilt by association, E for computer error.'

All these possibilities lay at the back of my mind, ready to rise up whenever I felt weak. I got up.

My flat was neutral but there were a few objects in it that I had once shared. The time had passed when they still had any sympathetic magic, but the things that were worthless to me in that sense were, I now realized, very valuable. There was a stone Khmer head that I loved, a good-looking Bluthner piano that I couldn't play and two large rugs that I'd come to appreciate long after taking them from the matrimonial home. The few pieces of furniture I'd removed were probably quite good too, but then almost no one had seen them, so no one had been able to tell me. They were the last booby prizes of my ignorance and gullibility: they took a lot of polishing.

By 6 o'clock on Saturday I had had enough of being alone and I called one of the people who'd left messages on my answerphone. Guy Tufnell was a musician I'd known for a long time; he had recently abandoned an unhappy struggle with heterosexuality.

'Appalling timing,' he used to say bitterly. Guy was one of my walkers, just as I was one of his. Society women aren't the only people who need moral support from presentable people of another gender.

Guy wanted me to go with him to what sounded like an arty party in Chelsea. He tried to persuade me that it would be fun, but it didn't sound like my kind of thing.

'Anyway, Walkers' Rules,' he said firmly down the telephone. 'I particularly want to go to this.'

He took me to a large Edwardian studio in Chelsea. It was full of people that I wouldn't have been able to talk to at all if I had come as myself; as Guy's walker I found it quite easy to go up to them. I saw that Guy too, as my date, was less troubled by shyness. Besides, my presence gave his interests a slight camouflage.

Walkers' Rules also mean mutual protection. Guy came up to me later, as I was standing on my own with a nearly empty glass.

'Can I get you another drink?' he asked.

'No, thanks,' I said 'but point some people out to me. Who should I talk to?'

'What sort of person would you like to talk to?'

'Male,' I said.

'Darling heart, most of the men here are of my persuasion. Would you call that male?'

'Crested, not cloven, is what I mean,' I said.

'Well,' said Guy, 'there's Jonathan. He's quite sweet, he's a musician too. The man next to him is Martin, he's a set designer. Actually I don't think you'd like him – rather lesser-crested in my view. Those two over there are straight, but rather dull.'

'Don't be so nasty,' I said. 'I thought you were enjoying yourself.'

'I am.'

'Who's that?' I asked, pointing to a handsome three-quarter profile. We were interrupted by a woman dressed as a maid carrying a silver tray of well-made canapés. Guy and I helped ourselves to as many as we could in the time it took the maid to start disapproving of us. Another advantage of going out with a trusted walker is that you don't have to disguise your minor weaknesses.

'That's Duncan Lloyd,' said Guy. 'But you won't want to talk to him.'

'Why not? He looks rather interesting.'

'He's terribly glum.'

'Interestingly glum?'

'No, not really. Just another paranoid.'

'I'm surprised at you, Guy. Throwing the word paranoid around like an old-fashioned trendy.'

'It's not just my opinion, dear. Lots of people every bit as literate as you think he's paranoid. Clinically. He believes literally that everyone's against him, that his prospects have been deliberately blasted and so forth.'

'Well, perhaps everyone is against him. You seem to be.'

'Oh no, I'm not. I just find him rather tiresome. He's completely obsessed.'

'What does he do?'

'He's an art historian. He used to be quite a star.'

'And what happened?'

'I never knew exactly. It was a long time ago. He used to specialize in seventeenth-century French painting – maybe he still does, for all I know – and he got very worked up about some attributions, about one painting in particular. You know how people are. There was quite a scandal about it at the time. It was hugely valuable. Anyway, he took against this painting but everyone that mattered was for it – he isn't the only connoisseur around, after all – and he got very hot and cross about it all.'

Guy paused to make a sign to one of the maids to come over and refill our glasses, and while he watched her he continued, 'It didn't do Duncan's career any good. Practically finished him in fact. But then you'd have to be slightly mad to take on the art establishement in the first place, right or wrong.'

'Who was the painter?' I asked.

'Georges de La Tour,' he answered. 'You probably know all about it. There was quite a fuss,' he said a little absently, beginning to look attentively round the room.

'What a coincidence,' I said. 'I've just come back from Georges de La Tour country.'

Guy was hardly listening.

'Now are you going to be all right? Because I want to drift round a bit.'

'Just introduce me to Duncan Lloyd and those people with him first. Please. At least I'll have something to talk about.'

I don't think Duncan Lloyd liked Guy very much. He certainly gave him an unwelcoming look and avoided saying hello to me. He immediately picked up the conversation I had interrupted, which I could not follow, and half-turned his back to me. I had almost turned away myself when suddenly all three men with him moved off, leaving me alone with Lloyd.

'Do tell me,' I said, wincing at the tones of my early training, 'what *The Flea Catcher* in the museum at Nancy is really doing. And how many fleas there really are?'

Lloyd looked at me with dislike, and was silent for quite a long time.

'I'm no longer very interested in Georges de La Tour,' he said.

'You can't really have lost all interest in him,' I said. 'Not in the mysterious *Flea Catcher*, anyway.'

'It's hardly for you to say what must or must not interest me,' he said, with a small smile.

'Of course not,' I said hurriedly. 'It's just that I've recently got back from Lorraine and it's very hard to escape the subject – it's like Thomas Hardy and Dorset. You know, Thomas Hardy tea-towels, Georges de La Tour Christmas cards.'

It was obvious that the man was not enjoying my company, and I was certainly not enjoying his, but the more I wanted to walk away the faster I talked. Early training in cocktail party drill dies hard.

'I don't know which is worse,' I hurried on, 'except that even Dorset could not produce a hotel as depressing as the one we stayed in. Do you know the Choucroute in Nancy? Presumably you've been to Lorraine quite often for research. I imagine you must know it well.'

'Hardly at all. I haven't been there for years,' he said, very rudely, and then his manner softened. Perhaps he felt that such rudeness was wasted on me.

'What were you doing there?' he asked.

'I was there with a film crew. We were making a documentary about the German occupation.'

'Which one?' he asked, more, I thought, to show his feeling about Germans than to prolong his conversation with me.

'1940s' I said.

'I'd be surprised if you get very far with that,' he said.

'You're right. And not only that. Not only did the programme fall through. We had a very unpleasant experience in the departmental archives.'

'In the archives?' he asked, surprised.

'Yes, in a very old vault where most of the manuscripts are kept. There were various documents from the early forties we wanted to film and we wanted some atmosphere. In fact we got a great deal too much. I almost tripped over a body – a very dead body. Rather smelly, with its head beaten to a pulp – brains and gore and splintered bone. Apparently it was the caretaker.'

I have never seen a man turn white so quickly. It seemed as if he were on the point of fainting. My first thought was that he must be unusually squeamish. But then I realized I had spoken very stupidly.

'I'm sorry,' I began to say, but he had already turned unsteadily away.

I had been both boring and tactless and I longed to go, so I was very glad to see from Guy's face across the room that he'd had enough too. We found our host, talking with alcoholic vigour in the minstrels' gallery, and said goodbye. Guy and two of his friends took me for an Indian meal in Pimlico, and after a while, and a few more drinks, I forgot my embarrassment. Walkers need thick skin. But, of course, if they had thick skin, they wouldn't need walkers themselves.

10

After a few days at Wireless House, doing very little, I got Dan to authorize another trip for me to Nancy. I didn't admit to the apparatchiks that the police had warned us off; in any case it was now nearly a fortnight since they'd begun their investigation. I still hadn't heard from Mr McAusland, and Marie-Blanche had nothing new to tell me. Dan took very little interest.

'When this programme wins an award for investigative journalism,' I said to him in Hank's cutting room, 'I am going to be the one whose hand gets shaken.'

'Fine by me,' said Dan. 'My own wrist will be limp from hours of handshakings and congratulations on my Wagner film.'

'Both very much in the planning stages, as of now, wouldn't you say?' said Hank, sitting at the picture synchronizer.

I laughed, but Dan became irritable.

'Do what you like,' he said. 'Anything, as long as you stay in France for a long time.'

So I found myself in Nancy again, in a bedroom in the Hôtel Choucroute. Despite my written requests to our production assistant to avoid the Choucroute she had booked me in there again. Perhaps it was the best our budget would stretch to. Perhaps, despite appearances, Dan was being careful. If anything the Choucroute was even more depressing than before; the management was modernizing and had decided to rip apart the front lobby and reception area, which almost completely obstructed the stairs.

'Change and decay in all around I see,' I thought immediately. That's the trouble with an old-fashioned Anglican upbringing; always a cheap sentiment ringing in one's ears. My thoughts are often disturbed by lines from austere hymns, or irrelevant exhortations. 'Fight the good fight. Who sweeps a room as for thy laws . . . What profit is there in my blood? To him that overcometh on earthly battlefields, to him that hath, from him that hath not, faint not nor fear, abide with me, fast falls the eventide.' That was true enough, I thought, looking at my cocktail glass. The Hôtel Choucroute didn't offer much, but it did serve good dry Martinis, which seems to be unusual in France.

It must have been about 7 o'clock and you don't need an Anglican upbringing to tell you that it's better not to drink alone. I went downstairs and sat at the bar. No matter how much practice I get, I cannot get used to sitting alone in a bar, and after half an hour of feeling both neglected and harassed, I went back to my room. I ordered a sandwich from room service and ate it in front of the television.

It was still raining the next morning and I got lost in the heavy traffic in my hire car. Finally I found what I was looking for: 6 rue de l'Echelle. It was the address of the caretaker's sister which the director of the archives had given the police. The house was a tall, elaborately decorated Belle Epoque building, typical of that part of Nancy. I thought in passing that it was probably unique and would make a good documentary.

I rang the bell marked Joly and after a long time the front door opened. I saw a plain, elderly woman wearing an apron. She seemed a little out of breath.

'I have come to offer you my condolences, Mademoiselle Joly,' I said. 'I am sorry to say I am the person who discovered your brother's body in the archives.'

She said nothing but moved her head to acknowledge what she'd heard and she held her mouth closed firmly, but whether it was an expression of grief I couldn't tell.

'I am so very sorry,' I said.

'The police have told me not to speak to anyone,' she said at last.

'Of course,' I said. 'They've told me exactly the same thing. They've been very kind, but unfortunately, as I am a complete stranger here, I was unable to help them at all. It's just that I was very sorry to leave Nancy without paying you a visit, and as I'm passing through again, I thought I might come now.'

Her immobile face gave me no encouragement but I persisted.

'May I come in?' I asked.

'Yes, certainly, come in,' she said, apparently unable to think of a good reason why not.

She walked in front of me, up four flights of stairs to the top of the house, and let me into her flat. It was very modestly decorated and very clean. On her own ground Mademoiselle Joly became talkative.

'What will you take? Will you take a cup of tea? The English always drink tea, don't they?'

I followed her into a small kitchen and listened as she moved around preparing tea. Her accent was slightly difficult for me to understand, unlike the clear, witty voice of Claude Mesnil.

'It must have been nasty for you too, very nasty.'

'I am really very sorry,' I said. 'Were you very close to your brother?'

'Of course I was, certainly, he was my brother, what do you expect? Of course that's not to say we saw eye to eye on things. We didn't. And what I regret is that I didn't see very much of him, one way and another. I blame myself for that.'

'I am sure you shouldn't blame yourself,' I said, without sincerity.

'To think he died with no one in the world but me, and if I saw him once a month it's as much as I did.'

'I am very sorry,' I repeated.

'And what are the police doing?' she asked aggressively. 'There's plenty of "don't leave the town" and "don't touch his belongings", but what have they got to show for it?'

'I'm sure they're doing their best,' I said.

'Maybe they are,' she said. 'That's not the same as having common sense, is it? I can't for the life of me think why they bother themselves with the war, that's all over long since.'

'With the war?'

'Oh, yes, if you can believe it. "Had Monsieur Joly any enemies from the time of the occupation? Had Monsieur Joly any secrets from long ago?" I ask you. And these young men were not even born at the time.'

'Surely the two senior detectives, at least, are older?'

'True, yes, they must be.'

The caretaker's sister put two cups of tea and some biscuits on a tray and took it into the living room.

'Anyway, I don't know why they can't leave it alone. It's true Bertrand never had many friends. He was always a bit of a loner, I don't know why. But I'm quite certain it has nothing to do with the war, with anything during the forties. Who here isn't guilty of something? But my poor brother never had the nerve to take anybody's side.'

I was nodding encouragingly at her, unnaturally fast, like a radio interviewer.

'He was always a solitary person?' I asked.

'Oh, yes, poor man. He never married. And he was a lonely boy too. He was never particularly happy, always complaining, but I think he was quite content at the archives. I suppose lately he started complaining at bit more, he was getting a bit fed up. I think his memory was going; he couldn't adjust to all these new systems, especially recently. He was never a librarian in the first place, always being sent all over the shop to find papers and documents, things being sent up to Metz and back, and they're not light, some of those books and files they have. Of course he was never healthy, we never ate good food when we were young, the way they do now. In the war it was desperate of course, there was real hunger, you can imagine the Boche almost starved us. So if you smuggled some eggs or some butter, well, one's got to live. Everyone did that.'

Having started to speak at last, she seemed unable to stop. She repeated the same thoughts again and again. It was not just her brother who had been lonely, I thought. After a few inconclusive attempts to leave, I stood up almost rudely and she finally showed me to the door.

As I walked down the stairs with their elegant iron banisters I was both encouraged and discouraged. I was discouraged by the narrow images of Mademoiselle Joly's life; I was even more cast down by her insistence that her brother could not possibly have been the victim of some long-standing grudge from the past. But I was very much encouraged to think that the police were still interested in that possibility. It would be such an easy way to make a film; to tell the story of the murder and its investigation. That by itself would make a shape for a documentary.

My next appointment was with Claude Mesnil. After a lot of

misgivings I had called him the night before. I had been worried that he might feel he ought to report my presence to his friends in the police. Equally, I thought he might be persuaded not to. So I had arranged to meet him at the Café Saint-Roch, which is near his faculty at the university. He was already sitting at a table waiting when I walked in. He made me welcome, standing up in his English Burberry and holding a chair for me.

'To what do I owe this pleasure?' he asked, because I hadn't explained why I had come back. 'It is journalistic persistence?'

I was uncertain how frank to be.

'Yes, I suppose so. Just one last attempt to resurrect our programme.'

'I'm afraid you may have had a wasted journey,' said Claude. 'All the contacts and interviews you set up are even less likely to materialize now than before. I mean, everyone is even less likely to cooperate with you.'

'Why?'

'Of course, I myself find it difficult to understand,' he said, laughing at me with charm. 'But unfortunately you personally, and the Corporation team as well, are associated in people's minds with this terrible murder, with publicity, with everything that no one wants. The papers have been full of it, as you can imagine.'

' Yes, of course,' I said.

'It's unfair, of course,' he said. 'I am sure you and Dan would have done a very good job, would have been unbiased. I really have done my best for you. I have great faith in your ability, if I may say so. But, as I said, I think you are wasting your time.'

'What about the murder?' I asked.

'How do you mean?' he asked in return, with a slight expression, I thought, of distaste, or something like it.

'I mean, is it still a mystery? Any arrests? What do the police think?'

'It seems from the papers that they incline to your view.' He smiled faintly. 'But of course they're being very discreet.'

'Would you advise me to talk to them?' I asked.

'If you want my honest opinion, no. They were quite pleasant on the morning you discovered the body, but I can't imagine they want to see more of you or any journalist. If you want, I'm quite prepared to speak to Monsieur Drouet on your behalf. The senior detective.'

'I've already been warned off, actually.'

'Oh,' he said. 'Well, I don't suppose they'll have changed their minds. How very frustrating for you. Have you got any other interesting projects in mind?'

It irritated me that Claude Mesnil should assume that that was the end of the subject. I certainly wasn't defeated yet. After we had said goodbye I went into a pharmacy close to the café and bought a small haircomb and some tinted glasses. In the car park, looking into the mirror of my hire car, I used the comb to pin my hair up very tightly, and I put on the glasses. It seemed to me that I looked quite different or at least older. I felt rather foolish resorting to these amateur sleuthing tricks, in a cold and windy car park in provincial France. But I wanted to visit the archives without being recognized, and I couldn't think of any other way.

The building was a short walk from the car park. When I went through the glass doors into the reception area and saw the door to the vault on the right, I had once again the feeling of playing a child's game of pretend in a world that was unpleasantly grown up. That is an occupational hazard of working in television.

I walked on towards the modern section: it was full of quiet readers, mostly middle-aged or elderly. The air was hushed, thickened with that unconvincing respect for learning that you get in libraries. I began by going to the newspaper stand. From there I could look at the recent coverage of the murder in the local papers and I could also try and make some sort of plan. What I wanted was to look at the visitors' book, if they had one. I had never seen one on my previous visits, but then I had come with various letters of introduction and perhaps it wouldn't have arisen.

The local newspapers had indeed been full of the murder. There were even pictures of Dan and me and the entire film crew which had been taken when we first arrived: but among all the big headlines and the statements from officials there was very little information. Bertrand Joly was much as he had been described to me already. He had lived in a little flat attached to the main building of the archives. Nobody seemed to have any opinions about him. The few fragments of his life gave me the same impression of sadness and solitariness as meeting his sister had done. The time of death was thought to have been late at night on 14 February.

It seemed to me that there was a chance of learning something from discovering who had been the last to visit the library before the murder. To the obsessive mind it was a long shot; even if there was a visitors' book, it didn't follow that everyone signed it. It was very unlikely that the murderer would have signed it, even assuming he was an outsider in the first place. But it was possible that the people who saw the caretaker in his last hours at work might be able to reveal something. And it would almost certainly put me on the same trail as the police.

To start with I had to have a good excuse for being in the library at all. I tried to think of some completely non-controversial subject that someone might reasonably be interested in. There are so few. After a while I thought of pottery. Lorraine has some well-known faience made in Lunéville and Saint-Clément and it probably does interest some people. I went up to the woman at the desk and explained that I was curious about the local faience industry and its history. As I spoke I noticed that there was indeed a large visitors' book on her desk.

The woman was encouraging and offered to explain the library's index system to me, so that I could look up whatever I needed. She led me to a long row of wooden cabinets in the centre of the room and I had to wait, only half listening, while she kindly outlined the system in simple French. I spoke very little in what I hoped was a slightly disguised voice, with some success; the woman asked me whether I was American or English.

'I come from Wales,' I said, lying.

'Oh, how nice,' she said.

After a while she left me to the index by myself and I started watching and waiting. Occasionally I pretended to write something down. It must have been over an hour, certainly nearly lunchtime, before the woman was called out of the room. I quickly went over to her desk, put my notes and papers in an untidy pile and pretended to wait for her to come back. Behind my pile of papers, hoping that no one was interested, I opened the visitors' book and looked at the dates. There was nothing at all listed for 14 February, nor for the 13th or 12th. So much for that, I thought with disappointment and an exhausted frustration that came from years of dead ends like that.

Then I remembered the strike. Of course it was not mentioned in the visitors' book and the newspapers had obviously been playing it down too, or I wouldn't have forgotten. The strike had ended the day before I found the body, on the 21st, and must have begun, I supposed, on the last day for which there were visitors' signatures. If so, he had been killed late at night two days after the strike had begun. And I had found him a week later.

I tried to imagine his life. With the entire building closed, with nobody officially there, he must have been off duty, only there because his home was there. I wondered whether from his flat the emptiness and sombreness of the old buildings was palpable. As I stood by the desk I copied down the names of the visitors in reverse order, going backwards in time for several days. It is quite difficult when you are reading upside down. Mostly the same names came up several times. French names from Nancy or Lunéville or other nearby towns and villages, as far as I could tell. There was one German-sounding name, Bob Kitzinger; its owner had been there all week and had given simply the name of his town, Resolution City, USA.

I had finished writing and had almost shut the book when the librarian returned.

'I'm sorry to keep you waiting,' she said. 'I do apologize. We have a few staff problems, somebody new.'

'Not at all,' I said. 'I've only just finished for this morning. Should I sign your visitors' book?'

'Oh no,' she said, 'that's not really necessary. Not unless you actually place a request for books to be fetched, or need to go to the shelves yourself. We just like to keep a record of it.'

I thanked her, picked up my pile of papers and left.

In the hire car I took off the uncomfortable glasses and looked at the map to see how to get Vic-sur-Seille, where we'd all had dinner the night before we went to the archives. I had made an appointment by letter to see a woman in Vic I knew nothing about: before I had first come to Lorraine, I had put together a list of people to contact and she was the only one left that I had never seen. Someone – I could now no longer remember who – had recommended her very highly. My notes simply said she was a housewife in Vic, worth visiting, but no reason was given. At least she didn't know me from before and she might, conceivably, be able to help me learn something about the people who'd signed the visitors' book.

Her name was Madame Cernay. I stood for a long time in the porch of her house, waiting for someone to answer the bell. It was a large, slightly shabby house, covered in old creepers and surrounded by an austere small garden with a dying palm tree and a wooden bench. At last a pleasant-looking woman of about sixty-five came to the door.

'Oh, hello,' she said, trying at the same time to keep back two lively dogs. 'You must be the lady from the television company. I've been expecting you. Please come in, this way. Don't mind the dogs; they're very sweet-tempered really, just a little rough, that's right, yes, come in, come in.' She talked so fast and was so preoccupied with the dogs that she didn't give me a moment to speak. Her French was exceptionally easy to follow but she spoke in a very heavy accent which I had never heard before. I thought it might be German.

'It's very kind of you to find the time,' I began, but before I could finish she started laughing and interrupted me.

'Who'd have thought it?' she said in a pronounced Lancashire accent. 'I was expecting a Frenchwoman. From the name, you see. And you're as English as I am. I'm a Lancashire woman, born and bred. How funny. I thought the television people would be sending one of their French representatives, or whatever they have. Anyway, come in and tell me what I can do for you.'

'What is a Lancashire woman doing in Vic-sur-Seille?' I asked.

'In the back of beyond, you mean?' she asked with good humour. 'It does seem a little like a ghost town, doesn't it? But it was an important place, a few hundred years ago. It's rather lovely, isn't it?'

Madame Cernay took me into the house, pressed me to have a cup of tea and went away to the kitchen to make it.

'In some ways,' she said, when she came back into her sitting room, 'I've become completely French. If I say it myself, I don't think you'll taste better quiche lorraine than this anywhere in France. But I've never really lost my English accent, and I always say that tea isn't tea if it isn't English.'

She gave me a cup of strong Ceylon tea with milk and sugar. She was right about the quiche; it bore no resemblance to what usually goes by that name: eating my quiche and drinking my canteen tea, listening to Madame Cernay's pleasant north country voice, I saw through the window the floodlit ruins of a sixteenth-century castle keep, overgrown with weeds. That was one of the more subtle pleasures of Corporation life, a recurring sense of pleasant absurdity.

Madame Cernay told me that she had first met her French husband by post. They had been pen pals as teenagers before the war and they had met in England during the war: he had come to London to join the Free French and he'd brought her back to Vic as a bride after the war. I was moved by her story and more relieved than I could have imagined to meet an Englishwoman, so I told her much more than I meant to. She was kind in return, but impatient too.

'I know that everyone keeps on telling you to drop all this,' she said, finally, 'and it must be very frustrating for you. But all the same I think you should. Can't you see that it's never been simple, especially not here? If my husband were still alive he'd tell you things that would make a wonderful story, as you put it, but if you heard them I don't think you'd really want to repeat them. You may think I'm just a nasty old woman but I think there are only two reasons why people do things, when all's said and done – greed and fear. And if it's fear, and it almost always was, you know, as far as I can make out, why can't you be merciful? Do you think that you are above fear yourself?'

'No,' I said, 'but as you said before, things are never

simple. And I don't believe that anyone has to be merciful about killing an old man like that.'

Madame Cernay sighed. I knew very well that she meant something different, that she was concerned for the feelings of all the bystanders, of all those only marginally affected, who would be exposed, humiliated, forced to remember some minor ignominy, some failure of courage or loyalty, some old and terrible dilemma.

'Of course,' said Madame Cernay, 'nothing is simple. What is it you want?'

I must have expected to find someone who had lived in Lorraine all her life; at any rate I was disappointed that she hadn't and felt that she probably couldn't help very much. In herself she provided something surprising, something I had been missing, a refuge and a sense of trust, but I couldn't imagine how she could help me. All the same, I told her about my list copied from the archives visitors' book and, to my delight, a naughty expression appeared on her face.

'I won't tell,' she said, laughing. 'Let's have a look at it.'

I showed it to her, but she couldn't tell me much about it. She said the addresses were all local; those that were not actually in Nancy were in towns and villages not far away, as I had thought. Beyond that she knew nothing. But she made a suggestion which turned out to be very useful, in the end. She suggested that I should go and see Mademoiselle Autran at the archives in Lunéville:

'There's very little she doesn't know and she must be over seventy. If she likes you, she might help you. You can say I sent you.'

'Madame Cernay, I think I ought to tell you I'm going to use another name – my own might be recognized, especially in the archives – presumably they're connected to the archives at Nancy – and I've been in the paper.'

'Have you, love?' she said, clearing up the plates and cups, putting on a good performance of inattention.

'I must have missed that. And I missed what you just said,' she went on, straightening up and looking at me firmly. 'But don't let Mademoiselle Autran down, or you'll make me ashamed of being English.'

11

I drove into Lunéville late the next morning. At last the rain had stopped; the sky was still dark and metallic but the gloom was lifted by a wintry February light. I parked in a side street, found a side entrance to the gardens of the former ducal palace and walked that way towards the old centre of the town. The château had been built in miniature imitation of Versailles, but all its splendour had long since been lost: the gardens leading towards the ugly building were plain and bare, with empty fountains, deserted except for three workmen pollarding the trees in an alley of willows.

Dressed all the same, in French workman's blue, two held a ladder while the third chopped slowly at the stunted bole of the tree. They were so perfectly placed, and the uniform blue so strong against the dead colours of winter, that they appeared to be posing for a camera. I wished I had one. It is a disease of television, trying to frame reality into shots and then, because of that, finding it implausibly picturesque. The workmen in their formations of vertical lines and neat placements of colour seemed as if they were there for my benefit, to give a suggestion of symmetry and purpose to what was a very pedestrian and almost certainly pointless visit to some provincial archives.

The entrance to the Lunéville library is almost hidden in a little courtyard at the side of an ambitious baroque church, in a pleasant architectural jumble. I went up some wooden stairs like an Oxford college staircase and found myself in a very tall airy room filled with small children sitting at tiny tables and chairs. They appeared to be laughing and talking without supervision, but at the end of the room, serenely ignoring the noise, was an elderly woman, who was obviously Mademoiselle Autran. She was a French version of the spinsters of my childhood, angular, clever and diffident, who somehow knew the score but didn't want to settle it.

I introduced myself to her, using another name.

'Madame Cernay said you might very kindly help me.'

'Ah, yes, Madame Cernay. An old friend, and also English, of course.'

I suppose the world does divide into those you deceive willingly and those you can't. Mademoiselle Autran, with her expression of resignation and intelligence, was certainly not a woman to give a false name to, and I felt uneasy in her company, especially as she was generous with her time.

'Now, where can we go to have a little peace and quiet?' she asked, glancing at the noisy children and summoning a young woman from the adult section in another room.

'Come with me,' she said firmly, leading me into another, older room, equally high, with elaborate wooden book-shelves on all sides and a wooden gallery high up, through passages of stacked papers and documents on iron racks and finally into a tiny office. The library had an atmosphere of the past, as if there were all kinds of possibilities there; it had escaped the sacerdotal fug of most libraries. I asked Mademoiselle Autran if I might take her out to lunch and after some protestation she agreed: I wondered what she normally did.

We found ourselves in one of those small, serious-minded restaurants you always read about but rarely discover. It was quiet and smart, with a small menu and large linen table-napkins. Without embarrassment, Mademoiselle Autran considered very seriously what to eat and advised me carefully before returning the rituals of first meeting. I began by saying how much I admired the library, and how congenial the atmosphere was.

'Yes, well, we really are quite proud. It's not just a library, of course, we are the municipal archives. There is a great deal in the archives, they're really very rich. We still have quite a lot of material that has to be re-sorted: we've been having a reorganization of the system. And then of course there are quite a lot of documents that have never really been dealt with since they arrived.'

'What sort of things?'

'Absolutely everything, but what you might call little things – birth, marriage, death and property. Law suits, baptisms, engagements, communal expenses, taxes, epidemics. Of course you would have quite a lot of those things in your church records, but naturally we don't.'

My idea of the French Revolution doesn't go much further than old women knitting at the side of the guillotine, shouting 'A bas les aristos', but I could vaguely imagine how old church records had come into the hands of the state, along with the confiscation of the property of the church and of the rich. Stray thoughts about library life did not interest me very much, but Mademoiselle Autran was an enthusiast.

'Yes, we probably have more than we really appreciate. Of course, from time to time we do have little discoveries – nothing terribly important, perhaps, from the point of view of the outside world, but none the less, of great excitement to us, in the sleepy world of the archivist. In fact a colleague of mine discovered a document about our great local painter, Georges de La Tour – well, I suppose it must be ten years ago now, and actually it was in the Archives Départementales at Nancy.'

'Oh, how interesting. What was the document about?'

'It wasn't much really, in itself. It was a legal document describing a law suit that he had brought, or if it wasn't him it must have been someone in his family: it was all to do with someone who hadn't paid for a painting, or couldn't pay. It was a painting of the Magdalen, that I do remember clearly. So you see, that was really quite a find. And of course we always have one or two academic researchers, and the students from the university, the more serious ones that is. And then we have the mormons.'

Mademoiselle Autran wiped her long upper lip on her napkin.

'The mormons?' I asked in astonishment. I thought this must be a French word that I'd never heard, meaning something to do with research.

'Yes, certainly, the mormons,' she replied, delicately using a piece of bread to finish the sauce of her dish of mussels.

'You mean the American Mormons, the religious sect?'

'Yes, exactly.'

73

'What on earth for?'

'Oh, my dear, it's very odd, but they're so good about everything, so one can hardly complain. Very meticulous, scrupulously careful with all our things whether it's just a pamphlet or an old document. They're great experts and very easy to deal with, you see.'

'Yes,' I said,' but why are they here at all?'

'Oh,' said Mademoiselle Autran, 'I suppose we've got so used to it that I thought everybody knew. They're ancestor hunting.'

I laughed with pleasure at the thought.

'Oh no,' said Mademoiselle Autran. 'It's not what you think. It's not snobbery. It's a religious belief. According to their way of thinking, they have to baptize their dead ancestors, rebaptize them in the true faith, and for that they need to know who they were. Or anyway, something like that. For Americans they are extremely pleasant.'

Our next course had arrived and we thought about that for a while. We'd both chosen rabbit casserole and it had arrived on the local pink and white plates, with three different purées of vegetable, dark pink beetroot, cream-coloured celeriac and bright orange carrot. In the face of this tricoloured cornucopia, I began to think I should be back at Wireless House, instead of greedily feeding my fantasies at the Corporation's expense. Mademoiselle Autran pressed me to have some out-of-season new potatoes. When she'd taken some herself, we returned to the Mormons.

'Nice as they are,' she said, 'it can be a little inconvenient. They have to see some of the oldest documents and that takes extra time and attention. It's quite funny sometimes – we can't be in three places at once and it slows things down. It drives some of the historians mad. You see it's only quite recently that they've started coming. Professor Mesnil was very funny about it – perhaps you've heard of our distinguished Professor Claude Mesnil?'

'Yes, indeed,' I said.

'He was quite surprised when I told him they were coming. "What?" he said to me. "I thought they came, saw and conquered at least three years ago. Surely they're not coming again." When I assured him they were he said, "Surely even

for the Mormons the dead cannot miraculously multiply."
Miraculously multiply! Such a wit, the professor, and a
charming man. He'd never admit it, but I think he secretly
resents it. Anyway, he's a dear man, and a bit of a tease too.
"Ah, Mademoiselle Autran," he said to me, "now you have a
permanent excuse. If we find a little disorder in the archives,
we shall no longer say Mademoiselle Autran is taking long
lunch hours – we shall just blame the Mormons." Quite
unfair, of course, to me and to the Mormons, but the professor likes a joke.'

This was getting me nowhere, though I was touched,
briefly, by her susceptibility to the charm of Claude Mesnil.
But before I could start trying to manoeuvre the conversation
Mademoiselle Autran herself apologized suddenly for gossiping.

'You must understand,' she said, 'the archives have been a
life-long obsession. Now tell me how I can help you.'

I admitted to her much more than I'd planned, including
the fact that the police had told me to stay away from the
murder. I even confessed my lie and told her my real name.
That turned out to be a good move; for some reason she
became an ally, although she said she couldn't help me very
much.

I showed her the list I'd copied down. 'These are the last
outsiders who might have seen the caretaker at work,' I said.
'People who signed the book in the last few days before the
strike, and might therefore have had his help – either going
with him to the restricted shelves, or getting him to fetch
them something, possibly from the vaults.'

'If someone went in there with a guilty motive you'd hardly
expect him to sign the visitors' book,' said Mademoiselle
Autran.

'True,' I said, 'and of course it's unlikely that the murderer
went there at all. But something might emerge.'

Mademoiselle Autran looked sceptical, but she took the
list and read it carefully.

'All these I know,' she said. 'They're all regular visitors
here, too. This one is writing a book, had been for years, this
one is a teacher, so is she, and those are all from the university. I would bet my life against any of them having anything

75

to do with it. They're all local, and all much too young, in any case.'

The waiter cleared our plates and brought two menus again, but this time Mademoiselle Autran was too interested in our discussion to pay attention.

'The only one I don't know is this one, the foreigner with the German name. Kitzinger. It could be anything, a name like that. German, American, Jewish perhaps, from anywhere.'

She looked up at me above her silver-rimmed bifocal glasses. Her expression was mixed; I could see curiosity mixed with reluctance.

'It's not that I won't help you. It's that there's nothing I can tell you. You could go and see these people, I suppose. But seriously, the police know all this, it's a matter for the police. They've probably already spoken to all these people, and many, many more. And whether the police have got to them or not, I don't suppose any of them would talk to you. It's true there are quite a few guilty secrets – my own feeling is against secrets. I prefer the light of common day, as they say. But no one is going to tell them to you, not after a murder.'

We finished our delicious lunch, talking of other subjects. Mademoiselle Autran had a pudding made from chestnut purée and cream and I had some of the local Munster cheese. I walked back with her to the courtyard of the archives and said goodbye. As I drove back towards Nancy, I wondered why it is that people are always so persuaded that no one will talk. If they were right, the television screen and the tabloids would be empty; the truth is that most people want to reveal themselves in public – warts, excess body hair, guilty secrets and all. Even the police talk, sometimes.

On a brief wave of aggression and self-esteem I stopped at a bar on the outskirts of Nancy and called the police. It was a stupid impulse. I asked to speak to Inspector Drouet, but he didn't come to the telephone. Instead I got a man whose name and title I didn't quite catch; guessing, I decided he was superior to Monsieur Drouet. This time the police did not talk. On the contrary I was told, yet again, to go away.

'Could you just tell me how far you have got with your investigations?' I asked, thinking I had nothing to lose by being importunate. 'Is is true that you do not yet have a suspect?'

'I am not prepared to discuss this case with you, but before you work yourself up into a journalistic frenzy about the French police, I will admit that that's true. We don't anticipate an arrest at this point.'

I persisted.

'Why has there been so little coverage of this in the local press? And', I asked, guessing again, 'in the national press?'

I may have imagined it, but it seemed to me that the man at the other end of the line hesitated. When he spoke he seemed to be controlling something – anger, annoyance or perhaps fear. On the other hand he might have been eating a sandwich and pretending he wasn't.

'You've been asked once before to stay away from all this, and I'm asking you again. You realize that I have the power to enforce this request, but I'm sure that won't be necessary. The need of your organization for our good will and your own good sense will make you see that. Professor Mesnil assures me that you are a very reasonable person; let us leave it at that.'

There's a tradition of foot-in-the door insistence that I've always felt uneasy about, and for that reason I always force myself to it at the most inopportune moment.

'Can't you just tell me,' I asked, 'whether you suspect any connection with the period of the German occupation?'

'Goodbye, mademoiselle,' he replied politely, and put the telephone down.

Turning away from the telephone, I went up to the cashier and gave back two telephone tokens. The bar was empty, in the middle of the afternoon; the barman was silently wiping sugar and damp marks off the shining counter. He glanced up at me as though he, too, would prefer me to go away without bothering him. So I walked to the door, went outside to my hire car, and drove to the university, hoping to find Claude Mesnil to say goodbye. I suppose I also needed a little encouragement, a little flattery to lift my mood.

He was writing on a blackboard and talking to a small group of teenagers, who were taking notes. Perhaps it was from a motive like my own that he spoke to me in English: a man like that could hardly avoid indulging in a little vanity, especially in front of his submissive students. I was not surprised, but irritated, to discover that his English was very much better than my French, though perhaps a little too correct to seem fluent.

In any case his students were duly impressed. He turned back to them for a moment.

'Continue taking down the different forms of the letter "s" and notice the distinction between cursive script and print,' he said to them in French.

Switching back to English he spoke quietly to me. 'I hope it's nothing urgent.'

'Not really,' I said. 'Please forgive me for interrupting. It's just that I've finally had my wrist slapped by the police, and I've got to go home. I wanted to catch you to say goodbye before I go, but I should have telephoned: you're obviously busy.'

He shrugged very slightly, to convey many graceful meanings. Poor Geneviève, I thought. A charming husband is not always the best sort to have.

'Take care of yourself,' he said, touching my arm. 'Why don't you choose a more restful subject next time? You look a bit tired. Something with which I could help you. Modern history is not really my pidgin. And be sure to let me know if you come this way again.'

I thanked him again and we shook hands: as I walked out I saw him turn back to his class and to the hieroglyphs on the blackboard.

12

It was late in the afternoon when I got back to the hotel, the time that passes for rush hour in Nancy, and it was almost dark. The Choucroute itself seemed to be in a kind of electrical dusk; perhaps the rebuilding was creating problems and making the lights flicker at half strength. At the desk I told them I was leaving, but they said I had already missed the Paris connection to London. So I had to spend another night at the hotel. I pushed past the builders' equipment and went up the stairs to my room to pack; into the bottom of my case I put my Corporation tape recorder and Polaroid camera, my Corporation stopwatch and my Corporation red notebooks. On top of them I folded up the ambiguous collection of clothes which seem to deal with most of the situations I get into.

I'm used to lonely hotel bedrooms, or as much as I will ever be, but I could have done without the dim lighting that evening. The shadows in the room had changed and deepened, and touched on that despondency which is also just a loss of energy. I remembered something that usually only comes back to me in the open air – that I am afraid of the dark. The small bedside light was quite strong, but the main light finally gave out altogether and I found myself suddenly in the obscure lighting of Georges de La Tour's *Flea Catcher*; exactly like her, I was alone in a bedroom lit only by one small light, surrounded by deep shadows thickening into darkness. And like her, I suppose, I was contemplating, thinking about a combination of last things and domestic trivia.

The other La Tours I could remember were also lit in the same way, with a single candle and dramatic contrasts of light and shade. That sort of scene went down very well in the early seventeenth century, a very commerical proposition. It's still very popular today – accessible, as people say. Of course those La Tour effects are entirely fake. Rick, our cameraman, would have been able to say how he'd achieved them, how many other lights he would have needed to suggest the illumination of the single candle, how much infilling. For all Rick's faults, he certainly is one of the best lighting cameramen in television.

I went and sat at the dressing table and looked into the three-sided mirror to see whether I was still there and whether I looked any older. I was, and I didn't, but I was. All I needed was a skull under my hand and a candle – the biblical precious ointment was already there in the shape of my expensive moisturizer – and I would be a dead ringer for a La Tour St Mary Magdalen, contemplating her own mortality. I wouldn't have put my past quite in her bracket, but there was enough to regret to justify a few penitential wrinkles.

My face in the mirror was curiously opaque, as if I were holding out on myself. My expression offered me no clues of the sort I would have looked for in somebody else's face, to what I really wanted or really thought. I did not seem to offer myself any recommendations about the past or the future, as I stared at myself in the looking-glass. After a while I thought I'd better stop. Loneliness breeds self-regard; that's probably what happened to Mary Magdalen too, in her lonely desert.

The documentary was not, after all, completely defeated. There was still the whole question of the old Comte, and that perhaps, was a better story in the first place. And although I was quite prepared to give up on Lorraine, I could still contact the visitor who gave the American address. It might, just, lead to something, though it seemed unlikely. That could very well be done from London, where I could also expect to hear more about the Loire valley story. It was time to give up for the day, to find my detective story and get into a hot bath.

The thriller was very good, profoundly morbid and set in the fens in East Anglia. The Hôtel Choucroute had nice bathrooms, not too draughty and very clean, with a large stool for putting a towel on, essential for readers who have to dry their hands before turning a page, without leaving the towel itself in a position where it will get wet. These minor pleasures have their rigorous requirements too.

Unfortunately even the dankest fen could not distract me from the film. The thought that there was still something I could do about it would not leave me. Finally, irritated and dripping, I got out, put one of those small hotel towels around me and went into the bedroom to find the telephone. I wanted to ring the American. The list was at the bottom of my suitcase, among my Corporation notebooks, and I unpacked, quickly and untidily, to find it. At last I reached it, and, cold and annoyed with my own incompetence, found a dressing-gown. Holding the list and a felt-tip pen, I sat down at last on the edge of the bed next to the telephone and called directory inquiries.

I had never mastered the Choucroute telephone system and was never sure whether I could get a line to myself or whether I always had to go through the switchboard. After several calls to women who kept telling me that I ought to be calling someone else and who refused to acknowledge any responsibility for anything I needed to know, I gave up, defeated by French directory inquiries. I rang the Corporation reference library in London. One of the many oddities of the Corporation is that its librarians are expected to look up telephone numbers and actually possess rows and rows of provincial and foreign directories.

I got someone whose voice I didn't recognize.

'I'm calling from France, and trying to get hold of a number in America,' I said.

'United States?' asked the male voice, with a hint of reproach at my amateurism.

'Yes, Utah, Resolution City,' I said. The connection immediately went quiet. But before I had finally decided to ring up the desk and make myself unpleasant, the English voice was back on the line.

'I'm with you again. I've got the directory covering Resolution City. What was the name?'

'All I have is Bob Kitzinger.'

'Well, let's start with R,' he said. I heard the flicking of pages.

'Of course Robert may be his second name,' he said conversationally.

'There's always that possibility,' I said drily, sitting uncomfortably on the bed in my damp dressing-gown.

'Trying not to keep you,' he said, still turning pages. 'Ah,' he went on, 'you're in luck. There are only five R. Kitzingers. Do you want all their numbers?'

I wrote them all down.

'I wonder if they're all Mormons,' said the librarian. 'Funny lot, aren't they? Would it be a Mormon you're actually looking for?'

'What do you mean, Mormons?' I asked in amazement, for the second time that day.

'Well, that's Mormon country, isn't it?' he replied. 'Salt Lake City. Resolution City. They're all Mormons round there. It's not important, I assumed you'd know.'

'I don't suppose it is important,' I said, 'but thanks anyway. You couldn't tell me something about their ancestor-hunting, could you?'

'I don't think that's quite how they'd like to see it expressed, but I'll do what I can.'

I asked him to send anything that seemed interesting to my office in Wireless House, thought about ringing the five Kitzingers, thought better of it, got back into the bath and turned on the hot tap.

I got through to the right Bob Kitzinger later that evening. He was the third on my list, and had an attractive, well-mannered voice. He called me ma'am, which I liked, and gave me a lot of his time even though I had interrupted his lunch. Although his open manner made him seem slightly innocent, he was one of the minority who took the trouble to write down my name and number; there I misled him slightly. Obsessiveness, or an overdeveloped secretiveness, made me disguise the fact I was calling from Nancy: I somehow had the impression that it made me sound too interested, and I gave him my office number at Wireless House. Having politely checked on who I was, he asked how he could help.

'It is rather a long story,' I said, 'but, briefly, I've been involved with some documentary filming in the archives at Nancy, which was cut short by the murder of the caretaker there.'

'Yes, I was very sorry to hear of that. The Nancy police called me here long-distance some time ago.'

'I was there at the time myself,' I said, 'and of course the police talked to me as well.' Before I could go on, he interrupted me, in his firm, polite way.

'Of course, I don't know what your interest is, ma'am, but before you waste any of your time on long distance I should tell you there's nothing I know about it. Of course if I did know anything, I would probably have to get the agreement of the Nancy police, and I'd certainly have to talk to them before talking to you. But there's nothing I can tell anybody.'

'Oh,' I said.

'I'd been consulting the indexes in the departmental archives there for just a couple of days, when they were suddenly shut because of a strike. I don't believe I ever even met the poor man. I left Nancy just as soon as I realized that the strike could go on for days, or even weeks maybe, and I've been back here ever since. I was very surprised when the police called, very surprised indeed, and course I was very sorry to hear the news.'

'Oh,' I said again. 'Yes, I wasn't able to help the police at all either.'

That was true.

'Anyway,' I said, trying again, 'I've been spending quite a lot of time at the archives, and I happened to see your name in the visitors' book and that's why I've called. I wondered whether you had any personal connection with Lorraine.'

'No,' he replied, 'none whatsoever. Apart from a pleasant memory of a short trip.'

'What exactly were you doing there?' I said, without finesse.

'Oh,' he said. He sounded confused, as anyone might be, by the inconsequential presumption of my questions.

'I thought you were familiar with the nature of our researches,' he went on.

'Well, not very precisely,' I said.

I hoped it would end there, but for some reason Bob Kitzinger described to me in detail what he'd been doing in the departmental archives in Nancy: it seemed, from a tired and practised politeness in his voice, that he had long ago decided that it was probably worth the effort of explaining to the incredulous some of the Mormon beliefs. It was more or less as Mademoiselle Autran had described, and as he spoke he made me think that there were worse ways of spending the time than fossicking in provincial records.

Finally he finished. 'What exactly was your interest?' he asked.

I told him that we had been at cross-purposes, that I had made a mistake in calling him, that I'd been given the impression by a librarian that he was researching into wartime Lorraine, like us.

'I hope I haven't wasted too much of your time; it was very interesting for me,' I said. I thanked him and put the telephone down. At last I felt I had finished. I had, in effect, just wasted a lot of time, and although I still felt, irrationally perhaps, but strongly, that it was for me to unravel the mystery on to which I had stumbled, I was able at the same time to see how preposterous that was. Probably Dan was right, that I read too many detective stories. I put away my Corporation notebooks in the bottom of my case, and turned my mind back to the bleak East Anglian marshes, where, in the way peculiar to detective fiction, moral order was imposed through curiosity and pain.

13

On my desk at Wireless House, there were very few messages, but one of them was the one I had been waiting for. Andrew McAusland had sent me a letter marked private and confidential, which, curiously enough, had not been opened by anyone in the Corporation. At the beginning of my time in television some of the journalists in my chapel had protested formally to the management about the way our mail was often opened and read, and appeared late on our desks with clumsy Sellotape repairs.

'We don't read it,' said the apparatchik who had been chosen to receive our delegation. 'We just peruse it.'

McAusland's letter was the first ever sent to me at Wireless House that might have been worth opening. But it was still intact as far as I could tell and invited me to come to an address at Pont Street later that week. It sounded like a summons. On the appointed day a Corporation taxi took me down Sloane Street at noon, past the landmarks of my childhood, and turned right into Pont Street at the Cadogan Hotel, a wonderful red brick monstrosity, good for adulterous assignations, and the place where Oscar Wilde was arrested; it has been immortalized by the event and by the Betjeman poem. If you live long enough in a city, it becomes filled with landmarks, a private map covered with traces of meetings, partings, first beginnings; here an assignation, there a dress in a sale, a humiliating interview, a first job, a church service, the wedding of a friend, an enemy, a lover.

I found the right address and pressed a bell marked Meadows as instructed, thinking as I did so that they could have chosen a less obtrusively English name. The flat was in a very solid mansion block: the wooden doors were thick, the walls were thick and the wide hall and stairs were thickly carpeted in dark green. The noise from the street was completely muffled. An old-fashioned lift with folding metal doors gave the same impression of solidity and permanence. I wondered where I was going and who owned the flat, which part of the secret service. Perhaps it was simply Andrew McAusland's private address. Perhaps he really was called Meadows.

The place seemed, at least, to give him an individuality he'd lacked at our last meeting, the look of a man on his own ground. His manner was far more relaxed, closer to something I recognized, but couldn't identify. Previously I hadn't noticed his appearance: now I could see that he was not at all featureless. He had the remains of conventional English good looks, an out-of-date handsomeness which relied mainly on a straight nose, blue eyes and careful shaving. He had the ruddy, weathered look that immediately suggests gum boots and gun dogs and wet hay, to those who have a weakness in that direction.

'Come in, come in,' he said, smiling.

The smell of the flat had the same effect on me; it was an amalgam of decay, none-too-clean, faded chintz, poor food, good polish and old wood. To be perfect, this atmosphere needs a grandfather clock, which was lacking there, but otherwise the smell and the feel of the place pulled at powerful, forgotten attachments.

'You'll have a drink, won't you? What can I offer you?'

'What I'd really like,' I said, determined to ask for something incongruous and to see whether he could make one, 'is a dry Martini.'

'Ha ha,' he laughed politely, with practised irony. 'Shaken or stirred?'

He turned away to a Chinese or Korean cabinet, whose front fell forward to reveal a very large collection of bottles and an ice bucket. After a certain amount of dextrous fidding with a glass jug and some ice cubes he handed me a small crystal glass that was icy to touch. There was no lemon peel, no olive, just the oily, transparent look of a serious drinker's Martini. He smiled as he gave it to me. I was surprised at how good it was, and he looked as though he had some idea of what was going through my mind. He himself had whisky and soda. I saw that the decoration of the flat didn't match the smell; it was too new and too coordinated, all salmon-pink and *eau-de-Nil*, in the fashion of ten years before, with enough Indian rugs, Chinese lamp bases and prints of Burma to hint at past glories without precisely suggesting Empire. It was a decorator's job too. This was not someone's home and yet I associated the smell with people's homes, but in the distant past, and in the country.

McAusland invited me to sit on one of the large leather chesterfields, which had been authentically aged. The flat was very comfortable: at exactly the right place there was a little occasional table for my glass. I felt at home; the atmosphere was pushing me gently, with the dry Martini, into confidence and acquiescence.

'This is off the record, of course,' he said. 'And not just off the record. It's strictly between you and me. You know the form.'

I didn't know the form at all, but I could understand that. I thought, though, that talking to a Corporation journalist in that way was like spitting in the wind, and I was surprised he even bothered to say it.

'Oddly enough,' he said, 'you may well be right.'

I looked blank.

'About Hubert de Villancourt,' he said, as if I were being obtuse on purpose, which I was.

'It is true that there's quite a lot wrong with his past. He was, for an ordinary man, rather unusual. He got mixed up in all kinds of things during the Vichy period, any one of which might have justified some orphaned son or small industrialist in bumping him off at any time in the last forty years.'

'What sort of things?' I said 'And why didn't anyone?'

'I think the answer to both questions is much the same: so many people were involved. People were confused, frightened, hungry; most people were implicated one way or another. There's collaboration and collaboration. After all, what about the taxi drivers who drove the Boche around?'

'I'm not interested in that kind of question, in the compromises of ordinary people. I'm interested in what the Comte did. In particular I want to know what he had to do with the selection of Jews to be sent to concentration camps.'

'Ah,' he said. 'Now that was nasty. What do you know about it?'

'Not much,' I said. 'Except that his son was Jewish.'

'It wasn't quite selection that he was involved in. As you may know, the summer of 1942 was a particularly terrible time for Jews in France, especially for non-French Jews. Refugees. In the Nazi-occupied zone the Germans rounded them up and shipped them east to the camps, and as you know, in the Vichy zone they insisted on the French doing the same thing. They issued the Vichy government with quotas that had to be filled. There were mass deportations that summer, thousands and thousands of Jews dragged out of their homes in French towns and villages by the local police and packed into freight trains. The French were only too cooperative, I'm sorry to say, though one or two civilian observers kicked up a bit.'

'Who was responsible for all this?'

'The police handled it; it was all quite efficient, although the trains were often late, which used to madden the Hun. "The departure of the Israelites", they used to call it in their memos.'

'So what had the Comte de Villancourt to do with it? If the police were running it?'

'Well, first I should explain that there were quite a lot of French people who were brave enough to try and protect Jews. Particularly the religious houses and the religious schools. They took in a lot of children. Parents and children were separated in the round-ups anyway; the adults used to try to hide in the woods. That's what happened near the Comte's château. His lands were very extensive then, and some time in late August some mass arrests were planned. A lot of Jews went into hiding in his forest, and there were some children in a local convent. The Comte found out and he rang up the *gardes mobiles*. And they came and took them away. I think he actually believed in the final solution; people did.'

'How did he survive that? After the war, I mean?'

'He was very powerful, of course. And the fact is, dear girl, that people felt very differently about these things. A lot of people feared and hated the Jews in France, particularly the

88

recent immigrants. They really did hold them responsible for rising prices and food shortages and just about every other social evil. The French went even further in some ways than even the Germans told them to – shipping out the children, for example.'

I wished I hadn't ever begun on any of this.

'There is something else about that particular week in 1942; we had some of our people there at the time, trying to make contact with the Resistance, and they knew about it. About the arrests and about the fact the Comte was calling in the police to search the forest.'

'And they didn't warn them?'

'They couldn't. It was too dangerous. It would have revealed their presence to all kinds of people. They didn't think it was worth the risk of exposing themselves. Why didn't the Resistance warn them, come to that? The Jews couldn't have survived anyway, you know. They would have starved.'

Again I wondered whether the Comte's son knew that he was Jewish, and if so, when he found out.

'How did they know who was Jewish and who wasn't?' I asked.

'You're thinking of the son, I suppose? You could get a certificate of not belonging to the Jewish race. For that you needed baptismal records, which he would have had. So would his mother, of course.'

'What an amazing story,' I said.

He settled back in his sofa, looking down at me slightly, because his head was thrown back – a rather old-fashioned posture of manliness which you see in films of the forties and fifties.

'Yes,' he replied 'and I want you, as journalists say, to spike it. To spike your own story.'

We stared at each other for a while. He seemed to be half-smiling at me, expressing a kind of sympathy. We were both silent for a long time, and the flat too seemed to have become silent.

'Why?' I asked at last.

'It would be very embarrassing,' he said.

'Embarrassing for whom? For the government?'

'Of course not that, though it would be. I mean bad for the country in the long run. A bad thing,' he said, smiling as if I were by common consent on his side.

'What on earth has this got to do with anything? With contemporary politics? This is history.'

'Oh, my dear girl, don't force me to explain. Use a little imagination. You seem to have more than your fair share. If a very old, painful story is raked up, distraught Jewish children rounded up, locals turning a blind eye, ratting on their neighbours, and it comes out that some British agents knew, and did nothing to warn the wretched victims, it's going to stir up a lot of feeling.'

'So?' I said.

'Which will most inconveniently translate itself into pro-Jewish pressure and pro-Jewish voting; the very last thing we need at the moment.'

'You mean pro-Israel,' I said.

He shrugged to show that the point was obvious. 'Our cowboy cousins across the sea would be very put out; all their initiatives are working out very nicely, the international mood has swung just the right way, and more importantly so has the domestic mood in the States. Need I say more? A little grief like this and the whole thing could be ruined.'

The massaging of public opinion has always been a mystery to me, especially where Americans are concerned. I had no idea whether he was talking nonsense, or whether, on the contrary, it was possible that the reverberations of a forty-five-years-old tragedy in provincial France would be felt on Capitol Hill and in the Middle East.

'We cannot,' he insisted 'have an anti-Semitic scandal at this point. You must see that. Damn it, you work in current affairs. And there's no need to give me that "lest we forget" line. You can depend on the Jews themselves to keep the Holocaust alive.'

Apart from the smell of the flat and the cast of his face he had something else in common with my own background, or my memories of it; there was an unspoken assumption, an assumed position, so subtle that it could never be articulated though it was always present. It was so familiar to me that identifying it was an effort. No doubt he too recognized our affinities, no doubt he assumed that in the end, whatever might be on my computerized file and in my past, I would revert to type, and respond like him.

'It's going to come out anyway,' I said. 'Quite a few French hacks are on to it.'

'Let them do their worst,' he said. 'I bet they don't get it on to the box anyway. And at least it won't be a British story.'

I must have shrugged or shown some sign that I didn't think it would make any difference who got the story. It would come out in the end, and it would be on all our screens.

'I'd be amazed', he said, rather complacently, 'if they discovered anything about the British agents. That's the thing you know that they don't and which they'll almost certainly never discover.'

I thought about that for a while.

'But I certainly wouldn't have discovered it either, if you hadn't told me. I wouldn't have been looking. Why did you tell me?'

He looked surprised.

'Because we trust you,' he said. 'You wouldn't be here if we didn't.'

He stood up and removed the empty glass from my hand, as if I were a child.

'Spot of lunch?' he asked.

I should not have accepted. It's more or less against the rules, to be friendly with people who are obstructing the sacred work of investigative journalism. But I was very tempted. I was curious to know what he did, what sort of man he was, and besides he seemed to be offering not only lunch but a short time on the inside of a world which I had lost and from which I felt excluded. So I accepted.

I enjoyed it, too. He still had the old-fashioned English habit of not talking sense to women, but he took the traditional way out, of treating me like an honorary boy. He was also at a conversational disadvantage because he knew, and I knew that he knew, a lot about me. We could have none of the usual opening lines: 'Were you brought up in the country?' or 'You're not by any chance related to the

Dumfriesshire lot?' Despite all that he was very entertaining, a steak, salmon and ancedote man, I thought at first, rather than a gourmet conversationialist, but funny all the same. Maybe it's a technique to avoid self-revelation, but he told witty stories throughout lunch, so that I hardly stopped laughing. Perhaps that had something to do with the bottle of excellent claret he chose.

By the time coffee arrived, the world of television appeared, as he had intended, rather remote, and the whole programme had begun to seem quite puerile to me. Either the wine or his attentiveness had made me feel that I hardly needed to concern myself about a minor piece of sensational hackery; better leave it to others who had less taste and less sense of political responsibility. I felt that in the end it would be a far, far better thing if I forgot all about it and put my neck gallantly upon the guillotine of *Pop Goes the Weasel*.

When we came out of the Knightsbridge restaurant the day was still bright, though very cold. Andrew McAusland tried to wave down a taxi for me, but I said I would walk part of the way back, and crossed Kensington Gore into the Park. It was a little after 3, and I wanted what was left of the fresh air and the winter light. The Albert Memorial was on my left, a grotesque and encouraging monument, with the sun in the west beginning to go down on its far side. I walked slowly north between the bare trees; the park was almost empty. Ahead was another piece of Victorian self-assertion, the ungainly statue of Physical Energy; did they really believe then that they had got science and nature and posterity all so neatly sorted out? That virtues and aspirations and responsibilities could be identified and pinned down in stone?

The sentimental drift of my thoughts made me realize that I had drunk more than I'd intended.

> *You cannot hope to bribe or twist,*
> *Thank God, the British journalist.*
> *But seeing what the man will do*
> *Without, there's no occasion to.*

It took me a long time to walk the breadth of the park; it was cold and I seemed to have listed a long way to the east because I reached the Bayswater Road near the Tyburn shrine, and when I arrived there I found I had, along the way, changed my mind. Dry Martinis and flattery should not prevail. Perhaps I was inspired by all the martyrs who had died at Tyburn; those obstinate and marginal people who misunderstood their interests, but who would not be deflected; another alcoholic sentiment.

By the time I arrived back at my desk, my mind was completely made up. Lorraine might have proved a dead end, but the story of the Comte might really be the best thing I had ever stumbled across. I rang Marie-Blanche in Paris, resisting a temptation to boast about my discoveries with McAusland. Marie-Blanche had little to tell me that was new. She confirmed that it was true that the Comte had a reputation for collaboration, that had somehow been conveniently forgotten, perhaps because he had been gaga for a long time, perhaps because he was reclusive and perhaps just in the way that national disasters are overlooked in parts. She told me that a lot of journalists were nosing around, but that nothing very much had emerged, nothing that she had gathered anyway.

'But give me time,' she said. 'I think there really is something in the Jewish wife angle.'

'I want to come over,' I said. 'I want to see the papers, the registration of ancestry that they had to fill in, everything relating to the deportation of those particular Jews.'

'If it still exists,' said Marie-Blanche.

'What do you mean?' I asked. 'Don't you even know yet whether it still exists? Why all this delay? I think I'm going to come over tonight.'

'Come when you like,' she said, 'I can't stop you. But it's too soon.'

'Everyone else will be getting all this,' I said. 'While you're sitting in Paris, waiting for your contacts to drop a few crumbs, I'll miss the story. I'm getting the next plane.'

'Listen,' said Marie-Blanche. 'You would embarrass me quite a bit. After all, if it weren't for me, you wouldn't be interested in the first place. If I promise to go and do all the work myself, would you just stay away for a while?'

'You can't do that,' I said. 'You have to stay in the Paris office. I mean actually going down there, talking to a few contemporaries, looking at all the records, getting on to historians. How could you do all that?'

'You'd be surprised,' she said. 'By the way, there is one thing, though it's pretty trivial I think. There have been rumours that the Comte was going to have a sale – a formal sale of some of his things. Apparently he had some very good furniture.'

'Do you know when that was decided?'

'All I can tell you is, very recently. Apparently he called in one of the top auction houses here. Of course they won't say much. They're supposed to be ultra discreet, but it seems that a man from Huysmanns' went down to see him in November or December.'

'And sure enough, a few weeks later he was dead.'

'Exactly,' said Marie-Blanche. 'Probably meaningless.'

'I'm not surprised he was trying to raise some money,' I said, 'judging from the state of the château. Surprising he didn't get round to it before.'

'Who knows?' said Marie-Blanche. 'Anyway, I'm afraid that's all that new, and not much at that.'

It wasn't much, but, since it was all she was offering, I thought about it for a minute.

'Presumably there'll be a sale anyway,' I said.

'Death is always expensive,' said Marie-Blanche in her drawing-room manner. 'Ignoring it, I asked her to be sure to monitor the sale, if there was one, and to let me know the minute she'd discovered anything else.

'And if not I'm coming over. Soon,' I said.

14

I tried for more than a whole day to get hold of Dan Cohen: late the following afternoon I was still trying. As I sat at my desk, following him round the Corporation buildings on the telephone, always a couple of numbers behind him, constantly being passed on to props depots, computer graphics departments and freelance designers all over Acton and Ealing, the sun set across the urban wastes outside my office. The extravagant drama of the sunset from the west side of the Wireless House tower block is the only natural beauty for several miles in all directions, and an outstanding one at that. Finally it was dark. I ate a Corporation rock bun, still holding the telephone, and discovered at last that Dan was going to be in a video editing suite from 23.15 hours onwards that night.

'Can't I speak to him before that?' I asked a woman on the end of a line somewhere who seemed to claim responsibility for him.

'No. He can't be contacted'.

'All right, just tell him that I called and that it's urgent.'

'I'm afraid I can't do that.'

'Yes, I understand,' I said, 'But just give him the message.'

'He cannot be contacted,' she insisted, as if she were enjoying it.

'What a pity,' I said. 'It's just to tell him that his flat has been burgled.'

'Even if his flat's burned right down, love, there's nothing I can do. He's in Perivale, covered from head to foot in protective clothing and locked away in the film library there.'

'Protective clothing?'

'Yes, dear. It's to do with the asbestos. They've discovered the whole building is riddled with it.'

'Things don't get riddled with asbestos,' I said.

'You might if you didn't wear protective clothing. And they're not letting anybody in, it's all out of bounds to personnel, except people with special permission.'

'All right,' I said, 'I believe you. I'll wait until the video edit tonight.'

'What shall I tell him about his flat being burgled?' she asked maliciously. 'I haven't heard that one before.'

There are plenty of ways of killing time in Wireless House. That night while I was waiting I went to one of the biggest studios, and the assistant floor manager let me join the audience of a chat show. When it got to 11, I left and went looking for Dan's editing suite. There were several on three floors, all of them closed off by many double doors from the rest of the building, and all of them in windowless complexes. As I walked through the last pair of doors on the right floor, I was met by the dim hush and light of high technology. All around a central desk, like the emergency department of a modern hospital, was a circle of glass cubicles, with dim interiors that had banks of elaborate knobs and switches and screens, looking like the control panels of a spaceship. I could just see Dan in one of them, with one of those tight-lipped, censorious technical whizzes who edit videotape.

I went in and looked around quickly. I couldn't tell what was going on and I was pretty sure from Dan's expression that he couldn't either. He must have just arrived.

'What are you doing here?' he said, when he saw me.

'I need to talk to you if you have a minute,' I said.

'What does it look like?' he said. 'I'm in a highly expensive, late night edit with barely enough time to get through it all.'

'I've been trying to get hold of you all day,' I said.

'Well, Daniel – it is Daniel, isn't it?' asked the senior editor. 'Let's have a look at what you've got, and see how much time we need to get ourselves stuck into it.'

'You must have got a new researcher,' I said, looking at Dan's editing script. It was uncharacteristically neat and full, like several train timetables superimposed. The precise timings in and out of the different spools of videotape were neatly lined up with brief descriptions in words, and special effects were highlighted in yellow pen.

'Leave it out,' said Dan. 'I did it myself.'

'Glad to see standards are slowly creeping up,' said the editor. 'This will do nicely. We'll start lining up and we won't need you for a bit – feel free if you want a chat.'

'Well?' said Dan, walking out with me to a place where he could smoke.

I told him everything I'd found out, including my strange lunch with McAusland. Dan laughed at that.

'Quoting Latin clichés at each other,' he said, almost snorting with laughter. 'The net of the establishment draws closer and closer, doesn't it?'

'You're enmeshed in it just as much as me,' I said to him, 'since you want to be a big fish. Don't think that you've escaped.'

He laughed at me again, but he was at last quite impressed with what I told him about the Loire valley story.

'I always did think you were a clever girl,' he said. 'Despite everything. Go for it.'

'What about you?'

'You've got a project number,' he replied. 'What more do you need?'

'Stop dragging at your cigarette like that,' I said. 'It's you that's seen too many films, too many third-rate existentialist movies in your youth.'

'Now, now. Calm down. Let's just leave things as they were before. You can see I'm busy. You carry on, pull out all the stops, and if you get anything together, I'll put myself back in the picture to take the credit. Fair enough?'

He turned away and walked towards a box of sand, stubbed out his cigarette and disappeared into the darkness of the editing suite. He was the kind of man who leaves an absence behind him, and besides, he had disappointed me.

However, a little encouragement, even from Dan, goes a long way, and I went straight back to my office to make a list of everything that needed doing. When I had finished I put some of it into a letter for Marie-Blanche, which I sent by the special Corporation messenger. I had decided to give Marie-Blanche three days to come up with some sign of real progress. I put a lot of unanswered mail into a full tray marked pending, put the playwright's mail into a tray marked filing, gathered together all my notes about the story, turned out the light and went home.

It was still dark when I got up the next morning and made some Kenyan coffee and unappealing wholemeal toast. I turned on the light in the big sitting room and sat in the armchair by the window. After a while some grey light came up across the river and made me realize it must be about 8 o'clock. I went down the iron warehouse stairs to the ground floor and was met as usual by the smell of spice from the outside air, this time turmeric or some kind of curry spice. In my mail-box were several letters and a slip from the porter saying there was a package for me in his lodge.

When I went into his tasteful modern cubby-hole, my package and my newspapers were lying ready for me in a pile on his desk.

'Good morning,' I said.

''Morning,' he replied. 'What do you think of today's olfactory sensation?'

'Cinnamon is my favourite,' I said. I didn't smile, because the porter preferred an atmosphere of lugubrious disgruntlement: it was his protest against his disappointments in life, whatever they had been, and against being a porter despite his command of English.

'Special delivery. Very expensive, the postage on all that, I should say,' he said, nodding from behind his hippy's whiskers at my heavy package.

I looked at the stamps and saw that they were French: it was a package from Marie-Blanche.

'Yes, very,' I said, and almost ran out, into the damp air and up to my flat. Outside it began to drizzle, while I looked for a knife or a pair of scissors. I opened the envelope and pulled out a large glossy catalogue of a sale at Huysmanns. There was a Corporation compliments slip inside: the Paris office was the only one that had engraved slips on high-quality woven paper. On this piece of extravagance Marie-Blanche had written in her well-brought-up handwriting, 'If it's of any interest, there is going to be a sale of some of the Comte's things in early June: see lots 125–300 in the catalogue, from page 19.'

The Huysmanns' catalogue also contained an impressive compliments slip sent to Marie-Blanche from someone called

J-F. All it said was, 'Here's the catalogue – what's your interest? Do tell. J-F.'

The catalogue itself was beautifully made, with a glossy photograph of a nasty piece of Empire furniture on the front. Inside, on shiny pages, were long lists of objects, all of them 'important', 'very important' or, rather less confidently, 'remarkable'.

The Comte's collection was more appealing to me than the rest. Most of his things were high-quality furniture; over-polished, overfed-looking pieces, with too much gilding and slabs of marble in unlikely places. But there were some more entertaining things too. Someone in the family must have had an Oriental period: there was a long list of netsuke, some ivory carvings and a folio of Chinese erotic paintings on skeleton leaves, a curiosity I'd seen once before and which had struck as a monstrous joke. I was reminded of the curious smell and ornate tastelessness of so many Chinese artefacts, and wondered why nineteenth-century and Edwardian Europeans had so much liked these convoluted curiosities. If you want to understand decadence, you only have to look at a couple of recent centuries of Chinese ornaments.

None of this had much to do with anything, but I was enjoying it, reading all about the Comte's objects, surrounded by my own, also quite important or remarkable, at least to me. There was nothing among his possessions that I would have swapped for any of mine, except possibly the skeleton paintings, as a memento mori. Certainly among the lesser 'interesting' pieces there was very little. Several correspondences and documents, autographs, letters from famous generals and diplomats, and medals, as if you could sell a fleeting personal distinction.

There was one lot that caught my attention – some very old recipe books. One was the private collection of a late nineteenth-century Comtesse de Villancourt, dictated to her cook. I could imagine the scene, in the gloomy basement kitchens of the château, with someone, perhaps like the woman who had shown us round the château, laboriously taking down the details of *tripes à la mode de Caen* and *petits coeurs à la crème*. It was probably her mistress or her master

99

who'd had an anglophile period: there was a long run of *Punch*, some of the volumes still uncut, and a large collection of old English lace.

The flotsam and jetsam of time, supposed to be so full of meaning, in fact do nothing but hint at conventions. These objects, curious and valuable as they were, only pointed to a standard history of a certain class, not to the peculiarities of this family, these people. My own things, too, reflected only the taste of a certain income bracket, and that in itself was misleading, since my pieces of virtue were really only salvage. It would be nice, I thought, to have an object of significance, not just of importance. A Vermeer, for instance. But that, too, would tell only about itself. The meanings we invest in things last only a short time, the period of a shared experience.

Most of the furniture in the sale looked or sounded vaguely familiar: a lot of it had been on display in the house when we had been there. The rest, all the lesser stuff, I hadn't seen. None of the things had been around in those oddly placed glass cases, or if they had I hadn't noticed. In any case Dan wouldn't have allowed me to dawdle over collections of clocks and Fabergé eggs. I wished, seeing the catalogue, that I had noticed more, and I looked up the date of the preview of the sale, in case I might be in France at the time. It wasn't until the 10th of June.

The Huysmanns' catalogue left me feeling slightly irritated and restless, as if something were unfinished. I suppose I'd hoped for something more from a special delivery from Marie-Blanche. She'd probably made no real efforts. Probably, in her place, I wouldn't have done either. I made myself some more coffee and looked at the catalogue again. One of the things I would have expected to have seen was the document about the La Tour painting: I hadn't remembered seeing that on display in the château either. It probably hadn't been considered interesting enough for the usual day tripper, but in an experts' market I should have thought it would have been worth something. I looked again in the list of documents and letters, but as far as I could tell it wasn't in the sale, unless it was one of the assorted documents of historical interest, which weren't individually listed.

There were several telephone numbers on the back of the catalogue and on an impulse I called Huysmanns' in Paris, at the same time turning on my call timer for claiming expenses. Whereas in England I might have called a famous auction house and been patronized for twenty minutes by some débutante on the front desk, at Huysmanns' I was connected immediately with the man responsible for the catalogue. He told me after only a very short delay to look at his files, that there was no La Tour documentation in the sale and suggested that I should call the château. But when I asked for a telephone number he politely refused to give it to me. Hacks would get nowhere if everyone were as professional as that.

Spurred on by opposition I began looking for a number at the château and started with the Guide Michelin, which gave one. I dialled it, and let it ring for a long time. As I waited I wondered where in the château it would be ringing and what had happened to our querulous guide. After at least a couple of minutes the telephone was answered by a woman. She sounded businesslike. I told her that I would like to speak to the executors of the estate of the late Comte.

She told me I'd called the wrong number, that I had come through to the main part of the house which was now completely empty; she was secretary to the executors, and she was working in another wing.

'I wonder if you could help me,' I said. 'I'm ringing up about the sale in June. It's about a document that interests me.'

'Yes?' she said, not very encouragingly.

I realized that I was going to have to provide a very respectable reason for my interest: the intonation of her yes was of the kind that tempts journalists to fib.

'I'm working for an antiques dealer here in London, at Abercrombie's, who specializes in the seventeenth century, particularly in signatures, documents, seals and so on, and he understands that among the late Comte's papers there was at one time a document which had to do with Georges de La Tour.'

'With who?' she said.

'With Georges de La Tour. The painter.'

'Oh,' she replied. 'Georges de La Tour. Yes?'

101

'I had been hoping that this document, or documents, might be in the sale. I have the Huysmanns' catalogue here, but it doesn't seem to be listed. Could you possibly let me know whether the Comte's estate still has the document?'

'Well,' she said briskly,' I'm afraid I don't know, off the top of my head, just like that. There's an enormous amount of stuff here, you know, and it's still going to take a lot of sorting. I shouldn't wonder if they didn't have another sale later on. It was with a view to purchase that you were inquiring?'

'Yes,' I said.

'If you'll excuse me for a moment I'll see what I can find out. They've only just finished doing the final inventories.'

She asked me for my name and for information about the document. I couldn't remember many details from the clippings, but I told her what I could.

'Ne quittez pas,' said the efficient woman.

That should be every journalist's motto, I thought.

After a long delay, which began to look very expensive for the Corporation, she came back on the line.

'I'm very sorry, I've searched everywhere, but there's no record of it. Just to be sure I've asked the two gentlemen who are in charge of the collection, for the executors, and they assure me it's not in the inventory – the inventory-taking has been very thorough, you know, and they tell me all the papers have been sorted.'

'But it was there once, wasn't it? Not so long ago?'

'Yes, you are quite right. Monsieur Roux, who I was talking to, remembers something about it. Something like that was discovered here but he didn't say when it was. Anyway he says there's no record of a previous sale, but it isn't here now. Perhaps the Comte gave it away; if this Georges de La Tour was an important painter, the Comte might have given it away for research or something. Between you and me I think it could easily have got lost. I'm told the late Comte was really not himself in recent years, and when we arrived things were in terrible confusion – attics and cellars full to bursting with all sorts of odd and ends. And it's all got to be cleared away because of the sale.'

'How do you mean?'

'Well, the château is going to be sold.'

'So there are no heirs to come and live in it?'

'Oh, no,' she replied. 'No heirs. There are some distant relations, and a lot of different bequests: well, I don't suppose it can do any harm, just to say that much.'

'You've been very kind,' I said. 'I have just one more question. Do you suppose any of the staff would know anything about it?'

At that point the secretary had clearly had enough.

'It's all in the hands of the executors, mademoiselle. There really is nothing further I can tell you.'

15

My call to France had taken twelve minutes and forty seconds and I wrote it down in my Corporation expenses book. It was now 9.30, still the middle of the night on the East Coast of the United States. So I went to work and waited until 11.30; then I dialled a Corporation stringer in Washington, Quentin McNulty. I told him before he asked me that I knew what time it was.

'But it's too late for a man of your age to be asleep,' I said. 'Are you busy?'

'I'm always busy,' said Quentin. 'I don't have the dozy third-world approach to life of the British. What do you want?'

'First of all,' I said, 'how's your general knowledge?'

'Second to none,' he replied.

'In that case, is Georges de La Tour's most recently sold *Repentant Magdalen* in Washington?'

'Yes,' he said. 'What's your next question?'

'My next question is, where in Washington is it, Quentin?'

'It's in the Rensellaer. Third floor as far as I remember.'

'You have hidden depths, Quentin. I thought you were only interested in Capitol Hill.'

'Man cannot live by graft alone,' he said. 'Now, what did you really ring about, because actually I am busy.'

'Really about the picture,' I said. 'Could you possibly make very discreet inquiries for me? It's about a letter which more or less goes with the picture. I don't have the details here, and you probably won't need them. If you do, call me at Wireless House, or telex. Anyway, this is more or less the story. The *Magdalen* was sold to America, to the Rensellaer evidently around 1980, 1981. It's an acknowledged masterpiece, of course, and I suppose it doesn't really need a pedigree, but anyway there was this letter, which was very important in authenticating it apparently. Actually I think there were two or three letters, fragments of a correspondence between the monks of a Franciscan monastery in the Loire valley and a satellite monastery in Lunéville, in Lorraine, where La Tour worked: a commission for the painting is mentioned. Anyway, these seventeenth-century fragments were found years before in a château close to where the monastery used to be. Or perhaps the château was built on to the monastery. Anyway all that is pretty unimportant. What I want to know, without getting anybody interested, is this: does the Rensellaer own this document as well as the painting? Please be discreet.'

'No problem,' said Quentin. 'I have a friend who's an assistant curator. By the way, how could it be sold out of France, a masterpiece like that?'

He was right, of course, and he reminded me how little I knew about painting and art dealers. But I didn't want him to know that.

'It wasn't. You really will be discreet?' I asked again.

'Yes, of course,' he said. 'If it's important. Is it?'

I told him that I was doing a programme about the Nazi occupation of France and collaboration.

'Yes,' he said, 'I thought you were in Current Affairs. I didn't think art was your bag. But how exactly does this painting link up with collaboration?'

'Wait and see. Time will tell,' I said, not having the slightest idea myself.

'And one last thing,' I said.

'Yes?'

'What kind of name is Quentin for an American?'

'Look me up when you come over next, and I'll explain.'

The Corporation's American employees and stringers confirmed all our clichés, and their own, about the American work ethic. Quentin rang back at 11 a.m. his time, which was around 4 in the afternoon at Wireless House. He had been to the Rensellaer already.

'It's good to have an excuse to go there,' he said. 'My friend was very helpful. He actually seemed to know all about it, although European old masters aren't his thing. He says they definitely haven't got the document; the curators very much wanted to buy it at the time they bid for the painting itself, but it seems the owner wouldn't sell.'

'Which owner?'

'The French guy who owns the place where it was found – I've got the name down here somewhere. Hubert de Villancourt. Apparently he refused all offers. Somebody went over to speak to him in France, but he couldn't be persuaded. Actually the museum wasn't really that concerned; it just would have been nice to own some of the circumstantial evidence, but it didn't matter much either way. By the way, have you ever seen the *Magdalen*? I've just had another look at it. It's really something. What a piece of ass! Wasn't the seventeenth century great?'

I said I hadn't seen it.

'Well, it certainly "vaut le voyage" as the guide books say. I think it's the best of all the La Tours we've got over here.'

'You've got too many of them over there,' I said, but in fact I had no idea how many there were in America.

On the way home from work that day I stopped at Notting Hill for a drink with Guy to listen to his new hi-fi equipment and exchange a little panic and consolation. We didn't drink because we had both independently decided we liked it too much.

'Alcohol's better than Valium, though,' I said, as we stood in his immaculate small kitchen and I watched him put lemon slices and ice and angostura bitters into our mineral water, to distract us from its lack of alcohol.

'Yes, but far worse for your appearance and for your innards. You should be careful. You won't look young for ever, and alcohol will speed up the inevitable.'

'You're always so encouraging,' I said to him.

'Now, here is something that can defy time,' he said, taking me into the sitting room. 'The compact disc.'

We listened for a while to his latest acquisition, but after a time, without realizing that I had become restless, I found I had got up and walked across the room to his wall of bookshelves. Among the tall books at the bottom there was one that caught my attention.

'Can I look at your La Tour picture book?' I asked.

'Of course,' he said. 'Borrow it.'

I took out the book and went back to sit in Guy's comfortable sofa. Guy was right. On his carefully chosen sound system, the compact disc made it sound as though Schubert were playing the piano himself, in the same room. You could even hear the pedals, and the rasp of the player breathing. It was obviously one of Guy's favourite pieces of music; he was listening wholeheartedly, without noticing anything else. But I, distracted, soon found my attention wandering and I opened the book on my lap and started looking at the pictures.

They all shared an unusual quality; they are instantly recognizable whether you've seen them before or not. It's partly the colours – terracotta-red, cream, beige and flesh tones and the many different kinds of black that make up the obscurity and shadows of La Tour's night paintings. I noticed a few daylight paintings too: a wretched poor man playing a lute, with a twisted leg and deformed mouth and teeth, staring blindly upwards; a beggars' brawl in which the misery of their lives was translated into terrifying greed and violence and mad, blind smiling. In a different mood there was a severe old saint, kneeling calmly among desert rocks with his back to the painter; at his feet lay a rope scourge tinted red with implausibly bright blood. His was not the only scourge; at least one of the many Mary Magdalens had a little knotted rope coiled round her night-light.

The curious thing about them all, as I turned from page to page, was the contrast between their quality of serenity and detachment, and their subjects. Despite their tranquillity the themes were of great intensity – betrayal, remorse, birth, poverty, martyrdom. Among them was the most famous one, the Christmas card *New-born Child*, which several generations of Santa and Rudolf the Red-nosed Reindeer had not yet robbed of its innocence and incandescence; a flat-chested girl in a tight red dress, with a peasant face and the brown hair and long nose of North-eastern France stares in astonishment and tenderness and sadness at a pink, pig-like new-born baby, in all its translucent ugliness and mystery. I had not realized Georges de La Tour was in that league: people are always enthusing about painters who mean nothing to me.

Not all the pictures were of that quality; many seemed much clumsier, much more wooden, almost as if they were the work of another painter. He must have been through an astonishing development, I thought, turning the pages. In the middle of the book was an identical pair of pictures, or so it seemed at first. In fact there were many small differences, but the subject was the same, a man cheating at cards. In most of the other pictures the characters look inwards or away or elsewhere. In this pair the cheat leans back and looks outward to the world outside the painting, defying us, disguising his cheating cards from his companions but not from us. They both had the feel of a portrait, a self-portrait perhaps, introduced, as painters often did, in disguise. But what a choice, for the painter of those meditative, penitential pictures – the personage of a card-sharper. There was an ambiguous expression on his face, perhaps regret, perhaps anger, perhaps that pained desire for recognition expressed by people who don't really expect it.

'WHAT'S LOVE GOT TO DO, GOT TO DO WITH IT' roared Tina Turner at top volume, angry and raw, from Guy's sound system. The sudden noise shocked me badly. I started and my heart began to beat unpleasantly fast. Guy was standing at his control panel, staring irritably at me. He turned the sound down.

'You deserved that,' he said. 'I'm very cross with you. You are not to use Schubert as background music. Listen or don't listen. This coffee table mentality is not all right.'

'I wasn't listening at all,' I said. 'I was really only absorbed in this.'

'Very pretty,' said Guy, looking for another disc.

'No, not very pretty,' I said. 'That's not what they are.'

'Well, anyway, a bit popular. Rather Christmas card.'

'You're quite wrong, Guy.'

'Since when were you a picture fancier? I shouldn't have thought there was much of a circle of connoisseurs at Wireless House.'

'Of course I'm not a connoisseur. I'm just telling you something that is inescapably obvious, that some of these paintings are very powerful. Christmas cards don't prove anything one way or the other.'

'The truth is', said Guy, 'that I haven't looked at that book much. Someone left it here. One of my transients. Those shelves are full of unread books, I'm afraid. Do take it.'

That was as close as he ever got to apologizing. I thanked him and went home.

16

When I arrived at my flat I was hungry. It was already nearly 10 o'clock. For supper I ate some muesli with milk, some dates and a vitamin pill. Finally I made some strong coffee and, resisting the desire for background music, sat abstemiously in my armchair looking out across the river with the La Tour book on my lap.

I had not realized how interesting he was, but there was little I could learn about him from Guy's book, apart from looking at the reproductions, because it was in Italian. From the Latin I had learnt at school I could understand a little of the text, but without any pleasure because it was so laborious to decipher. At the back there was a long catalogue raisonné, listing the histories of all the pictures, and the current owners – current, at least, at the time of publication of the book. Not only was it difficult to follow the Italian, the old documents cited were quoted in archaic French, many of them from the seventeenth century, and seemed comprehensible without really being so. In the end, despite my increasing interest in the painter, I gave up and got myself a small glass of whisky and my detective story.

It was raining again the next morning and Wireless House, obscured by drizzle and surrounded by the high winds raised up by its own hugeness, was at its most depressing. Inside, the indiscriminate cheer of the doorman added to the gloom. Upstairs in my office, my playwright colleague was back, making up for his absence with a thick atmosphere of noise and smoke, and monopolizing the telephones. As soon as I'd found out there were no messages, no note from *Weasel* and no progress, I went back to the reference library and once again took out the cuttings about the discovery of the Rensellaer *Magdalen*.

This time I paid more attention and read all the details carefully. I didn't in fact learn much more than I'd assimilated before, but I found what I was looking for: the name of the man who'd discovered the documents in the château nearly ten years ago. At that time he'd been a student at the Owermoigne Institute. His name was Simon Cadwallader. According to the cuttings he'd been on an academic visit, researching French furniture collections, and he had found the La Tour document entirely by accident. I also discovered that the Rensellaer *Magdalen* had been sold by Bruno Schwab, the well-known French dealer, and it had been discovered not in France, but, according to the rumours of the time, from a source in East Berlin, which Schwab's had been unable to disclose.

I needed a telephone, and Peter kindly lent me one of his extensions; I took it on its long flex to a slightly more private place behind the stacks and sat on the floor. The Owermoigne switchboard couldn't tell me anything about Simon Cadwallader, but offered to pass me on to their registry. The internal telephone rang and rang, but the registry did not answer and I gave up. When all else fails, try something obvious, according to one of Dan Cohen's many laws of television, and after a while I thought of the telephone directory.

It's not always right to assume that a number is unlisted, or out of date or lost among hundreds of identical ones: Cadwallader is a fairly unusual name, and I got out the A–D, resenting again the loss of the plain old directories in favour of the new and ugly 'phone book'. I was right. Simon Cadwallader was listed, at a Chelsea number. It would not have been difficult to guess his background, given his name, his early interest in expensive furniture, and his affiliation with the Owermoigne and the better part of Chelsea.

When I dialled the number he answered himself, almost at once. I explained that I was interested in the Comte, and that I understood he'd done some research at the château. A couple of minutes on the telephone is not much to cajole or bully someone who only seconds ago was thinking of something quite different. But the magic power of the Corporation's name usually does it.

'Yes, I did know him slightly and I do remember the house. But it was nearly ten years ago. What do you want to know?'

'We are preparing a historical documentary and it's rather lengthy to explain. Very roughly, it's about collaboration in occupied France. What I'm hoping is that you might find time to see me.'

'Yes, I don't mind. I rather like the telly, actually, despite what everyone says.'

'I suppose you couldn't possibly manage some time today?'

'I'm afraid not. Not really. I'm just leaving for Gloucester-shire for a long weekend. Well, after lunch.'

'Could I come and see you in Gloucestershire?' I asked, surprising myself.

He seemed surprised too, but agreed quite easily and gave me some very clear directions. He must have done map-reading in the Corps, at Eton or Harrow perhaps.

'I suppose you realize', he said, before he rang off, 'that I know absolutely nothing about occupied France'.

On Saturday morning I arrived at a stately pace in Moreton-in-the-Marsh, on a slow train. During the journey it had seemed to me as if the train had been taking me back in time, to a childhood journey into Gloucestershire, for some unremembered reason. Certainly I had passed the station sign for Moreton-in-the-Marsh before. Instead of a bare, bright winter day, it must have been high summer, as it always is in childhood, with the chestnut trees green and the hedges filled with elusive scents that would turn into nos-talgia and never smell the same.

But Gloucestershire does not change and decay – I suppose that's why it's so expensive: it could have been twenty or thirty years earlier that I argued with an unfriendly taxi driver outside the station. In the end, having nothing else to do but his job, he drove me to the address Simon Cadwallader had given me. It was a perfect Queen Anne manor house, stand-ing in parkland at the end of a short drive. A haha at the end of the lawn separated the croquet from the cows. In the park there were stands of mature oak trees and there must have been elm trees once, and Queen Anne's lace in summer: all along one side of the drive was heavy ploughland, falling away in the distance, full no doubt in summer months of wavy corn. Sheep may safely graze in a place like that: it was all about security and harmony and well-pruned beauty.

I imagined it was Simon Cadwallader's parents' house, but it seemed that I was wrong. He came out on to the front porch, looking like something from a Noël Coward weekend farce, blond, well-made, well-dressed and astonishingly young-looking. I had worked out that he must be over thirty and yet his small features and clear eyes were almost unmarked by lines. He had kept an earlier fashion for short hair and loose-tailored trousers, and it made him look like one of the generation that was butchered in the First World War, a collector's piece himself.

There was no sign of any parents; he seemed to be alone and very much at home, but without the proprietorial air that kind of house usually produces in its possessors; when we talked he seemed too interested in money to have any of his own. I guessed that he was kept by a rich friend, but I never found out.

The house was perfect inside as well as out, very carefully furnished, which was not surprising as Simon Cadwallader told me he'd left academic life and gone into the furniture trade. He took my coat from me in the hall and led me into a well-proportioned drawing room with sash windows looking over the lawn. Incongruously, the room was painted a deep peacock-blue, against which the few exquisite pieces of walnut stood out, but which also emphasized some indifferent paintings in handsome frames.

'Academic life can get very tiresome,' he went on. 'And there's absolutely no money in it.'

'So what exactly do you do?' I asked. These were preambles while he sized me up, but I was interested too.

'I'm an exporter,' he said. 'A wholesaler. To America mainly but also to Germany. I just fill up containers and pack them off to the land of the free.'

'What kind of thing?' I asked.

'Oh, mostly second-rate. But good second-rate. Top-quality nineteenth-century reproductions, heavily restored pieces, early English oak, which I absolutely loathe actually. So lugubrious.'

I asked him whether he ever had any reservations about stripping England of her few remaining assets.

'Good heavens, no. What does it matter? We used to despoil our Empire after all, and now we despoil ourselves. Rather curious, really. Anyway, I'd much rather some unknown American had my good pieces, than some dreary little upstart in Esher. I really don't think the English deserve real furniture any more, do you? Let them have pine.'

He smiled with an expression of such beauty that I was unable to concentrate on what he was saying. His gold hair and pale features stood out against the dark blue of the walls and his eyes seemed almost violet.

He invited me to sit down on a sofa covered with ivory raw silk. Another expert in comfort, I thought, as the thick cushions formed a support for my back.

'Tell me about your programme,' he said, sitting down opposite me.

I told him a little about our original brief on collaboration, extending it to the Vichy zone, which included the Comte's château.

'So I want to get a better idea of what the Comte was like. I gather from the newspaper cuttings that you actually stayed at the château. How did that happen?'

'It was for my PhD. I was looking at a lot of pieces in private collections for my thesis. It was an unmemorable work on patronage, and I had to go to all sorts of places, to look at various private papers. The Owermoigne is quite good like that.'

'Like what?'

'Oh, getting you introductions to people, getting you on the right circuit. I stayed with lots of people in the Loire valley: I had a sheaf of letters and they all passed me on to each other. After they'd met one, they realized one was going to be all right. I can't remember how I got to the Château de Villancourt actually, and it wasn't very useful to me, but I remember it very clearly because of the other documents I came across. Which you obviously know about.'

'Yes, what happened?'

'I don't know if you know the château. I was mainly working in the library, but in the end I was allowed up into the attics. I was looking at bills of sale for some pieces of virtue of my period, details of commissions. It wasn't terribly well-organized up there: the Comte seemed to have lost control completely.'

'Was he senile?'

'Oh, no, I don't think so. Rather vague and extremely rude, but marbles still in place as far as I could tell. I didn't like him at all. Mind you, I've never felt very much at home with French aristos. They're so frightfully middle class. Always thumbing through the *Almanach de Gotha*.'

'But he was quite helpful, at least? I asked.

'I suppose so, in a way. He wasn't exactly forthcoming, but he gave me the run of the attics. He didn't have much idea what was there, so he wasn't much use.'

'So what exactly did you discover?'

'Not a lot really. I came across a small box of assorted papers, some of them obviously very old, too old for me to have been interested. Some of the others were very useful, letters from architects – does all this interest you? The details are tedious beyond belief, though no worse than VAT returns, I suppose.'

I nodded and smiled.

'As for the La Tour documents, at the time it wasn't all that exciting. It was among the older papers, the ones I had guessed were probably seventeenth-century. I suppose one gets a bit blasé, having seen so much of that kind of thing. Anyway, the script of the time is extraordinarily hard to read; I had a bit of a go at it, and couldn't make it out at all. But as some of the other things were definitely of interest I asked if I could take the box back to London and have some of them copied and professionally deciphered.'

He stopped, and lit a pale mauve Balkan Sobranie.

'And what happened?'

'At first the old boy said yes. We used to have these rather glum dinners, just him and me in that perfectly horrible dining room, Frenchified hunting lodge, and the first time I brought it up we were both quite well oiled. He did have a marvellous cellar, you can at least say that for him, and he was quite generous with it. People always know when one appreciates things,' he said, with slight self-mockery, smiling his violet smile. 'Anyway, by the next day, he'd thought better of it, and he wouldn't let the box out of the house. But he did agree to some experts coming to look at them and he allowed me to photograph all the ones that interested me.'

'What sort of experts?'

'I don't really remember. Several of them, two or three, and quite distinguished as far as I remember. Or from the right places. From the Louvre possibly, or from some university. I can't remember whether I was still there when they worked out that one or two of the seventeenth-century papers had to do with Georges de La Tour. Anyway, I was credited with the discovery – God knows why – and featured in the press. 'Jeune connoisseur britannique' and rather a good photograph. Some rather nice people I'd met sent me a copy.'

'How did it get into the English press?'

Simon Cadwallader looked a little sheepish. 'I think I must have mentioned it to some journalist friend. The odd discovery doesn't do one's career any harm.'

'What were the other documents, apart from the ones that interested you?'

'I'm afraid I can't remember. There must have been scholarly monographs on it at the time. I'm sure the Corporation library could whisk them up for you.'

'What really interests me is the Comte's character.'

'What more can I tell you?' he asked, standing up and walking towards the window. 'It was a long time ago. He did strike me as a complex man, rather embittered even, but then it can't be much fun growing old, can it? As for the German occupation the subject simply didn't come up. It wouldn't, would it?'

'Oh, I don't know,' I said. 'Perhaps in connection with furniture and paintings and valuable things that were stolen during the war.'

'I suppose you're right. Yes, it's true that some families do talk about that, but he didn't. Presumably, if you're right about all this collaboration, he might have been protected in some way, and might have had rather a good reason for keeping quiet about it. In any case, I was twenty-one or something and he must have been well over seventy, it wasn't all that easy to talk to him and at the time I knew almost nothing about the occupation of France. It's amazing how little history one learns, which is why we keep repeating it, or so they say. I'm sure if England had been occupied it would have been just the same here. That kind of family rather liked the Aryan myths, soil and soul. I know my own did, probably yours as well. My papa had lots of German friends before the war and my dear mama spent every summer somewhere very Hunnish. In Lederhosen no doubt. And all quite anti-Semitic, of course, that generation.'

There was nothing new in any of that, so I came back to the document I couldn't find.

'Has the Comte still got it?' I asked.

'Why don't you ask him?' he replied. 'I don't think he'd have let it go. He wasn't exactly interested in all his possessions, they didn't seem to give him very much pleasure, but I do remember he wouldn't let me take all those papers away.'

'Perhaps he was hoping that they'd turn out to be valuable.'

'I shouldn't have thought so. But maybe. The only one of any interest as far as I can remember was the La Tour document and that has no real merit in itself.'

'Forgive the ignorance of a hack, but why then did it make the news?'

'That was later, of course, when an interesting La Tour emerged, one that some American gallery bought.'

'The Rensellaer *Magdalen*?' I asked, knowing the answer.

'Yes, I think so,' he said. 'I'm fairly sure. They keep coming out of the woodwork, don't they? I mean, even here in England there was the one that was found in a museum basement in Stockton-on-Tees and one in a country house in Leicestershire or somewhere. Anyway, that document from the château was a useful piece of authentication for the *Magdalen*.'

'Would you explain to me, in words of one syllable,' I asked, 'how a picture is authenticated?'

'Certainly,' he said, 'though people would talk about attribution rather than authentication. As you know, old masters are not my thing. Would you like to have some lunch, and then we can dispose of the subject? After that I'm afraid I'll have to put you in a taxi, because we've got guests.'

The other part of the 'we' did not appear for lunch. Simon took me into a kitchen lavishly covered with terracotta and cream marble. In that offhand way that female cooks rarely achieve, he made an excellent Spanish omelette, and put some interesting-looking leaves in a Perspex salad bowl. We took the dishes into the dining room, whose shape matched the drawing room. There were no pictures on the pale yellow walls and I asked why not.

'Too expensive. It would cost at least a couple of tons of furniture shipments to get anything that we'd like to hang. I'm not interested in numbered prints or the anonymous ancestor trade. One's own are all right, I suppose. But the prices of real paintings are quite insane.'

'So to go back to what I was asking,' I said, 'if I were going to spend a lot of money on a picture, what would I do to make sure it was worth the price?'

'In practice you'd trust your internationally famous, utterly charming dealer, or perhaps a couple of connoisseurs you might happen to know, if you were that rich. In the past that was always what happened. The attribution of a painting used to be an art, and like all art it was sometimes inspired and sometimes pure invention. It was an art that was very easily exploited by the cognoscenti. Bernard Berenson is the classic example, of course,' he said, tossing the salad.

'How do you mean?' I asked.

Simon Cadwallader smiled. 'As you'll remember,' he said, 'Bernard Berenson practically invented early Italian painting – if that's not an unfortunate way of putting it. He used to rule the art world from his villa full of acolytes, in the hills above Florence – the villa I Tatti, a mecca for aspiring connoisseurs. His opinions were law, and he did have a wonderful eye, wonderful judgement. But he suspended it sometimes.'

He passed me the salad of lamb's lettuce, radicchio and walnuts. This strange documentary had had, if nothing else, an accompaniment of good food.

'Berenson was in cahoots for years and years with an English dealer and he and this man Duveen passed off really inferior work on rich American collectors. They both made a fortune. Berenson alone made several millions of dollars.

And that was then. In the first quarter of this century,' he added, seeing that I didn't know.

'And it was such a subtle thing, too. Nothing crude like fakes, just creative restoration and optimistic attribution. So an anonymous triptych with some featureless saints suddenly becomes a glowing little school of Verrocchio, with an encouraging little accolade from BB.'

'I find this difficult to believe,' I said.

'I thought it was common knowledge,' he replied coolly. 'Anyway, those were the good old days, when attribution was an art. The connoisseur could recognize quality, through intuition and experience. Now everything is much more scientific; first of all there have been decades of serious scholarship, serious research on all this information has been widely published or computerized – it's easy to get at. Far more is known, there's much less room for guesswork, in theory anyway. Ideally a painting should have a proper provenance – as long a history as possible, preferably going back to the atelier of the painter. This history might be records of a commission, of a sale, an entry in an inventory of someone's collection, or a reference in the settlement of someone's estate after death. There are even cases of pictures being portrayed in other people's paintings, or in a few cases, in marquetry work on panels in furniture. Some of this evidence is circumstantial, some is direct, and the more the better. A genuine signature would help, for instance.'

'But is there really a lot of this kind of evidence?'

'Of course, lots of important paintings have very little such evidence behind them, but there are all kinds of other studies that are relevant, and which have been very highly developed. Iconography for instance – a knowledge of which subjects and symbols a painter couldn't have used, or almost certainly would have used. Then it's fairly well understood when certain subjects and effects became technically possible, or fashionable, and so on. Which is enormously important, especially in negative judgements. Do you really want me to drone on like this?'

I nodded.

'Don't think I'm rushing you, but I'll just go and make some coffee.'

He went out and came back quite quickly with a small tray.

'Decaffeinated and instant. I hope you don't mind. Do you know, it's really quite amusing, I believe Bernard Berenson actually stooped to calling himself Doris, in his coded cables to Duveen. Perhaps he had a sense of humour. Anyway, *revenons à nos moutons*. Finally,' he said, sitting down, 'there's science proper. Canvases can be tested. X-rays, pigment analysis, all that kind of thing. Paintings on wood can be tested with dendrochronology, which can establish the age of the wood from evidence of the growth of the original tree.'

'I can see how all those things might establish the date of a painting, but can they establish the identity of a painter as well?'

'No. Not as far as I know. But they can often establish that a certain picture couldn't be by a particular painter – you know, so-and-so couldn't have had a certain pigment with lead in it from mines in one part of Europe because it wasn't available in another part of Europe.'

'But presumably forgers know a bit of useful science too?' I asked.

'That is why the professional connoisseur is still not redundant,' said Simon. 'Now, is that roughly what you wanted to know? I'm afraid I can't get any more scientific than that.'

'Yes, absolutely,' I said, 'and you've been very generous with your time. I'm very grateful.'

'It's been a pleasure,' he said, 'but not entirely disinterested. It's always useful to have allies in television.'

I got the violet glance again.

'I'm sorry I couldn't have been more help about the Comte. But you know, you should have come clean in the first place, and told me you were interested in Nazi art thefts.'

I tried to look rueful, and we said goodbye.

I was sorry to leave that beautiful house with the ghost of summer lurking in the wet beechwoods. I was sorry too that I'd been so cautious with Simon Cadwallader: there hadn't really been any reason to disguise from him that the Comte was dead and that the document had been mislaid, as far as I could tell. But then, I couldn't tell.

17

On Monday morning I arrived at Wireless House so early that the doorman asked me whether anything was the matter. I needed to know a lot more about the background of expensive pictures, and I needed someone to point me in the right direction. I had heard once that somewhere in the bowels of Wireless House there was a formidable woman who knew about everything and everyone in the world of painting. After several telephone calls and a look at the arcane rubric which is the Internal Directory, I found her. Her title was AHSR6 Tel – Assistant Head of Specialist Research, Section 6, Television – and her name was Rosemary Meacham.

Her office was in the second basement, a place without any natural light. She had two underlit desks for displaying transparencies, and a huge collection of picture books.

'Don't think you can borrow any of them,' were her words to me. 'I've lost too much already.'

'I wouldn't dream of it,' I said. 'I'm not looking for books or transparencies.'

'Ah, transparencies I do lend,' she said. 'If it's really necessary. Because although it is expensive, they can be replaced. I mean, not outrageously expensive, though the inconvenience is something else again. If you had any idea of the time and the paperwork and the sheer frustration of getting replacements from some of those galleries, you'd think twice about taking any of them out. But I do lend them. When it's absolutely essential.'

'Oh no, it's not necessary at all,' I said.

'I don't mind,' she insisted. 'So long as you sign for them.'

'Actually there really aren't any I want, at the moment.'

'Well, if you don't want books and don't want trannies, why are you here in the first place?' she demanded.

I tried to begin again.

'I need advice,' I said.

'I don't know why you come here,' she replied angrily. 'I'm just a librarian, a shuffler of card indexes; do people imagine that I have any expertise after a mere nineteen years of getting their finger-marks off transparencies? Of course they don't.'

'I've come to ask your advice. I've been told to consult you.'

'Why on earth didn't you say so?'

'It's about Georges de La Tour,' I said.

'Yes?' she replied. '1593 to 1652. Overrated, in my opinion. What do you want to know about him?'

'Well, it's not exactly about him,' I said, hesitating.

'You haven't the slightest idea what you want, have you?' she asked.

She was very nearly right, but I persisted.

'I want to know about the provenance of a particular painting, and about the subject in general – I mean the subject of attribution.'

She walked to one of her well-filled shelves.

'For any particular La Tour you want this,' she said, holding up a large volume in a classic art series.

I looked carefully at the title.

'But you can't have it,' she said.

'I've already ordered a copy from the Reference Library, some time ago.'

'Oh well, then,' she said, slightly put out. 'You should find everything in that. It was republished last year, so it's pretty much up to date, though there may have been a little research since then, or a minor sale, though I don't remember anything. As for the subject in general, given that you don't seem to know much already, I suggest you go and see Anthea Himmelfarb. She talks so much that she won't realize what you know or what you don't. And she loves talking, or so I'm told.'

I was disappointed. Anthea Himmelfarb was a well-known radio personality, indispensable to chat and joke shows.

'I had meant somebody in the art world,' I said.

'Anthea Himmelfarb knows the art world inside out,' she

said coldly. 'But there's no reason why you should take my advice. I just catalogue transparencies.'

'I'm sorry,' I said. 'Is there anybody else? As well, I mean?'

'If you really knew your subject,' she began, but my irritation must have shown at last.

'Don't misunderstand me,' she said, collapsing as irascible people do. 'I mean, if you were a bit more of a specialist, I'd probably suggest someone who specialized. But at this stage I think you should start with Mrs Himmelfarb.'

Anthea Himmelfarb lived in North Kensington, on the fringes of the Caribbean district, in an area that was run down and covered in graffiti. Her house was in a mid-nineteenth-century terrace, partly covered in white stucco, where it wasn't coming off in large flakes. The paint on the front doors was peeling and the ornamental plasterwork and railings had fallen off or been taken away. I was surprised at the address until I found myself in Anthea Himmelfarb's enormous hall.

The house was not one, but three knocked together: the nineteenth-century shapes of the rooms had been lost and instead I seemed to be in the middle of a 1960s picture gallery.

'Early 1960s open plan,' said Anthea Himmelfarb, as if I had asked her a question. 'Pure vandalism, of course. But you could get away with it then, and my late lamented was really rather a vandal.'

She clearly did like to talk. I had not yet even had time to say who I was. I offered to shake hands, which seemed to be introduction enough. She had been expecting me. The feel of her hand, with its dry skin, made me realize that she was older than she looked. I supposed she was about fifty-five.

'Of course he was quite right, in a way. It is perfect for hanging pictures and he had so many. You must come and see them all later on, and tell me what you think of my latest acquistion. Now, let's go into my study and you can tell me all about what you want me to say.'

I followed her into another room, this one long and low, filled like a time-warp with 1960s colours, khaki and maroon.

'How long have I got?' she asked with a cooperative air.

'As long as you can spare,' I said, unused to this approach.

'Oh, I could go on for hours and hours, as I'm sure you know, darling. How long's the programme, and is there anyone else on it?'

'Oh yes, quite a few. We haven't finally decided yet. At least ten, I should say. The whole thing will probably be about fifty minutes, and then there'll be five or six minutes of film archive.'

'Film archive?' she asked, clearly astonished.

'Yes,' I said.

'On the wireless?'

'Hardly,' I said, trying a smile.

'Well, what are we talking about then?' she asked irritably. 'Are you or aren't you producing a new series of *Ask Me Another*?'

'I'm so sorry,' I said. 'There must have been some confusion. I'm nothing to do with radio.'

'Well, what are you doing here then? I'm expecting someone from the Corporation.'

'I am from the Corporation. But from the television side. From Current Affairs.'

She laughed the self-indulgent laugh of a fat woman who considers herself a character.

'I'm afraid it's out of the question, absolutely out of the question, darling. I never do telly. I did it once before and never again. A very nasty make-up girl made me look like a ghoul. A monster. The answer is no. Absolutely no.'

I've never found a simple way of disabusing people of their assumption that they're wanted on screen; their insincere refusals to appear are often very premature.

'None the less,' I said, 'there are several things I'd like to ask you about, if you would simply give me some of your time. Perhaps I should begin at the beginning.'

'Why not?' she said. 'Nothing wrong with the obvious.'

In fact I could not have begun at the beginning, even if I'd wanted to.

'The truth is that I've come to you for your help; it's nothing to do with your appearing, at least not at this stage. I want to test a guess on you, against your knowledge of painting and the art world. I know almost nothing about that world: I work in Current Affairs, and I've been involved in a programme about collaboration in France during the Second World War. I've come across something slightly odd, perhaps very odd, and there's a lot I need to know before it will make any real sense.'

She was listening to me carefully, smoking almost continually, her malicious eyes shining.

'What I'd like to do is not tell you my guess, but just ask some questions. Just ask you to talk, in fact, about the art world.'

'Only if you promise to tell me later.'

'I promise to tell you, but not necessarily today.'

'All right,' she said, putting out her cigarette and lighting another with her chubby hands. 'The first thing to tell you about the art world is that it stinks. And I should know. I've been sleeping with painters and dealers and connoisseurs – those that were that way inclined – since I was seventeen, and if I'd had any children I'd have made them take up forestry or tennis coaching. Luckily I've been frightfully rich for the last twenty years so I can afford to be rude to all of them. And I have been, darling, I have been.'

She leaned forward and gave me a roguish look which had probably got her a long way when she was young enough to get it right.

'I made a very sensible marriage. I loved painting but I did so hate all that gas ring and tin opener caper that arthurs used to go in for in my day.'

'Arthurs?' I asked, imagining it was some sort of fifties slang.

'Artists, darling,' she said. 'You know, from J. Arthur.'

I still could not understand.

'Wankers. From rhyming slang. J. Arthur Rank. Anyway, I didn't like all that squalor, except for a seedy night out now and then. My late lamented was extremely rich and also a connoisseur, as it happened. A real connoisseur. Unlike all those poseurs and frauds you meet in Cork Street. Some of them are lots of fun, of course, and frightfully clever. But there really are very few people who love painting. Who know how to look at a painting. That's the second thing you should know about the art world. What is it you actually want to know?'

'That's what I want to know. How to judge a painting.'

'I can't tell you that. No one can. It comes of being seriously interested and having a gift for looking.'

'No, I don't mean how someone ought to judge a painting. I mean how people generally speaking do.'

'Badly, badly,' she said loudly. 'Most people are liars and philistines. When they're not vandals. Most people wouldn't know a good painting from an out-and-out fake, let alone a bad or not very good picture. Personally I love fakes. I've got several myself. I've got two van Meegerens and a couple of de Hoorys. I always thought Keating was overrated but I've got one from a very embarrassed friend, who'd bought it as genuine. And I've got a David Stein Renoir which is absolutely delicious.'

'Go on talking about fakes,' I said.

'Oh, darling, how wonderful. I do hope you've found an absolutely marvellous one, and you promised you'd tell me first, didn't you?'

'No,' I said.

She laughed.

'Well you promised to tell me about your guess.'

'Yes, I did, but not necessarily today,' I said. Applying charm or flattery to women is one of the trickiest of all the forms of deceit required by Corporation life. However, Anthea Himmelfarb didn't need it. She was already completely in love with the drama of her own life.

'Fakes are one of my obsessions, I admit. One must have obsessions, don't you agree? I mean, they're so stimulating. Almost as good as having someone to hate. Fake paintings provide me with hours of harmless indignation. The odd thing is how many there are. I'm not talking about paintings which get attributed to the wrong arthur or even contemporary imitations or school-ofs. I'm not even talking about creative restoration of the kind Berenson went in for.'

At that point I was able to nod knowledgeably.

'I'm talking about deliberate frauds – nineteenth- or twentieth-century paintings specially done to mislead and to make money. All the big galleries have got them you know. There are thousands of them, all over the place. Of course people think I'm completely off my trolley – ask anyone and they'll tell you I'm hopelessly unreliable. But I'm right, you know.'

'The major collections all contain fakes? I find that very hard to believe. How did it happen?'

'Often in the most innocent way, because of gifts and bequests. It's often happened that a major collector decided to give his entire collection to, say, the National Gallery or to the Metropolitan. Now obviously no one's going to look a gift horse in the mouth – if there are a few duds among the rest, they can simply be put in the basement to gather dust. People have been making generous presents to public galleries for centuries. Often a painting is just quietly reattributed or someone discreetly adds a little disclaimer to the notice – "school of" or "attributed to". But there are important fakes on the international market today and museums and galleries do bid for them. Especially the Americans. There's far too much money pursuing too few masterpieces, and too many museums. That's what got poor old BB going, that and arrogance, I should think.'

You mean modern fakes? Successful ones?'

'Yes. Recent deliberate fakes. Made to commission. You see there are still to this day great master forgers for hire. But don't look so astonished, my dear girl. If van Meegeren could get away with it, as near as dammit, why shouldn't someone today? If he hadn't tried to sell a "Vermeer" to Hermann Goering he'd probably have got away with everything.'

'But how would it be possible now? Surely the scientific testing they can do today would make it impossible?'

'It is, of course, very much more difficult. But the forgers are scientists too. They read all the learned journals. They go to enormous lengths to get contemporary canvases, to use all the right elements in the pigments, to use modern heat treatment to create the craquelure.'

'Are you saying', I asked 'that someone could commission a fake old master which would pass every scientific test?'

'I wouldn't go quite that far,' she said, blowing smoke in her own face. 'No. But you could certainly get a fake through a lot of them. And people don't always do all the tests. Or do the ones on which a painting would be weak. But you have to take into account a particular feature of the world of art

connoisseurs (and this is the third thing you ought to know);
it's a world consumed with vanity.'

'What do you mean?'

'I mean, darling, that most of these poseurs have an exag-
gerated respect for their own aesthetic judgement. Look, I'll
show you what I mean. Come with me.'

She moved fast, for a fat woman, and hurried me out into
one of the rooms that formed her own gallery. We passed
some curious pictures; on one wall were a group of Balinese
primitives which looked to me like airport art, and nearby a
couple of landscapes, which looked as if they'd come from
the Sunday pavement merchants outside Hyde Park.

'Come along, come along,' she said, pulling me with her,
to stand in front of a painting of a woman in a Dutch interior.

'Now. What do you think of that?'

It seemed vaguely familiar and yet it made a curious
impression, as if something had slipped.

'Well?' she asked triumphantly. 'What do you make of it?'

'I don't know. Do you mean, do I like it?'

'No, no, no. You couldn't possibly like it. When do you
think it was painted?'

'There's something rather odd about it, but I suppose it
must be mid-seventeenth-century.'

'Exactly,' she said, 'You've proved my point. This is a very
good van Meegeren Vermeer, painted some time in the
1930s. I told you I had one. When it was put on the market all
the cognoscenti loved it. You couldn't see then what you can
see so clearly now, the flavour of the period in which it was
painted, the anachronisms. Look at the hair, and the glass on
the table. Of course this is a particularly good example of the
phenomenon, which is why I bought it. It's not always nearly
so obvious.'

'I still haven't understood what you are explaining.'

'Can't you see? My point is this. When connoisseurs or
dealers or whoever decide that a painting is a genuine whatever, a genuine Constable, say, that's what everyone sees,
and if it has a provenance that is remotely respectable, or if it
comes from a reputable dealer (or a powerful one), or if a top
scholar is all for it, I don't think they'd bother to test it. They
are vain enough to think that their own judgement is more

reliable. I could quote you hundreds of cases.'

'What would happen to someone who did question it?'

'It would depend who he was. Or she was. He'd have to be very brave. Only a child can get away with saying the emperor has no clothes. A child or someone who doesn't matter. I don't think anyone with a career to make could take on the art establishment.'

'And then, you see,' she went on, 'after a painting has been around for a while, the incentive to test gets rather weak, to put it mildly, when people's reputations are on the line. Especially when there's a lot of money involved. For instance, that Georges de La Tour in the Metropolitan in New York, the one there was all that fuss about. That was sold for a small fortune in 1960, $750,000, according to gossip, which would be – what? – about $7 million in today's money. As it happens, I don't think *The Fortune Teller* is a fake, or at any rate I'm sure it's a seventeenth-century masterpiece, and it is after all signed. But you take the point. The Met paid a lot of money for it. It would have been terribly embarrassing to discover it had been put together by a professional forger and deliberately unloosed on to the market.'

I wished I had read the La Tour cuttings more carefully, but they had seemed so peripheral at the time.

'Presumably they've tested it, though,' I said.

'Oh yes, and as I say, I think it's genuine. But there are still a few rumours that won't lie down and die.'

'Like what?'

'Oh, you know. Which tests it actually went through and so on. Besides, even the tests are open to interpretation. But the whole point is that no one likes to have egg on his face, especially not in the aesthetic world. And at that level, at the very top, it's a very small world. Everybody knows everybody. And now, darling, what's your secret guess?' she asked, turning upon me.

'It's only the possibility of a secret,' I said, 'and it's too soon to say.'

'You promised,' she said with a sulky look which was an anachronism on her face. 'I shan't show you my paintings!'

'I'll tell you as soon as I can,' I said.

'Well, I'll show you my pictures then, and not before.'

So I never did discover why she had the Balinese airport art or the nasty English landscapes.

She relented enough to give me some herb tea and to tell me about some of her sexual adventures at the Slade, more than thirty years before. At another time I would have been interested; women so rarely tell the truth about sex and she, if not frank, was at least forthright, but I was anxious to get back to Wireless House before the main point of the story escaped me yet again.

18

On my desk at Wireless House was a copy of the big picture book about Georges de La Tour that Rosemary Meacham had shown me. As she had said, it had been republished the previous year. It was one of those exhaustive, quirkily written books that the English still think they do best. Also on my desk was a demand from my personnel officer to inform her of my movements, and a note of congratulation from my head of department, thanking me for my important contribution to the collaboration film and exhorting me to keep up the good work. I smiled. I owed that, presumably, to diplomacy from Dan, and I gratefully photocopied the note and sent the duplicate without further comment to Staff Mobility.

It was early afternoon and I settled down for the first time in a long time to spend several hours reading an academic work, something I prefer to leave to academics. The book had plates of all La Tour's pictures, some of them in colour, a lengthy bibliography and reference section and a catalogue raisonné at the back listing references, some of the past owners and other documentation; it also had a long introduction and a new preface. I decided to start at the front: as Anthea Himmelfarb had said, there's nothing wrong with the obvious, and conversely, I thought, there is something perverse in always trying to avoid it. I did, however, skip the preface.

In an effort to be businesslike I got a notepad, and hurried into the life of Georges de La Tour; he had had the misfortune to have been born in interesting times and the book gave elaborate accounts of the Wars of Religion, the Thirty Years War, outbreaks of plague, famine and witch-hunting, the passage of armies and refugees back and forth across Lorraine. But there was not much known about his personal life.

He had been born a baker's son in 1593 in Vic-sur-Seille, where I had had quiche lorraine and sweet tea with Madame Cernay, and he had somehow managed to marry an aristocrat's daughter when he was twenty-four – clearly a boy who knew how to hustle. He and his wife settled in Lunéville, where I had had such a pleasant lunch with Mademoiselle Audran. I realized why Vic and Lunéville had seemed like ghost towns: they had been enormously important in the early seventeenth-century but had been in decline for a couple of hundred years.

I hurried on through the baptisms of La Tour's children, his niggardly contracts with boy apprentices, his official recognition as a painter by the duke of Lorraine, his tax avoidance, his growing wealth. His behaviour became more thuggish or more seigneurial as time went by, depending how you looked at it: he was a man who beat up a trespasser so badly that he had to pay for his treatment, left rubbish in the streets at a time of plague and let loose his hunting dogs on the peasants' corn; rather odd, considering the unearthly simplicity of his paintings.

After this long narrative, the author apologized, unnecessarily in my case, for the scantiness of the account, and said that there was very little remaining evidence. It seemed strange that after considerable success in his own lifetime, Georges de La Tour had been quickly forgotten. Both he and his painting had fallen out of the bottom of history, into a kind of limbo. Perhaps that had happened to a lot of painters, I thought, but it seemed odd to me. In the middle of all this I got a call from Dan.

'Hello,' I said. 'Thanks very much for the PR job on HCA.TV.'

'Any time,' he said. 'I'd hate to see you sink without trace into kiddie programmes.'

'Where are you ringing from?' I asked.

'From Hank's cutting room.'

'I don't want to sound contrary, but whenever I really need you I can't find you, and now I'm very engrossed in something, you find me.'

'Still as encouraging as ever,' said Dan. 'What is engrossing you?'

'I'm not sure exactly. The beginning of a guess.'

'Oh. One of those. Why don't you take a break and come down and talk to Hank and me? You can even tell us about it.'

'I'd like to,' I said. 'If you'll listen.'

Both Hank and Dan looked more relaxed than usual. They'd just put a programme to bed and the assistant was clearing up and labelling film cans. They were both smoking and Dan was writing something up on Hank's chinagraph joke board.

'By the way, I've just seen the Lorraine rushes,' said Dan. 'I would have asked you to come if you'd been here this morning.'

'What are they like?' I asked Hank.

'Good,' he said. 'In themselves. The answer to a film editor's prayer. You can say what you like about old Rick but he certainly is the best. That stuff will cut together like the proverbial. Nothing wrong with Rick.'

'Just a minute,' said Dan. 'Who directed it, I'd like to know?'

'Be that as it may,' said Hank, trailing his voice peaceably.

'Anyway, I've fixed a viewing for you tomorrow in theatre R7,' said Dan. 'Since you weren't here today.'

'What for?' I asked.

'What do you mean?' he said. 'You're supposed to be the one who's interested in this film. Not me, sweetheart.'

'Now, now, children,' said Hank.

'I am,' I said, 'but not in Lorraine. It's the Comte and the Château de Villancourt that interest me. That's what I wanted to tell you about.'

And I started. They weren't very impressed that the document was missing.

'You mean you can't locate it, after a few phone calls,' said Dan. 'Just because you can't find it doesn't mean it's missing.'

'No,' I said. 'But it's odd.'

'Why?'

I explained how reluctant the Comte had been, according to Simon Cadwallader, to let it out of his house, and how the Rensellaer had tried without success to persuade him to sell it.

'Just a minute,' said Dan. 'Why would the Rensellaer want it?'

I began to despair. There was so much to explain and it was such a long shot.

'They wanted it because they'd just bought a previously unknown painting – a night scene of St Mary Magdalen – and the letter was the only surviving evidence supporting the attribution to Georges de La Tour.'

'How could it possibly be the only evidence?'

'Quite possibly with Georges de La Tour. Not one of his paintings has a proper history and not one of them can be traced directly back to him. He disappeared for a couple of centuries, he was completely forgotten and so were his pictures.'

'Is that unusual?'

'I think so, but I don't know. What do I know about art history? All I can tell you is that the one the Queen's got at Hampton Court has the longest history of any of his pictures – it probably arrived in the Royal Collection in the 1660s, but they don't really know where from.'

'OK, then, what's unusual about this picture only having one piece of supporting evidence? What is it, anyway?'

'It's a letter, part of a correspondence from a monastery in the Loire valley to a monastery in Lunéville, and it mentions the commission of the painting. A penitent Magdalen.'

'Well, what's wrong with that?'

'Nothing. Except I can't find it. It's rather a good piece of evidence.'

'Really dear,' said Hank, 'I do sometimes wonder. Time for a holiday, do we think?'

'No, no, I'm fine,' I said, thinking.

'Hank,' I suddenly said, hugging him and laughing, as I finally got the point, 'what's the difference between a document and a painting?'

'I don't know,' he said, humouring me, 'I haven't heard that one. What is the difference between a document and a painting?'

I was very excited.

'With a picture you look at it,' I said loudly. 'With a document you look at the words.'

'My, my, my,' said Hank. 'Your Pulitzer prize is getting nearer and nearer.'

'Jesus Christ,' said Dan angrily, knocking a can off the work-bench and spilling coils of tangled film around his feet, while the assistant looked on contemptuously. 'If you can't talk sense, you'd better go away. There isn't room here for all four of us and your crazy fantasies.'

'But what it means,' I said, 'or what I think it means, is that no one ever checked the documents themselves. With a painting, the thing itself, the quality of the work, the pigment, all that you look at closely, you judge on its appearance. But a document you see differently. You judge it on its sense.'

'Well?' said Dan.

'So if I found some documents and they were modestly interesting, and there were no reason to doubt their authenticity, there'd be no motive to test them exhaustively for forgery. Especially if there were no motive for forgery. And especially if some experts came along to decipher them and raised no objections. Especially if most of the documents were in fact genuine.'

Dan's irritation had reappeared.

'Imagine that exactly this had happened at the Château de Villancourt. Then of course if a painting appeared later, a masterpiece from a reputable dealer, its authenticity would be enhanced by an obscure document whose authenticity was already accepted. Because the document had been found years before anyway, and none of the people involved were in any way concerned. Not only that. The painting would in some way be expected to reappear one day.'

'Do you know who was involved?' Dan asked. 'What's this got to do with the Nazi occupation? Who, for instance, was the dealer?'

'There's a lot I still don't know,' I said. 'That's what I mean about having the beginnings of a guess. For instance, I'm assuming the Rensellaer would only buy from reputable dealers.'

'Still this touching faith in the establishment,' Dan said, and I thought of Anthea Himmelfarb.

'12.25,' said Hank firmly. 'If we don't hurry we'll be late for the bar.'

So we all went to have lunch in the crowded, subsidized canteen complex which serves to feed about 5,000 Corporation employees and prevent them from having anything to do with the world outside. We didn't talk about La Tour any more. I think Dan would actually have walked out if I'd tried to.

We came out of the canteen at about 3 and walked across to the other side of Wireless House just in time for a departmental meeting. These are monthly rituals, to be missed as often as possible, except by the unproductive. Dan and I were conscious that we hadn't been achieving very much and so we went and sat in a windowless conference room for two hours or so, to appease the managers.

There was a lot of indignant talk from the apparatchiks about our failure to stick to our budgets, our failure to warn the police about parking crew cars, our failure to send in the appropriate forms for holidays, sickness, transfers and all the rest. While these reprimands were being delivered, people at the back of the room played noughts and crosses or worked out their expenses. About halfway through two tea ladies came in with a trolley and passed round biscuits and lukewarm tea. The atmosphere was that of a talk on team spirit at a second-rate public school; television viewers might have been surprised at the institutionalized, adolescent behaviour of some of the nation's top newscasters and commentators.

As soon as the last speaker had drawn to a close, there was a general rush towards the club, only two floors up, where drinks are served from 5.30 onwards. I stood with Dan at the bar, talking to people I knew and trying to give the impression that our collaboration film was still making progress. But I overheard Dan saying to someone that he was dropping it. I turned towards him and saw that he was talking to a man I recognized, the editor of a minor documentary series.

'Dan is just saying that,' I said, interrupting, 'to conceal from the world that we might have stumbled on a scoop.'

Dan smiled.

'How do you induce this zeal, Dan?' asked the other man.

'It's not zeal,' Dan said, 'it's monomania, and it's self-induced.'

The other man smiled at me, but Dan did not introduce us.

The room soon filled up with people drinking spritzers and mixed fruit juices, looking continuously around to see who was coming in and who was sitting with whom. It was restless and uncomfortable, and not a good place to be when your work is not going well. Dan continued to talk to the same man, with his back three-quarters turned to me. He was famous for his rudeness; I often told him he was the only man capable to unconsciously forcing a woman off the pavement and into the street. That evening I thought it was probably deliberate and therefore a sign of interest. After I'd had enough of the smoke and the noise and my own thoughts, I asked him to give me a lift home.

'A lift home?' he asked, looking around at me over his shoulder. 'I live in Islington and you live in the East End, don't you? Isn't that a little out of my way?'

'It depends where you're trying to get to,' I said.

Dan turned round fully then.

'I suppose I might make a detour,' he said.

We left soon afterwards and walked through various different buildings and courtyards to get to the car park.

'Well, well, well,' said Dan as we got into his car. 'I'm not quite sure where I'm going. You'll have to give me directions.'

'Oh, it's pretty straightforward,' I said. 'Not really very far.'

'Perhaps we'll get on better without the Guide Michelin,' Dan said.

It was very cold when we arrived at my warehouse, and cold inside the hall. We walked up the open wrought-iron stairs which had been part of the original building and which the architect had painted a bright red, to clash fashionably with the tall expanse of brick wall. If Dan was impressed by the beauty of the building he didn't show it. He said nothing when we walked into the wide space of my flat, but, with unusual politeness, took off my coat for me.

I went to the kitchen end of the room to get some ice from the refrigerator.

'What would you like to drink? Whisky, bourbon, beer?'

He came across to where I kept bottles on a butler's tray.

'Bourbon,' he said, 'since you have Jack Daniels.'

'We globe-trotters,' I said, feeling silly. 'And ice?'

I had vodka and ice, thinking that if I had any sense I would be having fruit juice.

'Where's your sound system?' he asked, walking over,

without waiting, to the place where it was most likely to be, next to two sofas and the Cambodian stone head. He bent down slightly to look at the shelf on the wall which held the amplifier and pre-amplifier.

'How did you get this kind of money?' Dan asked. 'This is the best. But you're always trying to cry poor, aren't you?'

'It would be pointless to try to explain to you,' I said.

'No need,' said Dan, grinning. 'The bad faith of the ruling classes. Quite simple.'

'You sound very old-fashioned. Very sixties. People don't apologize about privilege any more.'

'But they still feel guilty, don't they?' said Dan with pleasure.

'I don't want to argue with you. If you want to fight those fights pick someone else. And don't drink my Jack Daniels.'

'Sorry,' he said. 'Only teasing.'

'But it isn't funny. These assumptions, this inverted snobbery, is not funny.'

'I should have your problems,' he said, looking closely at the sound system, which was English and, as he said, the best. He put on a disc of Ella Fitzgerald singing with Louis Armstrong.

With the music my irritation lifted at once.

'Would you like me to cook you some supper?' I asked.

He sat back in one of the sofas, put his head back on the cushions, smiling unkindly.

'Yes,' he said. 'I would. What have you got?'

I looked in the fridge. There was some very good cheese, enough leaves of various kinds to make a salad, and not much else.

'Eggs and bacon,' I said, not wanting to come across too obviously.

'Omelette soufflé,' he said. 'I will make it myself. Have you got any dried mushrooms?'

'Funghi porcini, of course,' I said, getting them from a cupboard.

So we had supper together, looking out over the Thames and watching the barges going slowly past. I opened some Californian red wine.

'This is good,' said Dan accusingly, when he tasted it.

'You have expensive tastes yourself,' I said.

'Ah, but I've acquired mine through honest labour. How did you acquire yours?'

'It's true that honest labour had little to do with it,' I replied, wondering when the temptation to talk about oneself begins to wear off.

'Tell me about your early struggles,' I said instead. 'Your deserving family, the first glimmerings of recognition, the formative years of student politics.'

'No,' said Dan. 'There wasn't really any picturesque hardship, although my grandparents were poor. My grandfather was a tailor, in the classic tradition. But my parents weren't poor. Or specially deserving.'

So we didn't talk about ourselves, even though autobiography is the easiest seduction technique. Instead we talked about the Corporation, that adult playground where the rules are really only pretend. After dinner we felt less self-conscious and went to bed, though it was not late.

Later in bed Dan asked me, predictably, how I'd acquired my flat.

'A lot of this is loot. The spoils of marriage. I'm divorced.'

'Oh yes, somebody said you were married before. You must have been quite young.'

'Yes, it was a university romance.'

'An Oxbridge romance, no doubt.'

'Yes, Oxford.'

'Of course. Well?'

'Well, I got married and then I got divorced.'

'And he had a lot of money.'

'Yes, he did. I didn't think about it at the time.'

Dan smiled.

'I mean, I didn't wonder about it. Or realize how much he had. He was part of a group of people, some of them quite a lot older, who lived a very flash life in London. I thought they were paying, a lot of the time. He was supposed to be doing a PhD on some American poets. He was quite a lot older too. I liked all that glamorous stuff. Not so much the parties as eating in good restaurants, going to France and to New York. Some of his friends were seriously rich, with big boats in the Caribbean. All that.'

'So what made you throw it all in?'

'I suppose I was too young,' I said.

'Now, come on,' said Dan, 'you can do better than that.'

'Not much better,' I said, 'and you can't smoke in my bed.'

'If I put my cigarette out, you must tell me the whole story. Otherwise it's a few more puffs of Marlboro Light and then goodbye to the East End boy. And no more filming in France.'

'All right,' I said. 'Voyeur.'

I got out of bed, wishing I were one of those women who can walk around naked with pleasure, and fetched two glasses of bourbon.

'You're a nice shape,' said Dan, like a friend. 'Enjoy it. Now, begin at the beginning.'

We leant back against the big pillows and he looked as if he were really curious.

'Why are you interested?' I asked.

'Why are you prepared to tell me?' he said. I decided to ignore that.

'I was very slow on the uptake. I just enjoyed our expensive life, being expensive. Students weren't serious in those days – it must have been well after your day – but finally, after a while it dawned on me that he, my husband, hadn't got all his money from his loving parents. He was dealing. That was the point of all the travel. At first I thought it was just grass, cocaine perhaps, which doesn't worry me. But in the end I realized he was doing smack. I had just begun to quarrel with him about it when he was arrested. Several of them were. You might remember the trial.'

'So many socialites get done for drugs, don't they?' said Dan. 'I probably wouldn't remember.' But I knew he would look it up when he got back to Wireless House.

'So I left him.'

'And you returned to the bosom of your outraged but loyal family in – let me see – a Gloucestershire manor house?'

At that I kicked him.

'You know, this class stereotyping is just a sign of age. You're getting old. What's more, you belong to the privileged classes yourself. Don't bully me with these tired old clichés. Not every woman with a public-school accent is stupid, whatever people pretend to think in the Corporation.'

'I've never pretended to think you were stupid.'

'But you certainly think I'm undeserving.'

'If it comes to deserts, who should 'scape whipping?'

'Dan! Shakespeare yet!'

'I'm not entirely a philistine either. None the less, there is a section of society that should be whipped first.'

'And which is that?'

'Your section. Your daddies in the City.'

'Now listen to me, you shit. There is no daddy in the City, no mummy in the Cotswolds, no brothers in banking. There is just me and my brains. And my divorce settlement.'

'You poor little rich girl,' he said, putting his hand over my mouth to stop me talking.

'You know, for a rich girl you try quite hard,' he said in the morning, as we lay in bed.

'I'm going to go and try hard with some coffee,' I said. 'Would you like some? I suppose you want it black, with a cigarette?'

I got out of bed, less self-consciously this time, and went and made some strong coffee. I brought him back a cupful to drink in bed.

'I may have some expensive possessions,' I said, 'but the world still feels very draughty to me. Usually.'

Dan stared at me. I don't think he was listening. Then he stared out of the window, finishing his cigarette. He stubbed it out on the saucer of his coffee cup. Then he seemed to regain consciousness of where he was, got quickly out of bed and started to get dressed.

'Now shake your ass, honey,' he said. 'We've got to get to work.'

'You *have* seen too many films,' I said.

'Too many for what?' he asked.

19

In the great lobby of Wireless House we parted and I went to see his Lorraine rushes in viewing room R7, since a booking had been made for me. Rick's moody pictures were beautiful, particularly the ones that had been shot outside the chemicals factory in the light of the oncoming storm, but there wasn't any obvious shape for the film. The interviews that we had lost had been essential, and we hadn't replaced them. Those we had were good, but insubstantial by themselves. We didn't have nearly enough to construct a documentary, not even with cobbling together some library film.

I was glad to get back to my office and the big picture book. It took me all afternoon and some serious concentration to work out what I wanted to know. After a while I took the book home and went on working in my peaceful flat, with the rain still coming down on the short afternoon outside. I took down a few notes on my computer.

I'm not used to reading through the small print of a catalogue raisonné, with all the tedious detail: *generally accepted as 1640 or 1641 but believed by H. Awonohara (Tokyo 1934) to belong to the earlier, daylight period. First listed in the inventory of the duc de Choiseul in 1825, attributed to Shalcken.* I had no idea how fragmentary and disconnected the history of paintings could be; some appeared for the first time in the lists made immediately after the French revolution, one arrived in a London sale room in 1842, sold and bought anonymously. It was then not heard of again for a hundred years, when a Miss Annie Clephan left it to the borough of Stockton-on-Tees in 1930, where it lay, forgotten again in a basement, until 1972.

Often it was quite unclear whether everyone was really talking about the same picture; they often disagreed on either the subject, or the painter, or both. Was one painting Job mocked by his wife, or St Peter delivered from prison? Paintings now considered unmistakable La Tours were once thought to be by Shalcken, Honthorst, the Spanish School, in the manner of Albrecht Dürer, Andrea Catalani, Ribera, Seghers, Velàzquez and even Rembrandt. And yet many of these had since become acknowledged La Tour masterpieces.

They're all just amateurs, I thought, amàzed. The connoisseurs are just a set of stylish chancers. One particularly thin story was attached to the Lvov painting, *The Payment of Dues*; in 1970 a Russian academic interested in a candlelight painting by Theodore Rombouts came to the conclusion it was really a La Tour. The picture was exhibited in Paris, and the connoisseurs agreed. As for its past, it had probably come to Lvov, then called Lemberg, in about 1810, and moved from one museum to another, as a Honthorst, or a picture of the French school. Finally in 1940 it was placed in the new Lvov picture gallery, newly attributed to Rombouts. Most of this information was the result of a conversation with the Russian museum curator in 1972.

The Rensellaer *Magdalen* seemed much like the others, with little history other than art historical speculation. The relevant part of the letter from the Franciscan abbot was quoted; he agreed to the commission from Georges de La Tour of a penitent St Mary Magdalen 'en nuict', as most of his pictures were. The abbot specified the Magdalen's jar of ointment, with which she had traditionally anointed Christ. After three hundred years of oblivion, the picture had been bought by the Rensellaer Collection in 1981 – acquired, as they say – but the catalogue didn't name the dealer, Bruno Schwab. If anyone knew how it had arrived in East Germany, the theory didn't appear in the catalogue raisonné.

La Tour had done many Magdalens – she was clearly a commercial subject in the Counter-Reformation – but only this one had the traditional jar of ointment. The painting was widely considered to be a masterpiece of the late middle period, according to a brief description. For the rhapsodies I would have to read the main text.

The one thing that art books like that don't mention is the vulgar question of money. I wanted to know what the Rensellaer had paid for their La Tour – and what other paintings sold around the same time had fetched, for comparison. I checked my notes; doing that kind of thing on a data base gives an encouraging impression of efficiency: I just chose the 'FIND' instruction, typed in the dates of a couple of years either side of 1981 and suddenly, from the mass of my aimless notes, they appeared highlighted on my screen, one after another. I used the cut and paste editing commands and within seconds had a list of all the La Tour paintings sold during that time.

Although it was by then past 9 o'clock I called the Corporation main reference library and asked for Peter.

'Yes?' he said, without any attempt at chat.

'I want to know the prices paid by various galleries for four paintings. I assume you've got a pencil.'

'A pentel, actually,' said Peter. 'Standard issue.'

I spoke to him in list form, which is our most successful form of communication.

'De La Tour, Georges,' I said.

'*Job Mocked by his Wife*, bought by the Brown Museum, La Jolla, California in 1978.

'*The Penitent Magdalen*, bought by the Rensellaer Collection, Washington in 1981.

'*The Choirboy*, bought by Leicestershire County Museum in 1984.

'*The Deposition of Christ*, bought by the Manhattan Museum, New York, also in 1984.'

'This may take some time,' Peter said.

'It's urgent,' I said, 'and I'm almost sure all these sales would have been in the news.'

'Of course you appreciate that if it's only news clippings the information may not be 100 per cent accurate,' Peter said indifferently.

'It will be accurate enough,' I said and asked him to call me at home.

He was, as usual, very quick. The telephone rang only twenty minutes later. I found when I picked up the receiver that my hand was trembling.

'Peter from Reference Library here.'

'Any luck?' I asked.

'Yes,' he said. 'In the order you asked me the prices are as follows:

'*Job Mocked by his Wife*: $7 million.

'*The Penitent Magdalen*: $7.6 millon.

'*The Choirboy*: no information.

'*The Deposition of Christ*: $9.2 million.

'Would you like conversions into sterling at today's rate of exchange or at the rate of exchange of the time of sale? I have them here.'

'No, thank you, Peter. What about the Leicestershire one?'

'There's no mention in the press of a price. I asked one of my colleagues to check out our catalogues collection; she found a very good catalogue for an exhibition in the Leicestershire County Museum, which mentions the sale directly from the country house where the painting had been seen and reidentified. Quite frankly . . .'

I waited with interest: he was about to risk an opinion.

'If the Leicestershire Museum could afford it, I shouldn't think it cost very much. Not in these times of austerity.'

That was what I thought too.

'But nearly $10 million for a La Tour,' I said, impressed and slightly incredulous.

'I don't see why you should be surprised,' Peter said. 'The Getty apparently paid over $7 million for a Dieric Bouts in 1984. And that was only Bouts.'

I thanked him and rang off.

It surprised me then, and it still does, how much people are prepared to pay for important paintings, and I looked up the plates in my book to see again what it was that cost so much money. The Leicestershire one interested me least; it was a full face portrait of a choirboy reading by a candle which appeared to illuminate the darkness in which he stood. To me it seemed a little wooden and very like one I'd seen in Nancy, that hadn't appealed to me.

But the others were remarkable. They had the quality that all the best La Tours have; they are instantly recognizable as his. It isn't just the technical trick, bordering on the sentimental, of using candlelight for emotional effect. It is a kind of mood, a kind, I would say, if the word came more easily to me, of spirituality. In all of them something serious is going on, but not in the form of activity or drama, but as profound meditation, lit by a slightly theatrical light. The staginess is accentuated by a persistent sense of the ambiguity of the paintings. They are irresistible.

I was finally beginning to be interested in the oddity of Georges de La Tour; a hot-tempered social climber who could paint these works of solemnity and modesty, a man surrounded all his life by violence and disasters who expressed the most moving tranquillity. Late though it was, I began to read the critical section of the book. There was no doubt about it: La Tour had lived in unpleasant times; he had seen all four horsemen of the apocalypse, including some of the biggest witch-hunts in seventeenth-century Europe.

> *Until recently,* wrote the author, *those commentators who permit themselves to speculate on what an artist ought to have done have asked why so little of this social reality was recorded by a painter fêted above all as 'peintre de la réalité'. Ignoring for the moment the issue of whether such questions are legitimate in themselves, these ruminations are answered, in our opinion, not just by the existence of* The Beggars' Brawl *and* The Hurdy-Gurdy Player *but also by that of the New York* Job, *the middle-period* Deposition of Christ *and the Rensellaer* Magdalen. *These canvases convey the painter's profound, if oblique, concern with the human drama immediately around him.*

Art historians seem to have a special language, to prevent you from thinking that just anyone can look at pictures. I was almost deterred, but I read on.

> *Above all the Rensellaer acquisition can be seen in this light. This sublime* Magdalen *has also been called the* Profane Magdalen, *referring, in our view, not just to the overt sexuality of her loosened hair and parted legs, common enough after all in the painterly tradition of the Magdalen and in La Tour's other work, but also to her so-called scourge, which is in reality an* aiguillette, *or witch's knot; in his own hermeneutic convention La Tour has provided us with a clue to a second meaning to this canvas, the ambiguity so dear to him and so profound a part of his artistic response. The Rensellaer* Magdalen *is in effect a witch, and a witch of the kind that was*

*burned in hundreds and thousands in the Lorraine of La Tour;
a countrywoman, not obviously beautiful, no longer young,
yet retaining great sexual power. Is it purely imagination to
discern in the form hidden beneath the Magdalen's skirts the
outlines of a toad, well-known familiar of witches and
warlocks?*

In the midst of my astonishment, I wondered whether this
remarkable style was a translation, but to judge from the
writer's English name, he was just suffering from rampant
francophilia. But what stuck in my mind was not the witch-
craft angle, though I liked it, but the list at the beginning of
the paragraph. It was the same as mine, apart from the
Leicestershire boy with the torch. It was exactly the same as
the one I had put together on my database and read out to
Peter on the telephone. The *Job*, the *Deposition* and the *Magdalen*. The most recently sold paintings.

I summoned up my notes on my computer; they were very
scanty and I turned back to the catalogue raisonné. There is
something about computers that makes you unnecessarily
tidy-minded. My notes were neatly set out with automatic
tabs for each piece of information and so it came quite naturally to note down without noticing all the details from the
catalogue that I had ignored before. When I'd finished, I
looked at my list of paintings again.

There was something about them all which stood out very
clearly, though it wasn't interesting in itself, and which made
me feel as faint as Lloyd had looked that evening at Guy's
cocktail party in Chelsea. All three of the paintings had
almost no known history of previous owners. But they had
each been anticipated, so to speak, by one or two important
pieces of documentation. The document for the *Magdalen* had
been in the Château de Villancourt-le-Chapitre. And the
other papers, the documents for the *Job* and the *Deposition*,
were listed as being in the Archives Départementales de la
Meurthe-et-Moselle. That was the end of the beginning. I was
now in the middle of my guess.

20

At first I could hardly take it in. I read every detail again
carefully. The *Job* had been sold to the Manhattan in 1978
through an unnamed agent. The previous owner, also anonymous, was said to have been Argentinian. It had first been
mentioned in an inventory of the estate of a merchant from
Metz, resident in Nancy, who had several paintings. He had
died in 1691: this document, which had led scholars to anticipate the existence of the painting, had been discovered by a
librarian in 1967. That was eleven years before the emergence
of the painting, said to have been in a house in East Germany.

The *Deposition*, said to resemble La Tour's many St Sebas-
tians, also came from an undisclosed source. It had been sold
in 1984; its only real documentation had also been discovered
in the Lorraine archives in 1972, by a historical researcher.
That was twelve years before the related painting appeared.
In this case La Tour himself was suing for non-payment for
the painting; the heirs of the man who had commissioned it
disputed the price. I remembered that La Tour had sued
someone else for non-payment, and looked back at the catalogue. Sure enough, he'd had the same problems with the
widow of a man who'd commissioned a Magdalen and then
died. The papers of that suit were discovered by a woman in
the Nancy archives in 1976. It must have been that one that
Mademoiselle Audran had spoken of.

I looked again at the three plates. It was true that although
they were religious paintings, they had a lot in common with
some of La Tour's genre scenes. The *Job* slightly resembled
*The Flea Catcher*, with its hint of clumsiness. As well as the
traditional pot-sherd to identify him, he had a boil on his
upper thigh: that was traditionally the mark of St Roch,
patron saint of the plague. Conventionally the bubo was

modestly moved from the groin to the thigh. No doubt there was an elaborate literature on whether this boil belonged to Job or to St Roch.

The *Deposition of Christ* also had a slightly provincial feel about it. It was like the Louvre St Sebastian; a half-naked man with his head thrown back, held half-supported by three women in local dress. A single lamp on the ground threw up a ghastly light on their faces; the little group was surrounded by darkness, but the background was not quite dark enough to conceal something standing in the shadows. It looked more like a ladder than a cross. According to the text, the ladder suggests l'*épreuve de l'échelle*, being put to the ladder, a form of torture used on suspected witches at that time in Eastern France. Equally, it might not have been a ladder, but some other half-formed shape in the obscurity.

It was obvious that I would have to go, yet again, to Lorraine. This time I could not imagine any possible way of talking the Corporation into paying for my trip, and against every journalistic instinct, I decided to pay for myself.

I did not go back to the Hôtel Choucroute. I stayed the next night in Paris with a journalist friend near the eastern side of the *periphérique*, and left very early in the morning in a hire car to drive to Nancy, following the big signs for Metz and Strasbourg. Getting up at 5 on a cold morning in March is the kind of effort I've always hated, and this time it was made much worse by my state of mind, torn between incredulity and fear. But those feelings heighten the senses and I remember unusually clearly the drive along that flat motorway, and the taste of the croissant and bitter instant coffee that I bought after 6 o'clock.

As before, I went to the archives in slight disguise, though it was probably vanity on my part to imagine that the staff there would have remembered me. This time I had got my hair into a style with a middle parting, so that it fell over my face and inconveniently over the sides of a pair of glasses. As before it seemed rather futile, but this time I was really afraid of what might happen if I were recognized.

The letter of introduction I presented at the main desk had been written by my word processor on Cambridge University History Faculty headed paper, and said that I was working on

seventeenth-century French paintings in English collections –
a subject that would not endear me to most French librarians,
but then I didn't want to arouse any pleasant helpfulness and
chat. The obstacles I had imagined failed to materialize. I was
not referred to the director, who would have recognized me
and questioned the letter. I did not see anyone I recognized
and the librarian in charge of the reference room was a complete stranger to me. I handed her an impressive list of
documents whose reference numbers I had copied from the
exhaustive catalogue raisonné. To the two that really
interested me I'd added a random list of others.

The woman looked expertly at the list.

'Oh, yes,' she said. 'You realize that all this will take some
time to deliver. These are stored in several different places.
You see all these different serial numbers? Would it perhaps
suit you to come back in a couple of hours?'

'Yes, of course,' I said. 'Though I wonder, I don't suppose
it would be possible for me to look for some of them myself,
at the same time?'

'Oh, no, I don't think so. It would be most unusual.'

'I realize that. It's just that I'm not here for long and in any
case I'm sure your staff have many other requests.'

'It's true we're busy, but I really don't think . . .' she began.

'Would it help if I were to tell you I'm a friend of
Mademoiselle Autran at Lunéville?'

'Oh really, how interesting,' she said, and I could see it had
had the right effect. 'How did that come about?'

'Oh, a shared interest in history,' I said. 'I had to consult
her not so long ago about something; I remember we had the
most delicious lunch at the Relais de la Poste.'

'How nice,' said the woman. 'Well, I suppose it wouldn't
really do any harm if you were to help look for some of them,
though I must warn you to be extremely careful. Some of the
documents are very old and very fragile. I'm sure you understand, and I must ask you to leave your larger bag here, if you
would.'

She allowed me to choose the ones I wanted to start with,
so, given that time might be short, I chose a group which
included the documents I had actually come to see.

'Those, I think, will be in the vaults,' she said, looking at the numbers. 'You see those first two letters? Those stand for the vaults, and the following number stands for the aisle. The others are mostly upstairs.' She led me to the familiar stone archway, turned the key, pushed at the heavy wooden door and reached inside to turn on the light.

'There,' she said. 'You'll see the reference numbers quite clearly marked on the ends of the stacks. And don't worry, you'll be quite alone. There'll be no one to disturb you. Call me if you need help.'

I nearly called her back there and then and asked her to stay. The room was profoundly cold and, irrational though it still seemed, I felt afraid. I've never been good at finding my way around the most conventional libraries and this was necessarily quite different. The papers were kept in different-sized boxes and files and stacked in different ways on metal shelves arranged in long bays. Some of the shelves seemed to be filled with solicitors' boxes, some with large bound volumes. It was more a store room than a library. I tried for about half an hour to find any suitably marked files or boxes but it was difficult in my heavy coat and gloves and the light was dim. All the time I was there I was filled with distaste, at my memories, at my suspicions and at what I felt was my incompetence.

To double-check, I started looking for another reference number, which had been listed for another document which didn't interest me. After about ten minutes of looking without success for that, I gave in to the feeling I get so often in libraries, that something is being withheld from me. I was about to give up when at last I saw the number on a slim file. I took it out and carefully untied the linen strips which held the cardboard file together and the papers in place. All the documents looked much the same, closely and neatly handwritten on thick paper, almost illegible despite the regular script, apart from occasional phrases and names. Only the figures were clear and I could see that most of the documents were dated in the mid-1640s.

In some cases the library's reference numbers were pencilled on the documents and so after turning several pages carefully, I came to the document I had listed, a contract with a boy apprentice in November 1643. I knew roughly what the text should say, from the transcriptions in the catalogue raisonné, and could make out a few words: La Tour was described as painter in ordinary to the King; according to the contract he was taking on Chrétien Georges, undertaking to teach him the art and science of painting well and diligently, without hiding anything from him.

At last I saw his signature, bold and firm. George de La Tour. No 's' in Georges, I noted automatically. People get rewritten in even such small ways as that.

I tied up the papers and put the file back where I had found it. Obviously the shelving system was not beyond my modest powers and I started again to look for the documents I had come to find. I even went down the aisle in which I'd found the body and looked in all the shelves there. I began to lift up all the old boxes to see if anything were lying between or behind them. I looked as thoroughly as I knew how. Even bearing in mind the tendency of libraries to withhold the most obvious things from me, I was finally convinced. The documents were not there.

I pulled the great door towards me and went out, locking it behind me.

'Ah, mademoiselle,' said the librarian, 'we've located everything for you and we've put it all in a little room upstairs where you won't be disturbed. Did you find everything you wanted in the vault?'

'Yes, thank you,' I said.

I followed her into a modern store room on the first floor and pretended for an hour or two to look at the other documents. After a suitable length of time had passed I went downstairs to the librarian, to thank her and say goodbye.

I was hungry and perplexed but decided it was too late for lunch and I drove instead to Claude Mesnil's house; they were expecting me, because I'd telephoned that morning from the motorway. It seemed better not to cancel.

'What a pleasure to see you,' said Geneviève at her front door. 'And so you're on your way to friends in Strasbourg for the weekend?'

'No, Geneva.'

'Oh yes, Geneva of course. Just let me call Claude.'

I had the impression I had disturbed him; he came out of his study with a preoccupied look.

'How very good of you to look us up. Forgive my distracted air; I'm correcting some proofs.'

I didn't want to tell him I'd come to Nancy for the purpose of visiting the archives, but I did mention I'd been there. He looked astonished.

'Good heavens', he said, 'What on earth for? If my students spent one quarter of the time in the archives that you do, they might pass their exams. What was it this time?' he asked, passing me coffee in one of the pink and white faience cups that I remembered from the time before.

'You promise you won't tell the police?' I asked.

'Well, I'm sure you're not trying to get me to conceal a crime,' he said, smiling.

'The truth is, I haven't given up – but you know the police have asked us to stay away – and so I went back to look around, try and find the visitors' book. I even got into the vault again on the pretext of looking up some La Tour documents – what I really wanted was to have a proper look around. I also wanted to see that correspondence I told you about.'

'Oh yes, the Lorraine girl and the German boy in the middle of the war.'

'Yes. The odd thing is, the documents weren't there.'

'The letters?'

'No, I mean the La Tour documents.'

'How do you know they weren't there?' he asked, slightly impatiently, I thought. 'I mean, how did you know what you were looking for, if it was just a pretext?'

'Oh, I just looked up some references quickly in a picture book. Mind you, I said I'm not very good at finding my way round libraries.'

'Oh well,' he said, 'I'm glad it didn't really matter. Irritating, of course. But it is more a store room than part of the library proper. At any rate it isn't open shelving.'

'No,' I said. 'Besides which, it was too cold to stay there long.'

'You know it's not really open to the public. I congratulate you on gaining access. Between ourselves I'm afraid that the archives are not terribly efficiently run. Neither here nor elsewhere, in Lunéville or Metz. The people are charming, quite charming as you know, but I'm afraid things do get mislaid from time to time. Not only that: some documents are occasionally lent for various research purposes, and of course there are the Mormons.'

'The Mormons?' I asked.

'Oh yes, they do extensive research on family histories and some of their representatives have been busy here for some time. Inevitably it causes quite a lot of disorder – things have to be removed from one library to another, taken away and so on.'

'Oh well, that's probably what it was.' I said. 'No wonder I was defeated by the system. Fortunately it didn't matter. I found what I did want. Tell me, is there any news about the caretaker?'

'None at all, I'm afraid to say. I have to tell you that the police have asked me not to discuss this with the press. You understand, I'm sure. I really don't think you should persist; you might get into some real trouble.'

'Of course,' I said. 'It's just that I couldn't resist asking, as I'm passing through.'

I told him that our documentary had been cancelled and I was about to start work on *Pop Goes the Weasel*, and to exchange the world of warfare and murder for the peaceful environment of children's games.

'I'm afraid you will find the world of childhood no less violent and intense,' said Claude Mesnil, 'as you will learn when you have children of your own.'

He smiled with *gravitas*. I was slightly surprised that he was consigning me in his imagination to maternity, but then all flirtations, even the most trival, have their appointed end. I stayed talking for quite a long time, despite my impatience to leave; my suspicions had made me extremely cautious.

21

As I drove away from Saint-Symphorien, Mademoiselle Autran came into my mind, and the expression on her face when
she spoke of Claude Mesnil. Like her, I liked and trusted him,
and like her, I thought, I had been misled by the lack in my
life of a sympathetic and intelligent man. I had been taken in
by the seductive way in which he appeared to take people
into his confidence; the indirect compliments he perpetually
paid disguised, it seemed to me now, a certain deviousness.

It had been foolish of me to imagine that he had ever been
on anyone's side except that of the police. I was glad I hadn't
told him in advance that I was going to the archives, or, I now
realized, I'd certainly have been stopped. Mademoiselle Autran, too, would have been very disillusioned if she had heard
him talk about disorder and lack of efficiency in the archives;
she, who like me, had felt that he was a special ally, who
perfectly appreciated what she was and what she had
achieved.

I didn't share his opinion of the archives. To me they
seemed, both at Lunéville and at Nancy, quite extraordinarily
efficient, well run and pleasant to work in, apart from the
matter of finding a dead body. And free from bureaucracy. In
fact it simply was not true that they were disorganized; even
the Corporation libraries at their best had not provided me
with such fast and pleasant service. I felt slightly ashamed of
my amateur disguises and lies to the people at the archives.

'The people at the archives. I know them. Not well, but I
know them. I'll see what I can do there.' That was what
Claude had said, the day the Mesnils had given Dan and me
lunch. But it wasn't really true; it wasn't true that he didn't
know the people at the archives well. He clearly knew them
very well, I now realized. He knew the director at Nancy and

he knew Mademoiselle Autran quite well enough for her to be discreetly in love with him.

How could he fail to know the people at the archives, I thought, when he taught students to decipher old documents and personally sent them there for research? He must have known them all very well. So his offer to help us, to do what he could, was not particularly genuine, just an automatic charming response, to appear to cooperate. In fact he pretended that he had far less influence than he had, both with the police and with the librarians. And yet he was quite prepared to appear to be on my side, and even to criticize them. So what? I thought. Flattery costs nothing. A nice word finds a nice place, as the proverb says. It was no worse than journalists deserve, or give out. But I was sorry.

I drove back to Paris and to my friend's flat near the Place Gambetta. It was well placed for the motorway to Metz but otherwise not very appealing. There had been a time when I enjoyed stuffy Parisian lofts in buildings that smelt of urine, but those days were past. To make it worse my friend was out and had left a note saying he would be back late and asking me not to make long-distance calls on the telephone.

I thought of ringing up some of the people I had known in Paris when I was much younger, before I'd come to the Corporation. Probably some of them could have enlightened me about the Villancourt family; some might even have known something about old paintings. But I did not want to revert to that self, unless I could think of nothing else.

Finally I thought of Quentin. He might know. It was nearly 9 and late enough to ring the States. Quentin's answerphone played me a ridiculous message; he was out of town on an assignment. Then I decided to settle the question of the Mormons. I rang Bob Kitzinger in Utah, disturbing him at lunch again. I told him that I was ringing from Paris and that it was important.

'It may sound rather trivial to you, but it is very important to me. It's a long, involved story, and I could of course tell it to you, but will you bear with me and just answer a simple, non-controversial question?'

'Certainly,' he said, 'if there's no reason why I shouldn't. What is the question?'

He was extremely relaxed for a man who'd been interrupted at lunch.

'I believe you stopped working in the archives at Nancy at the time when the strike began.'

'That is correct,' he said.

'So is it true that since that day your research in the archives has been suspended?'

'I don't see why I shouldn't answer that,' he said. 'Yes and no. I myself left at that time, as you know, and I haven't been back since. And of course we didn't like to press for access while there was any question of getting in the way of the police or generally speaking being a nuisance. But for several days now, nearly a fortnight, two colleagues of mine have been working over there in Nancy, right there in the archives, and in some of the closed shelves in the upper rooms and in the vault as well. Does that answer your question?'

'Yes,' I said. 'Thank you very much. It was quite important to me to know.'

'I must confess,' he said, 'my curiosity is getting the better of me.'

'Of course I will tell you, if you insist. But the long and the short of it is that you've set my mind at rest about a little thing that was troubling me very much. You see, I was the person who happened to discover the body of the *gardien*, and the whole incident has been preying on my mind. It was an unimportant discrepancy. It had absolutely nothing to do with your church by the way, I promise you. It was a suspicion, and since I was wrong I'd rather not repeat it.'

I apologized mentally to Claude Mesnil for having doubted him. Nothing suspects like suspicion, and I began to think that it was time I had a rest and bowed to the inevitable. If Marie-Blanche came up with something interesting on the Comte I would work on that. Otherwise I would take some leave and submit myself to *Pop Goes the Weasel*.

The next morning, just for pleasure and with no trace of my previous obsessions, I went to look at the La Tours in the Louvre. I had never noticed them there before. One of them, *Christ with St Joseph in the Carpenter's Shop*, must be one of his masterpieces; a little child holds a candle in a dark room for the old carpenter to see by. Perhaps it's Christ and Joseph, perhaps not. The old man is working on a piece of wood in a way that reminds you immediately of workmen making ready the cross for Christ's crucifixion. The child's hands are pierced by the light from the candle he is protecting, and his childish fingers with their dirty nails are made translucent. The subtle light, the subtle expressions make that painting quite different from the others hanging there; the *St Sebastian* and the *Cheat with the Ace of Diamonds* could have been done by someone quite different.

I wandered through some of the other rooms, but the Louvre is too full of people and objects and noise. After a while, I came outside into the cold morning and went shopping. My holiday mood continued through lunch at a brasserie with my friend Anthony Mortimer, owner of the flat where I had stayed. He chose for both of us: calf's head in a cream sauce and some Chablis.

'You look dreadful,' he said. 'What have you been up to?'

I told him some of it, dwelling on the office politics. He was one of my favourite people to complain to.

'Flogging a dead horse.' he said, with his mouth full. 'What you should do, the classic move in your position, is to take a job abroad. Absence makes the apparatchiks grow fonder.'

'Of somebody else,' I finished.

'No,' he said, 'it will sort you out nicely. The dead end suddenly becomes a limitless vista. With overseas allowances too. Why do you think I'm here?'

'For the pleasure of living in Paris.'

'Well, yes, partly that. But also to make my masters at the *Intelligencer* more appreciative.'

'You don't need to worry,' I said.

'In any case, I don't worry. Nor should you. What is really on your mind?'

'I don't think you'd believe me if I told you. Some of it I don't believe myself any more. But I've been very frightened, I've been warned off something and I'm not even sure it's safe to talk about it.'

'I must say,' he said, swallowing a mouthful of frisée and goat cheese, 'what you lack in small talk you certainly make up for in theatricality. Are we being overheard? Spied upon?

Where is the man in the fedora and the co-respondent's shoes?'

'You're probably right,' I said.

He looked at me with kindness.

'Just because your life was once, briefly, rather fantastical, there's no need to see high drama, betrayal and crime all around you to this day. The odds are against it, unfortunately for the working hack.'

'I know. I know. You are right. And I'm having a holiday. It began this morning and it's been very nice so far.'

He told me, at great and indecent length, about his Algerian girlfriend. He treated me in effect like a male friend and an old friend too, and the tension of the past few weeks began to give way to the pleasure of his company and the fact that I was in Paris, in what was almost spring.

In my own mind my holiday was only going to last as long as it took Marie-Blanche to come up with something or make it clear that she couldn't. After lunch and some pleasant wandering around Paris, I rang Marie-Blanche's office to see whether she was expected back. The receptionist told me she'd said she would be returning three days later. I asked on an afterthought if there were any messages for me.

'Oh, yes,' she said 'one from a Monsieur Robert Kitzinger from the United States.' She read it in hesitant English: 'If still concerned as previously, suggest you call my colleague now at Nancy, Mr Owen Young.'

There was a telephone number.

'I'm coming in,' I said to the receptionist, following Cohen's fifth or sixth law of programme-making: always use someone else's telephone.

Of course when I arrived at the Corporation office and made the call, I got through to an hotel and Mr Young was not there. Probably he was at that very moment labouring away in the archives. I thought I'd call back at 6 and spend the time until then interrupting people in the office and aimlessly snooping, a habit of which other journalists are understandably both tolerant and suspicious.

I didn't find out much. One man on secondment from Belfast asked me what I was doing so I said I was about to work on *Pop Goes the Weasel*. He pretended briefly never to have heard of it, but the temptation to put someone down was weaker than the temptation to display knowledge.

'So you'll be going to New York,' he said.

'Probably,' I replied, mystified.

'I think it's absurd,' he said. 'American children are even more repulsive than English children. Still, you'll have a good time in the Big Apple, I suppose. Pity about the health risk.'

Personnel managers are oddly perverse. Mine would have got a lot further with me if she'd told me that *Weasel* was doing a summer season in the States.

'Well, one can't deny that the New York office is a little more lively than this one, AIDS or no AIDS,' I said.

And I was tempted to go. I would give Marie-Blanche her three days, I would ring up my Mormon, I would take in a little of Paris and that would be that.

At last I got through to Owen Young in Nancy. He was less open than Bob Kitzinger, but equally helpful.

'Yes, Bob told me you might call. He said you seemed anxious about something, and we might be able to set your mind at rest.'

I was touched at the kindness.

'Mr Kitzinger was very helpful, and I think that what he said was all I needed to know. I just wanted to find out whether or not it was possible or impossible for some documents to have been moved.'

'Well, if Bob has covered it ... What was the original question?'

'Just this. After Mr Kitzinger left, when did your work resume?'

'I see,' he said. 'Well, of course he told you. We took up from where he left off, on the morning of 5 March. At the moment we're concerned with nineteenth-century evidence; we still have quite a lot of work ahead of us. I don't know if this is relevant?'

'Yes,' I said. 'Thank you. Could you tell me, you mean that you haven't had anything to do yet with any earlier documents, eighteenth or seventeenth-century, or before?'

'Why, no,' he said. 'Not this time.'

'So since work has been resumed you haven't been dealing

with or removing any of the older archives?'

'No,' he said. 'We haven't even requested that that kind of material be located. As a matter of fact we haven't removed anything at all this time. And nor did Bob either. It's true we got permission for photography some years back and that entailed some removals and some inconvenience, but this time I don't believe you would have known we were there at all: the director of the archives actually said as much to us. Is there some problem?'

He was beginning to sound concerned.

'No. Please believe me. My interest has no bearing on your work, your church, your research or anything. I haven't any views one way or the other about the Mormon faith, except that its people have been good to me.'

'I'm glad to hear that. Is there anything else?'

'No,' I said. 'No, but thank you again, very much.'

At last there was one thing which was very clear. Amongst all the rest of the speculation and muddle it was quite obvious that whoever had removed the La Tour documents from the archives, it was not the Mormons. Perhaps it's an occupational hazard for godless hacks to sentimentalize people with organized faith and to believe them uncritically, but I was none the less certain someone else had moved the documents. My obsession had risen yet again from its own ashes, as obsessions do, I suppose, whether we wish them to or not.

22

I now had a powerful reason for going to the States, or so it seemed, and I wanted to fly home to London to arrange it. Anthony took me to the airport and told me he was flattered to see how much lunch and a pep talk from him had cheered me up.

'Telling me to go abroad was a very good idea,' I said 'I'm going to New York.'

'Be very careful,' he said as he kissed me goodbye.

'I certainly shall. I'm quite nervous.'

'You can do it,' he said as I was taken up into the crowd pushing towards passport control, and he disappeared from sight.

On the plane, I could not resist having one of those big Martinis that would sink at least two businessmen. For me it submerged my scepticism and undirected anxiety and sharpened up my thoughts, despite what the biochemists say. Skyborne and Martiniborne, I reflected for a while in that limbo where causes and consequences are indefinitely postponed.

History and libraries have always seemed to me frustrating in the same way. All those details and pieces of evidence, and coincidences – it's impossible to get anywhere near a beginning of knowing something. It's not even possible to figure out some workable system of cross-reference, or, having one, to use it effectively. I suppose I long ago gave up hoping to know things, or retrieve things. So on the face of it, it was not surprising that three paintings had lost some documentary evidence. The paintings themselves had been lost, after all, and there must have been much more lost about La Tour than could ever conceivably be found. Why shouldn't objects slip in and out of history, which is only to say in and out of people's perception of them?

All the same, it was odd. The Rensellaer *Magdalen*'s only piece of supporting evidence was lost and its owner was dead. The *Job* and the *Deposition*, both worth millions, had lost their only supporting evidence as well, and the caretaker was dead. These speculations were given a lot more force by my first irrational assumption that the body of the Comte and the body of the *gardien* were linked. They belonged each to a different class, a different country almost, their aspirations and connections could not, within one culture, have been more different. Yet these two men, these two geriatric corpses, had one thing in common. They were both extremely close to the documentation of the pictures.

Each picture had come upon the art world in a burst of plausibility, its authenticity recognized at once by connoisseurs and given particular point by the fact that it had somehow been anticipated. And anticipated because of some unimportant and really rather uninteresting documents. Looking at it back to front, these remarkable, valuable pictures needed documentation. It had all been discovered very innocently, but then that would be the way to have it happen, of course. Who could have pointed researchers in the right direction, if that's what had happened, in Lorraine? That was not difficult to guess. And which French aristocratic family had pointed Simon Cadwallader in the direction of the Château de Villancourt? Of that I had no idea.

The histories were almost too good to be true. I thought of Hank Bartlett's chinagraph board; true is merely true enough, but never too true. Completeness suggests design. It was a question not of one fake, but of three. The mistake, I thought, opening a British Airways plastic snack box and closing it again after smelling it, was to make the stories so credible. A lot of La Tours had very weak provenances; these paintings stood out a little with their plausibility.

But there were still the scientific tests the paintings had undergone in the United States. It didn't seem at all clear whether fakes could pass those tests, or whether all the tests had really been done. That was the point of going to America. 'Go in person,' which must be another of Cohen's laws of film-making. There was no doubt that I should go, except, if I was right, the subject might be getting dangerous. In my elevated mood I had very little real sense of danger, but the fact remained that two men were dead. I kept reminding myself that I should be careful, but I couldn't seriously believe that such a preposterous plot could have anything to do with reality.

The plane landed on time but I waited nearly an hour for my luggage to appear. Then I waited another twenty minutes for a taxi, without success, and finally took the Underground. The surly baggage handlers at Heathrow, the depressed Punjabi cleaners gloomily following outsized mops around the dirty floor and the seediness of London public transport removed the last effects of my dry Martini. It was cold, wet and late, and I was home.

My personnel officer welcomed me into her office the next day with practised blandness. I felt the usual temptations: it's always fun to startle the professionally unshockable.

'It's about *Pop Goes the Weasel*,' I said.

'Yes?' she replied carefully.

'Well, as you know, I've been very involved in this Current Affairs documentary.'

She had my file in front of her, and must have been reading it. She began to look irritated.

'And I think the Current Affairs claim on my time naturally takes precedence over any other. I'd like to say again that I've never been able to understand the Corporation idea that people can be shunted around like railway carriages.'

'That is not our policy, as you very well know,' she said.

'This rampant paternalism can hardly make for the best use of talent, the best return on capital invested in training us poor hacks.'

She stared at me.

'That is precisely what my job is – to make the best use of talent.'

'Don't you think it would be better to let the so-called talent make its own choices?'

'We do encourage personal choice, of course.'

'Well, in that case I would like to spend the summer based in New York on *Pop Goes the Weasel*.'

It took her a while to control herself and then she put back her personnel officer smile.

'I'm glad you've decided to see reason. *Weasel* is just the right career move for you at this point in time. I'd like you to go and see the editor, Edwina Skinner, as soon as possible and have a little chat with her. We're talking about an August run so you'll need to be there for the pre-production period, starting at the end of the month – very soon, in fact. There're lots of details to sort out. You should see various of the foreign travel and foreign accounts offices and don't forget health insurance – go along to the clinic on the nineteenth floor of the Wrightson building. I've got a little list for you.'

'Ah, a railway timetable,' I said, but she ignored me, already talking on the internal telephone to her secretary.

'Thanks so much for coming along. Lovely to see you,' she said brightly, as I walked out of her office. 'I do so hope you enjoy it.'

'I'm going to America,' I said to Guy when I saw him the next day.

'Oh, dear, have you done something very dreadful?'

'Certainly not. Except bowing to the Corporation inevitable. Before I go, are there any interesting things going on? Any parties we can swap?'

'I'm not sure. You realize you went away last time without saying and let me down very badly. A formal dinner.'

I said I was sorry, and he relented.

'Well, what can you offer me?' he asked.

'There's a Corporation middle-management do,' I said, 'very dull, and there's the documentary awards thing.'

'Yes please,' he said.

'And a rather alarming West London assorted party. Heartless glitterati, cheap champagne.'

'Definitely,' he said. 'Regardless of the date.'

I looked in my diary and told him the date.

'I'm leaving in ten days,' I said. 'What have you got before then?'

'Absolutely nothing, except a big drinks at the Owermoigne Institute. Not your tea, I shouldn't think.'

'What is it?' I asked.

'Oh, nothing much. Every term the senior and junior academics get together, plus suitable friends. You can wander round and look at the pictures. Come to think of it, I suppose you are suitable, in a way; you do know how to behave and you won't suddenly get earnest and sincere on anyone.'

'You know me,' I said.

'And don't think you're going to meet another Mr Wrong there,' he said with affection.

'I'm not looking,' I replied.

The party was in one of the most beautiful buildings in London, which houses part of the Owermoigne collection. We walked up a double-sided staircase under a dome into a wide room with two large Poussins on the wall in elaborate gilt frames. There were a lot of good-looking young men standing about, and the waiters were good-looking too. One of them offered Guy and me champagne.

'Who's here?' I said to Guy.

'Mainly Owermoigne types and hangers-on.'

He pointed out to me one or two people I'd heard of, a rich Labour peer, a well-known woman novelist, an American collector. There were also some faces I recognized from the Corporation, people from the more serious arts programmes.

Guy had a lot of friends there; men in their late twenties and early thirties doing doctorates on subjects so tediously arcane that I was reminded of the contempt of Simon Cadwallader. We spent at least an hour there, talking to people who shared an idiom I couldn't quite follow: there seemed to be a standard manner, both lackadaisical and sharp. I felt at last the alienness, the privateness of the world of art history and connoisseurs.

The woman novelist was talking to a tall, handsome man of about seventy. Between them they conveyed the impression that theirs was the only place in the room to be standing.

'What a pity the general standard of looks is not so high among hacks,' I said to Guy. 'Who is that striking man talking to Mary Strether?'

'That's Sir Miles Tremaine. He's the director of the Owermoigne. I do know him slightly, but I'm afraid I can't introduce you,' he said.

One or two young men had already noticed Guy and were coming over to us.

'To whom are you refusing to introduce this delightful creature?' asked one, dividing a mocking look between Guy and me.

'To Sir Miles. And I'm not sure I should introduce you to her, either,' said Guy, flirting.

'Well, we can introduce ourselves,' he said to me. 'I do want to know you. But you don't want to know the great man.'

'Don't I? Why not?'

'My dear, you look far, far too straightforward.'

'Don't be so patronizing,' said Guy, defending me. 'Appearances can be deceptive.'

'Oh goodness, who is she? Do tell.'

'For heaven's sake stop pooving about like that, Brian,' said Guy. 'It's very *vieux jeu*.' His friend was slightly drunk.

'Do tell,' I said to Brian, as he had. 'Why shouldn't I want to know him? Apart from Guy's anxiety that my philistinism might reflect on him.'

'Well, actually, I suppose you probably would,' he said. 'Everyone does. That's his thing. His forte, his fortissimo, being known to everyone.'

I looked at him again across the room.

'Well, why not?'

'No reason, in itself, except that he extends his acquaintance too wide. Far too wide. He takes the rough with the smooth, as it were. The cottaging with the country housing. And that is odd, when you think how viciously fastidious he is.'

'What of it?' I asked, touched all the same by the bitterness in Brian's voice.

'Well, my dear, if all his protégés were in this magnificent room together, instead of just an acceptable few, they might be very surprised. Astonished, in point of fact. The cultivated and the rude mechanicals, all hugger mugger together.'

Although I was extremely interested, I said I thought that was none of my business.

'It's just that I wouldn't want yet another nicely brought-up female being taken in by the well-worn charm.'

166

'How could it affect me?' I asked, but Brian had tired of the subject and of me, and had turned his attention, with the same bitter expression, to my friend Guy.

I asked someone else about Sir Miles, this time an admirer. I discovered something I should have known already, I suppose, that he was an expert on French painting and architecture. I was wondering how to organize an introduction to him, when Guy came up to me. Perhaps to get away from Brian, perhaps for some other reason, he insisted, against my protests, on leaving. But my party in Ravenscourt Park, which Guy had been so anxious to get to, was not very interesting. I left him there by himself and went home alone, with a feeling of discontent.

23

It took a surprisingly long time to prepare to leave for New York: the complications lay not in entering the United States, but in leaving the Corporation in the approved standard manner. I followed up the list given me by my personnel officer, and found myself wandering through half-forgotten passages to recondite offices which issued special press passes, medical examinations for special insurance, banking facilities, a Polaroid camera, a typewriter, maps of New York and its environs and a lengthy briefing on overseas expense claims, a climate briefing and a reminder of the limits of the protective clothing allowance. I received special Corporation cards for use in the States on which I was described as a senior producer: it seemed to be standard practice to elevate hacks on their foreign visiting cards. I was surprised in the end not to receive a Corporation leaflet on the most effective way to pack twenty-two kilos into a suitcase.

There were not many people I had to say goodbye to; I had become rather reclusive. One of those I arranged to meet was Helen Dunbar, an old friend of my mother's and one of my few links with her. I went up the steps of the Royal Academy, through the revolving doors, and looked round for her. She was standing by herself, a slim and well-dressed woman with thick white hair cut short and fashionably. She looked, despite her elegance, a little anxious, or perhaps a little out of place. Perhaps it was because of her elegance. She had lived out of England for too long to be as badly dressed as a real Englishwoman.

Her nervous expression disappeared immediately she saw me.

'Darling,' she said, holding out her arms and smiling,

'what a good idea this was. But how tired you're looking. Those dreadful television people.'

'They're really not as dreadful as they seem. Some of my best friends.'

She laughed, interrupting me, and taking my arm.

'Let's go and have a look at all this and then perhaps we could have some early dinner and catch up.'

The exhibition was a collection of eighteenth- and nineteenth-century animal paintings.

'This was a very good idea,' I said, 'though I am not sure any of these are really for me. Do you have a special interest in all this?'

'Not really, darling, but after all I am a member and one likes to come; in any case at my age it helps to fill the day.' She smiled with self-deprecation; she was being unnecessarily modest. But I wondered at what age women accept the fact of their own isolation. Husbands and children and careers come and go, as hers had, but the day does remain to be filled.

She had made supper for me in her tiny flat in Knightsbridge. She was, of course, an excellent cook. We had a soup of Jerusalem artichokes and scallops, and then some salad and cheese. We both resisted the temptation to talk about our personal lives; she had many of the best male habits, producing good wine and funny stories and that ability to leave someone alone, while understanding most of what is left unsaid.

'I went to a party at the Owermoigne the other day,' I said. 'I found it slightly alarming. Sir Miles Tremaine was there.'

'Oh, yes, a fascinating man.'

'Oh, do you know him?'

'Well, not really, darling, not any longer, though I used occasionally to meet him at drinks parties. So clever. You've probably read some of his books.'

'You mustn't assume I'm as well-informed as you.'

'I must lend you some. There's something rather arrogant about his style, perhaps. But he is quite fascinating.'

'When did you know him?'

'I first met him, briefly, in the war. Of course I didn't know then how distinguished he'd become.'

'You must have been a schoolgirl during the war.'

'No, I came out in 1939, the last season before the war. I must have been about nineteen or twenty when I first met Miles Tremaine. But it was terribly brief, it was only interesting later when I became interested in painting. Actually it was all rather cloak and dagger, if the station hotel in Aberdeen can be said to have any glamour.'

'What were you doing in the war? And what were you doing in Aberdeen?' I asked.

'I was staying near there, with my family, convalescing. As a matter of fact I was in Intelligence.'

I stared at her.

'Oh, Helen.'

'Only in a very small way,' she said, smiling.

'But Helen, what on earth were you up to, where were you sent?'

'I said, only in a very small way. You see, I spoke really quite good French and German, and I got a job at the beginning of the war which turned out to be for MI6. I was interviewed by a man who rather unimaginatively called himself Mr Smith, and then by someone who knew my father. I'd love to tell you about it, but we did sign the Official Secrets Act, and really that is that, I think, whatever anyone else may say.'

'But you can tell me what happened in Aberdeen, can't you?'

'Oh, yes, I think so, because it all came out later. As I said, I was convalescing at home. I think once you're in that sort of thing, you're in for life, though I disapprove of it except in wartime. But anyway, they all know who you are and they don't forget you.'

'So what happened?'

'Well, someone got in touch with me at home, someone from MI5. It was a dotty sort of job, a one-off thing, before I went back south to my real job. When I was recruited, I was interviewed by two men in the station cafeteria. Or at least we met there, and then we went on to one of those old-fashioned gloomy hotels they used to have near stations. They asked me all kinds of things; you see I wasn't educated – girls weren't in those days – so I suppose they couldn't have relied on someone knowing me at Oxford or Cambridge. And after a while they asked if I minded if a colleague were there as well, and they introduced Miles Tremaine. I though he was rather glamorous. I had no idea then that he rode under different rules.'

'A better expression than gay,' I said. 'But what was it all about?'

'I've no idea what he was doing there – I would have assumed with his perfect French he'd have been involved with MI6. But he was MI5. Everybody one knew seemed to be in Intelligence of some sort in those days.'

'So what did they want you to do?'

'They told me that a German agent had recently landed on a beach not far from the naval base at Aberdeen – this must have been about 1943 – and he'd been captured. They wanted me to give the sort of information he might have been able to get, if he hadn't been caught, so they could pass it on to the Germans as if it came from him. To give some genuine local colour to the disinformation they were sending.'

'What did you do?'

'I just stayed in Aberdeen, following people around on buses, listening to people's conversations, hanging around the naval bases. It felt very odd, pretending to be a German spy. I'm not sure that it was very useful and it didn't go on for long. I was rather glad to get back to my real job.'

'How is it that you've never told me before?'

'People seem to have stopped being discreet. Perhaps it's catching. Besides, everyone seems to misunderstand what went on. In all kinds of ways. For instance people always say the war was terribly good for us, but really it was just boring, even the air raids. Just not much of anything – men, food, travel, fun. There is one thing I rather like to remember.'

She looked at me shyly as though she ought not to tell.

'What is that?'

'It was the name they gave me in Aberdeen, my code name. It was rather flattering.'

I looked at her, waiting.

'It was Offenbach.'

'Why Offenbach?'

'After his opera, *La Belle Hélène*. It was a very long time ago.' She laughed.

'Of course. You were all very good-looking, all you Second World War lady spies. Still are,' I said, looking at the remains of what I now saw for the first time was her striking beauty.

If I needed any incentive to leave London, other than the heavy weather and my feeling of isolation, I was given one later that week. I left work at about 6 and went home on the Underground. It is an unpleasant journey on a bad line, followed by quite a long walk from the station to my flat. For some reason it seems to get darker south of the Thames, certainly in the area of disused and half-converted warehouses where I live. It was raining lightly and I wished I had the car: I took a short cut through some alleys. In the daytime the narrow streets between the tall buildings are picturesque enough to attract feature film crews but at night the Dickensian effect is a little too strong. Keeping my head down because of the rain, and absorbed with minor worries, I didn't notice that I was being followed by two men until they had caught up with me and tried to stop me.

Immediately I was annoyed, not frightened; annoyed that I had been so stupid and so unobservant. In the same instant I started to run, thinking that I might reach a lighted building. My heavy bag, slung across my shoulder, banged against my thigh, slowing me down, and within seconds the two men caught me and pushed me into a dark doorway. I assumed they wanted my bag and in the midst of my fear that made me very angry; there were irreplaceable papers and telephone numbers in it, as well as my passport, tickets and traveller's cheques.

At first I was too frightened to scream, but after a while I managed to start shouting. But the alley was completely deserted. I also tried kicking my attackers, because they didn't seem to have knives; there was a sour smell about them, of clothes not often enough washed, too much time spent close to frying food, and bad breath too. One of them was very overweight, but I couldn't see much of their faces. Quite quickly my courage left me. One of them kept hitting my face, and grabbing at me.

'All right, take my bag, take it!' I screamed, but I had dropped it, and in the dark I couldn't see it. I suppose they couldn't either. Anyway they went on hitting me in the face and punching me in the ribs and belly, and I fainted. I don't know what happened after that. Perhaps someone disturbed them, but suddenly they went away. They didn't take my bag. They didn't take anything.

After a while I recovered consciousness, lying half in the doorway and half in the alley, and very wet from the rain. I managed to walk to the nearest lighted building, a block of flats like mine, where someone ordered a taxi for me, and I took myself to the casualty department of the local hospital. I had been, as the police told me later, very lucky. I wasn't very badly hurt, though I had some painful bruises, and I hadn't even lost my bag. In fact I looked much worse than I felt, with swollen eyes and lips. Lying on a high bed in a side ward I was disturbed from time to time by the usual jumble of reflections; fragments of Anglican exhortations, many confused suspicions and some anxious thoughts about Corporation life. In the middle of this agitation I was touched by the number of visitors who came to see me. One of them was Dan Cohen.

'I'm glad to see you have some female friends,' he said when we were alone. 'I didn't think you did.'

'What on earth do you mean?' I asked, knowing very well.

'Perhaps they just like you better with your face smashed in.'

'Misogynist,' I said, without much energy.

'Is any of this damage permanent?'

'I don't think so. I think I'll be out of here very soon.'

'You were very lucky,' he said. 'It could have been a lot worse.'

'People keep telling me how lucky I am.'

'You know what Jack Nicklaus said?' Dan asked. 'The harder I try the luckier I get.'

'Well, I am trying hard,' I said.

Dan kissed my face, gently so that it didn't hurt.

'You don't suppose,' I said, 'that they weren't trying to steal my bag or even rape me? I mean that they were perhaps trying to frighten me?'

'Now you're trying too hard,' said Dan. But I wasn't convinced.

173

24

The New York Corporation offices are startlingly lavish. Someone in the 1970s, flushed with the American sense of prestige, had managed against all regulations and budgets to install his team into a large suite in the Rockefeller Centre. On Corporation hacks visiting from London it had an even more demoralizing effect than the shabby gentility of the Paris office. It made sense of all those American jokes about Britain as a Third World country. The grey silk walls, the powder-grey carpet and the sophisticated equipment made a depressing comparison with the badly painted passages of Vox Pop house, its risible attempts at designer chic in some of the modern blocks, its seedy hospitality rooms in which shabby MPs seemed content to drink themselves into indiscretions; all this seemed mildly amateur in contrast with the self-congratulation of the New York office.

My first day as a member of the *Weasel* team began at a conference round a table in the guest section. Between us we managed to look very out of place, arriving at 10, at least an hour later than the snappy American staff researchers, with our assorted bags and files, dragged in from cheap hotels in the wrong parts of town, and our tacky London street fashion. We had all sent down for sandwiches and coffee and doughnuts and they had arrived, excessively large, full and varied and accompanied by big pieces of pickle; even the Danish pastries seemed to be accompanied by slices of giant gherkin. It was very different from the poor coffee and shrunken scones of the Corporation caterers. I loved New York, its hustle and its anxious buzz, its swagger and its pseuderie.

The executive producer was a nervous, weary-looking Englishman of about forty. His name was Stephen and he introduced me without confidence to the rest of the team, a collection of men and women of my own age whom I'd never seen before. At first I had very little idea of what they were talking about as I'd never watched *Pop Goes the Weasel*, but it gradually emerged that everyone was talking about the filmed inserts, which were what I was meant to be working on. There were supposed to be some short ones of four or five minutes and some longer ones of twelve to fifteen minutes. It seemed that most of the filmed inserts had already been planned as the other directors were talking about exotic trips to the Rockies and to jazz festivals in the deep South.

'You'll be starting out with some New York shorts,' the executive producer said to me without much attempt to pretend he was doing me any favours.

'Oh good,' I said. I did want a reason to stay in New York; the prospect of two weeks on wild life in the prairies while I needed to be in the city was not appealing.

The producer looked astonished.

'Any ideas for subjects, team?' he asked.

The faces round the table looked blank; with their own excursions now arranged they did not seem very concerned with what might be cobbled together in New York; besides, it is a notoriously difficult place to film, and everyone was trying to stay away.

'I know,' I said cheerfully. 'What about a day in the life of a cockroach catcher?'

There was a noticeable pause.

'Why not?' I said. 'Vaguely scientific, vaguely comic, very New York. It would appeal to sadistic children – beetle's death agony in the Bronx. You could have a wisecracking pest control man going from the sweaty Lower East side to the chilly Upper West side, meeting all kinds of New Yorkers, maybe taking a child with him. A pest's eye view of New York.'

'Great,' said Stephen. 'We might even give it fifteen. Could be a useful standby item.'

Undeterred, I went on suggesting little stories. I even began to get interested in some of them, and finally I got round to what I really wanted.

'On the how-to theme,' I said firmly, 'what about an

occasional series on how to do all the things New York does best?'

'This is a family programme,' said one of the directors, and everyone laughed.

'How to make a pizza,' I persisted. 'How to choose a diamond on 47th Street, how to drive a taxi.'

'How to fill all those holes in the road,' a young man interrupted.

'How to run for mayor, how to restore a world-famous painting, how to . . .'

'Not bad, not bad,' said Stephen. 'Anyone want to have a crack at those? Could you do me a few short treatments by the end of tomorrow and then we can sort them out? OK, chaps and chapesses?'

The conference wore on. I couldn't tell whether the *Weasel* team was really uninterested in what was going on, or whether they were struggling to seem unimpressed with the excitement of a couple of months in America.

Our working idiom was quite different from that of the American staff in the office. Whereas we occasionally used to mention the possibility of making a few calls, our colleagues spoke of hitting the phones; cobbling together a treatment for a short film was storylining to them. We enjoyed the feelings of superiority our devious amateurism gave us, but we envied them their premises and their salaries.

When later I found an empty desk and hit the phones I called the Manhattan Museum's publicity department. It was very easy. I explained that the Corporation wanted to do a short film for children and teenagers on the scientific expertise needed in a great gallery – as in how to restore a famous painting. I asked if they had anything suitable being restored; it would all have to be quite simple, I said, and we'd like to film a few exteriors of the building and perhaps a couple of the most famous paintings already hanging, just to introduce the Manhattan. It would have been odd if we'd been turned down; it was easy publicity.

She did in fact seem very enthusiastic. Before I had had time to finish the request, she was sending schedules and details round by messenger and she arranged a meeting with the head of the restoration and conservation department.

I went to the Manhattan to meet him the next day at 6 o'clock. The imposing exterior was floodlit, the shining fountains playing in the dark; the breath of passers-by on the crowded sidewalks rose in the dim light like mist. I walked up the shallow steps and into the opulent lobby; a uniformed porter took me into a lift, and on to the office of the man I was supposed to see.

His name was Sam Bartoshick. He was older than I had expected. He must have been nearly sixty, an introverted man but with bright black eyes and a sad expression. He spoke with a slight European accent.

'Come in, come in,' he said, though his face was less enthusiastic than his voice. 'I've always been a great admirer of the Corporation. Please sit down. What can we do for you?'

I repeated what I'd said to the public relations woman.

'We'd like to make a very short film on how to restore a masterpiece – a quick look at the science of conservation. It's a children's programme, so it would have to be very simple. And for my benefit too.'

He smiled.

'You're in luck. We do have a couple of important paintings in the workshop. Tell me, how long do you think all this will take?'

'Only a day's filming,' I said, 'as well as the time you can spend talking to me now.'

'Our publicity department is very anxious that this be done, but as I'm sure you'll understand, I myself am unfortunately very busy.'

'But you'll be able to appear yourself – just for an interview and a sort of guided tour round one of the paintings?'

'Oh, no,' he said quickly. 'I'm so sorry. I couldn't possibly do it myself. But I'm sure you would prefer one of my young colleagues, Dr Burroughs. He is extremely competent, very articulate, really very fluent and as a matter of fact he's rather good-looking. And of course he speaks native-born American. I'll introduce you to him. But a guided tour for you personally I shall do myself. Please come with me.'

We took the lift to a vast room on the top floor of the building which had skylights in the ceiling, like an artist's studio. There were big canvases without frames on easels everywhere and two women in white coats were moving around among them, tidying up; it was clearly the end of the working day. The room seemed very empty and curiously lit; perhaps that was to protect the pigments.

'I shall have to send our cameraman to discuss lighting with you,' I said to Sam Bartoshick. 'Can you explain to me what happens here?'

'I suggest you make your film around this one,' he said. 'Do you know it?'

'Gainsborough?' I asked, not recognizing it.

'Yes, a recent acquisition. In what they call "country house condition". Terrible. Perhaps you remember the fuss when one of your English lords sold us three of his pictures?'

'I wonder whether a painting that has so recently left England is the best one to choose for our programme,' I said.

'Art is international,' said Sam Bartoshick, in his depressed way. 'Besides, surely your children are not political yet. Not in England at least?'

'I'm not sure,' I said. 'Probably.'

'Well,' he said, 'You could have this Boudin, or the Chagall over there, but neither would be so interesting to talk about from a scientific point of view.'

'What about that?' I asked, pointing to a miserable-looking triptych painted on wood, with a whey-faced Holy Family looking cold and hungry.

'Yes, that would be quite good, because you can discuss dendrochronology, the method of dating wood from the marks of the growth of the tree. It doesn't really matter to us, which you choose, but with the Gainsborough, because of the discoloration and the missing patch on the coat, there would be a lot to say about pigment. And there's another painting quite clearly underneath, which is always interesting. I can show you the X-rays.'

He explained at some length the difficulties simply of repainting the section of coat.

'I had no idea how complex it is. It sounds from what you say as if it would be impossible to forge an old painting.'

'Oh, yes, certainly very, very difficult. Impossible, I would say. But you're not interested in fakes, are you?'

'Not for the programme, no,' I said, 'but like everyone else, I read sensational stories in the newspapers. And coming here like this, seeing how far the technology of analysing paintings has developed, I can't help thinking about it. There are supposed to be so many.'

'Ah yes,' he said, spreading his hands and smiling.

'Presumably it's here, in this room, that you test pictures for their authenticity?'

'Yes, we do most of it here,' he said, 'though it's not very often really necessary. Very often it's really a matter of form. We do it for other people more than for ourselves, in fact.'

'I'd love to know,' I said, with perfect sincerity for once, 'what sort of tests a doubtful painting would have to go through before it was accepted as genuine.'

'Tests?'

'I mean scientific tests, objective tests, nothing to do with style.'

'That is a very big subject,' he said. 'So many new techniques have been developed since the war.'

'Couldn't you just give me some idea, in layman's terms?'

'I'm afraid you might find it rather boring; it's extremely detailed.'

'No, I would love to know.'

'Well, when we're testing a painting, it's still very hard, if not impossible, to prove that it definitely *is* by a particular master. What we can prove is when it couldn't be. And for that, mostly, we look for anachronisms, things that simply couldn't be in the structure of the painting, if it had really been painted at the time it was supposed to have been. We can look at the paint layers, at the undersketching or at the preparatory ground of the support itself.'

I could follow him that far.

'We take a tiny section with a scalpel across the depth of the pigment, mount it in resin, and inspect it under a microscope. Just by looking you can detect particles that shouldn't be there, that prove a pigment is too recent. Some modern synthetic pigments, for instance, you can spot at once because their particles are so uniformly round.

'But this is just a beginning. You can go well beyond what you can see. You can analyse pigment particles micro-chemically, and we now know so much about the history of pigments – of paints – that we can very often date them. Usually negatively – not before such-and-such a date. We can sometimes detect the place of origin, a particular mining region for instance.

'If you just take the colour blue: painters have used all sorts of different pigments, over the centuries, to make blue. Before the sixteenth century European painters depended on very expensive substances from exotic places: there was ultramarine, extracted from lapis lazuli, mined near the head of the Oxus river in Afghanistan, or indigofera plants from India. They also used azurite, imported from Hungary. But at the end of the fifteenth century a blue glass industry grew up in Saxony, producing the pigment smalt as a by-product; painters started using it immediately – the earliest known use was in a German picture of the early 1480s. Then again, in the early eighteenth century, a German chemist accidentally mixed up a pigment which became known as Prussian blue; the result was that in the eighteenth century painters virtually stopped using azurite and smalt and ultramarine. Later in the century two chemists produced cobalt blue, and in 1828 a Frenchman made an artificial form of ultramarine which cost almost nothing compared to imported lapis lazuli. And so on, into contemporary synthetic pigments.

'A huge amount is known about the development of pigment – all the attempts to make them cheaper, or more stable, or less poisonous and smelly. I could have told you the same kind of story about yellow and white. And this knowledge has uncovered many fakes and many misattributions, just through anachronisms.'

'But surely,' I said, 'this scientific knowledge is available to forgers too. Couldn't they just recreate the appropriate pigment – aren't there lots of old formulae and recipes from all the different periods?'

Sam Bartoshick looked slightly irritated; clearly I was overstepping myself.

'A forger would have to be some sort of chemical genius and he would have to spend a lot of time and money reproducing them. If you just think of lead white: the degree of zinc contamination in lead white has been changing gradually, but noticeably, over the centuries, depending on how the pigment was produced. You'd have to know what degree of zinc content to include and how to get it. And today we can measure this very minutely, using radioactive techniques. Not only that. There's quite a new technique, the radium lead disequilibrium technique, which gives conclusive results.

'Lead white is made from an ore called galena, which contains trace levels of uranium. I won't go into the details, but it's now possible to measure the age of the substance from the nature of its radioactive decay. We can also measure its lead isotope composition, and this would enable experts to know which mining region the original ore came from. Several fake Vermeers have been identified using this process. And even if the pigments happened to be all right, there's still the canvas itself, and the preparation on it. X-rays can show a discrepancy between the crackle on the surface and the crackle pattern in the ground layer.'

'Even if the forger had thoroughly stripped the old canvas of all its previous marks?' I asked.

'Very, very likely. Then there's infra-red radiography; with that you can see the undersketching. You can even tell whether someone was left-handed. Hieronymus Bosch was, for instance, which rules him out for right-handed forgers.'

'And Leonardo da Vinci too,' I said.

I got the look reserved by professionals for intruding amateurs.

'This undersketching must correspond with the known work of the master, which is often very distinctive. Then the ground – which was treated with chalk or gypsum – that is a very useful source of information for authentication. Until the mid-nineteenth century natural chalk was used and it contains fossil remains – these fossil fragments can be scanned with an electron microscope; under intense magnification the individual fossil species can be identified. And these different species are found in different places. So you could easily tell whether the chalk used to treat the canvas came from France, or the Low Countries, or America. Or, of course, whether it was synthetic and therefore post-1850.'

I was longing to ask him whether a forger who was also a

great scientist could none the less override all these problems; he would surely have to have analysed at least one canvas by the real master himself, using all these methods. But would it then be possible? I thought not. But I was, even then, afraid of arousing his suspicions.

'How fascinating,' I said. 'So major forgery is really a thing of the past.'

'It can't survive modern scientific detective work,' he replied, without much emotion. 'But look at the time,' he said, interrupting himself. 'If we don't hurry we shall miss Dr Burroughs and he will be on his way to Westchester.'

We hurried to his office on the same floor. Bartoshick was right. His colleague was extremely fluent and would be very telegenic. He was one of those serious-looking American men who look even younger than they are. He had large designer spectacles and an impeccable suit and seemed willing to appear on British television.

As most of the building seemed to be closing for the day, I asked them if they would both have a drink with me somewhere nearby, but Dr Burroughs was indeed hurrying away to suburbia, and I was left alone again with Sam Bartoshick, who seemed inclined to refuse. But he didn't. We walked together out of the gilded lobby and towards a bar I like at the bottom of a well-known hotel opposite, but he shook his head.

'I don't particularly care for this place,' he said. 'Let's go on a little further. Here's a cab.'

We arrived at a pleasant bar in the Village, not far from where I was staying, and found a quiet place to sit.

'Are you based in New York?' he asked me politely.

'Yes, just for the spring and summer.'

'Not the best moment to stay here,' he said. 'But the weather will be all right until June. But forgive me. I'm well aware that the British don't really talk about the weather.'

'What do we talk about?' I asked.

'Well, at least you don't talk about success all the time, as they do here,' he said sadly.

I laughed.

'That isn't really true any more. We do talk about success. But I think the national mind is more naturally drawn to failure.'

He smiled rather sourly.

'But your Corporation is something to be proud of. A lot of people all over the world have reason to be grateful to the Corporation.'

'You must mean radio,' I said, without reflecting.

'Yes, probably. The wireless. I don't watch your English historical dramas, which is all we get on TV over here. Have you been here long?'

'No, I arrived very recently. From the Current Affairs department.'

'So art and painting is not your field?'

'No, not at all. Nor children either, I'm afraid.'

'Ah,' he said, mystified.

A waiter brought our cocktails.

'To your stay in New York,' he said, raising his glass. 'May it be fully air-conditioned.' He smiled again, not like an American, I suddenly noticed.

'Our staff allocation can give surprising results,' I said. 'The truth is I didn't really intend to work on children's programmes, but I was shanghaied. Tell me, were you born in this country?'

'Why do you ask?'

'Just your use of the word native-born. In connection with Dr Burroughs.'

'Oh, yes. I am Hungarian. I was born in Budapest.'

'How long have you been in the United States?'

'Since 1956,' he said sadly.

'Did all your family come out then?'

'Escape, you mean,' he said. He looked at me with an expression I couldn't understand. 'It's a subject I prefer not to talk about.'

'I'm sorry,' I said.

I should of course have guessed that he was Hungarian; he had that sort of melancholy dash, not the more openhearted Polish swagger. I was unable to say anything, silenced by the possibilities of what he might prefer to forget.

Finally he rescued me.

'Of course I miss Europe,' he said quite lightly, and we had one of those conversations that Europeans enjoy, no matter how often they're repeated, about the heavy-handed literal-mindedness and ferocious, childish vulgarity of the Americans, an acceptable form of lament for our own societies. But it's a conversation better held outside New York where the glitzy pull of the hurry of everything that's going on makes these old world reflections tedious. Besides, Sam Bartoshick was very bitter, too embittered to make good company. And I didn't feel I could ask him any more about what I wanted to know, without arousing his suspicions.

25

I left the bar soon afterwards and caught a cab to a restaurant that was fashionable at the time, or so I assumed. I had been invited there by a friend of a friend in London, a man I did not know. The restaurant was austere and almost entirely grey; it was not the opulent pinkish-grey of the Corporation offices but a harsh, minimal grey. It was unrelieved by coloured objects; there were a few slate or black Japanese vases here and there bearing single white freesias. The people eating there appeared to be cluttering the place up, and quite a few of them seemed to sense it and were talking in hushed voices. Only the waiters were an expression of the designer's scheme, with their white aprons pulled taut across their minimal hips.

In one corner alone was the tasteful hush being disturbed; there was a large round table full of young men and women, talking very loudly with flushed faces. English, I thought at once, and then almost equally quickly realized this was the table of my friend's friend. He was called Harry.

He rose slightly when I was led to him by the head waiter.

'Hope you feel like a party,' he said. 'The evening seems to have expanded.'

He introduced me to a few of the others, but most of them were talking or listening too hard to take any notice.

They were nearly all English, all lively, all speaking at once. The conversation moved quickly between people I didn't know and places I hadn't been to; sometimes there was a name of someone I remembered, but whatever was said passed on so swiftly that they might almost have been talking a foreign language. If they had been a few years younger they would have been hurling bread rolls about at dances, and throwing people into fountains. But they seemed to have taken to more expensive pleasures; they all had the same high animation and drawn cheeks. I wondered what they were all doing in New York; most of them seemed to live there, but only one or two had jobs.

They were, unmistakably, what was then known as Euro-trash; a little band of expatriate Europeans, well-bred or seeming so, rich or seeming so, but all with expensive tastes and manners and a short-term view of life. Despite complaining about the bill, one of the quieter young men drove several of us away in a very large car which contained a chauffeur and a bar.

I didn't know whose address we were going to; when we arrived I had the impression it was not far from the river on the Upper East side, but by then I'd had a lot to drink. It was not a flat but a house, what in London would have been a medium-sized terrace house too, disingenuously modest. Inside an interior decorator had fully compensated for that misleading impression. The place was sumptuous in a way that was quite un-American.

Remarkable though it was, I began to wish I wasn't there. I had hardly spoken at all to Harry, and almost no one else had spoken to me. I wanted to call a cab, but there was no telephone in sight; I don't know why, but even there some fear of being impolite prevented me from asking where it was, so soon after I had come through the door.

The drawing room was a front and back room knocked into one, and had been painted with scenes of English country life, some of them moonlit scenes in a landscape garden. Everywhere there were delicate little tables with precious objects on them; the place looked ready for a photographer from a glossy magazine. A man came in holding a silver trayful of glasses of champagne; he was the chauffeur of the beautiful car, so the house presumably belonged to the man complaining about money in the restaurant.

He and his friends were by now draped untidily over the sofas and chairs, which like the chauffeur and the champagne and the silver salver were outstandingly good of their kind, overstuffed in canary-yellow velvet, the sort of furniture that would have made a perfect setting for Simon Cadwallader. They were discussing whether some woman had or had not inherited a fortune; someone was passing round *Country Life* with a picture of the house in question, a mausoleum I had seen once as a child. Someone else was finishing a very funny, vicious story about the woman: its real nastiness escaped me, but not them, and they laughed at great length.

They were gossiping together with a brutality I had always before then associated only with middle age; their cleverness was filled, unless I were representing them to myself in my own image, with a hateful nihilism. I felt a great revulsion, and I stood up to leave. But as I moved to the side of the room, Harry called me over. He was neatly dividing a little pile of shining powder with a gold American Express card; there was a perfection about the way he clicked the hard edge of the card on the harder edge of the marble mantelpiece, making exactly equal symmetrical lines.

'Have one,' he said, handing me a rolled up bank note. 'Have two.' I took the dollar bill and slowly breathed in one of the lines. I have always hated the first sensation, a suggestion of the beginning of drowning, but before long I had that feeling, irresistible despite all its banality, that I could do anything. I noticed, then, that some music was playing: some heavy rock from the sixties, which felt entirely appropriate, and yet I couldn't help smiling, couldn't stop smiling for pleasure. The world was a place of infinite possibility; the oppressiveness of the company was nothing.

I found myself, perhaps immediately, perhaps after some time, taking Harry by the arm with an expansiveness that's quite foreign to me. 'Come and sit with me, I want to talk to you.'

We fell together into a sofa with deep, down-filled cushions and lay back, laughing at each other. He had a hungry, foxy face with eyes that were probably quick, usually, but then were filled with the sly exuberance that I felt myself, the look of having a wonderful secret. Behind him, over his shoulders, I saw the chauffeur come in and help himself discreetly to a line from the mantelpiece.

I don't remember what we said to each other, but he seemed very witty: perhaps he really was. He was a commodities broker, and we didn't talk about that. He wanted to talk about people we might both know, and I avoided that. In the middle of something he was saying, with his eyes shining flatly, as if I weren't there, the sad, dispossessed face of the Hungarian came back to me, and almost superimposed itself on Harry's. The memory was out of place.

I have very few associations with Hungary – a few moments at a shabby trade fair in Earl's Court, fragments of black and white documentaries of the uprising, a troupe of girls in big petticoats dancing the *czardas* at the Albert Hall. The country is as misty to me as all the middle-European countries – Lithuania, Bosnia Herzegovina, Rumania, Ruritania. Most of them aren't countries any more, just part of Comecon. Whatever Comecon means. It's one of those suggestive acronyms, which is really meaningless. Communist economies? And then it dawned on me. Two, possibly all three of the new La Tours came from Comecon countries. Like Sam Bartoshick. And all, of course, would have been tested at the Manhattan.

'I've got it,' I said to Harry.

'Got what?' he asked, lying back on the cushions with that unmistakable foxed look, full of anarchy, and he smiled with joyfulness and malice.

'The explanation. One of the missing pieces.'

'Well done,' he said, imitating an American accent. 'I'm vurry vurry happy for you, truly.'

'I mean,' I said, wanting him to know what I meant, 'that I've understood what I've come here to find out. I've been sleuthing.'

As I said it I could not understand why I'd used such a stupid word.

'Detective work. Investigative journalism. And you've just had another inspiration. Well done, Miss Marple. Have another line, speedy Jane. Perhaps it will assist the process.'

'Perhaps it already has,' I said.

Harry seemed as incurious about my work as I was about his. He began talking about my former husband. So after a while I did at last go into another room. I found a telephone and called a cab to take me away. As I left the house I noticed that the chauffeur was watching me leave, from behind a half-open door in the passage.

26

I had to spend three weeks working in New York, putting in a lot of overtime, before I could get a few days off. I found it hard to wait to get back to England and hard to concentrate on the trivial film items that I had myself suggested. Finally Stephen gave me a short break and I left. One of the many things I wondered about on my way home on British Airways standby, enclosed uncomfortably in the stuffy half-light of a full overnight jumbo, was why Lloyd had turned so pale that evening in Chelsea, when I had mentioned the caretaker's body. His reaction was one of the few indications that I was not indulging in a manic series of fantasies.

It took me some time to find out where he lived and to get his telephone number. Finally I called and made an appointment. He had a flat in a building by a canal at the top end of Ladbroke Grove, on the outermost fringes of Notting Hill. You could see at once why he had chosen it: there were traces of a Dutch canal painting, from a certain angle, with a bridge and flat, shining water, sluggishly brown in this case.

'You look terribly familiar,' he said to me, as he opened the door. 'Haven't we met?'

'Really! What an unflattering suggestion. No one likes to have her face half-remembered,' I replied.

Female archness was clearly thrown away on Lloyd, but he did look slightly apologetic.

'Come in and sit down,' he said. 'What exactly did you want to ask me about?' He took me into a small sitting room, with a lighted fire under a marble chimney-piece that was too elaborate for the room.

'I'll admit it straight away,' I said, as I sat down on the sofa. 'About the painter, Georges de La Tour.'

'That's not what you said on the telephone,' he said

irascibly. 'You clearly said you were interested in my book on Counter-Reformation iconography.'

'Well, I am in a way, because of the subjects of some of the La Tours, that bother me. But I must admit to you that I was being deliberately misleading. I do very badly need to talk to you about La Tour.'

'I'd like you to leave,' he said. 'I never discuss La Tour, certainly not with people I don't know. My interest in him is completely finished, exhausted. If you know anything about anything, you'll know why. I'm certainly not going to explain. I'm not having all that dredged up again. I don't know how you have the nerve to come here like this.'

'Please be patient,' I said. 'I just want you to listen to something and then you can tell me whether or not I'm showing the first signs of insanity.'

'You ask me,' he said bitterly, and I felt I'd hit the right note.

'Please. I think you'll understand. It's about the New York *Job*, the *Deposition* and the Rensellaer *Magdalen*. I began by thinking the *Magdalen* was a fake. Now I think all three are.'

He stared at me.

'What, may I ask, do you know about it? Are you a judge of painting?'

'Not at all. I haven't even seen them.'

'I expect you know you're in a minority of one,' he said smoothly.

'Of one?' I asked.

He looked back at me with an expression of something that showed for a few seconds and then was quickly hidden.

'Certainly,' he said, but he had for a second been unable to resist the temptation of showing superior knowledge.

'Won't you just listen to my theory? Please. Assume they are all fakes, all from the same stable. They all, in fact, have quite interesting provenances, as you know: no recent history but some solid documentation at or near the time of painting. The documents for two of them are in Lorraine, in the Archives Départementales, and for the third, in the château of the Comte de Villancourt in the Loire valley.'

'Are you an art historian?'

'No, I really am a journalist.'

'I don't know which is worse,' he said. 'Anyway, as you say, I do know all that, unsurprisingly.'

'What you don't know, I imagine, is that all the relevant documents are missing.'

After a slight hesitation, he said with the same joviality, 'That's unsurprising too. French academics can be terribly untidy.'

'Maybe. Maybe not. But the Comte de Villancourt wasn't an academic. And he's just had a fatal accident. Nor was the caretaker at the archives in Nancy, and he's dead too. He was beaten to a pulp only a couple of days after the Comte died.'

'Your face *is* familiar,' he shouted at me. 'Who sent you? Who sent you?' He rose up and moved towards me in such a rage of fear that I thought he was going to hit me. I stood up too, to defend myself.

'No one sent me. No one at all.'

'What were you doing at that party, why did you come up to me?'

'I was brought by a friend. I didn't know anyone there. I didn't even know you had been a La Tour scholar until someone mentioned it.'

'I know nothing about this,' he shouted at me. 'Nothing. I never want to hear the name of Georges de La Tour mentioned again. Get out. Get out now.'

You see naked fear very rarely, except on the faces of actors, and I was amazed by his wildness. I must have looked as frightened as he was, and bewildered too. Because after a moment his manner changed.

'Forgive me,' he said, moving back and sitting down. 'I apologize for losing my temper. But as you must realize, the subject is a painful one to me. One can't help becoming paranoid – but perhaps you're too young to know.'

'No, I know all about that,' I said.

'Well, even though it was years ago, it changed the course of my life, of my artistic interests.'

Although he was smiling manfully, apologetically, I could see that he was sweating.

'And though the subject is closed, it's all over, it still makes me slightly irrational. Besides,' he said 'it was slightly unprincipled of you to pretend that you were coming to talk about something quite different, wasn't it? So you'll understand if I ask you again, this time rather more courteously, to leave me to my work. Unless you want to talk academic iconography.'

I had no choice but to go. When I shook his hand it was not damp but wet.

'These subjects are very touchy, and they do bring out the prima donna in one, rather,' he said lightly, but not lightly enough. 'If you want to go on a lunatic fake hunt I can't stop you. But you know you are quite mad. And it won't do your career any good. I'm sure the long arm of the art establishment stretches into the Corporation. And it's not just millions of greasy fivers involved in fakes, you know. It's face, or rather the loss of face, and that can't be permitted.'

'You're probably right,' I said. 'In any case, you think it's impossible that those three La Tours are not genuine?'

'The idea is absolutely dotty. I am absolutely certain,' he said firmly, 'that they're all genuine, and some of his best work at that.'

At last, having no less ambitious ideas, I summoned up the effrontery to write to Sir Miles Tremaine, to ask for his help. He replied very quickly, in a short note on thick woven paper, in attractive handwriting. He expressed himself with that simple, unaffected style that is the height of self-consciousness, making light of his tone of *de haut en bas*. He said that he'd be delighted to see me, if I really felt it worth my while to consult him about a subject on which there were so many distinguished specialists, but if there were some way in which he might help he would be only too glad. His various connections with the Corporation had always been pleasant and he looked forward to meeting me.

He invited me to come and see him at the Owermoigne, or, if I preferred to come sooner, to his home in Norfolk, where he was taking some time off to write. Reading this encouraging letter, I realized it had been stupid of me not to try to see him before. He was clearly not the sort of man to take a small-minded view of my ignorance. If I hadn't been so ignorant I would have known that, of course.

27

I don't know what draws intellectuals and artists of Sir Miles Tremaine's generation to the cold east coast of England. His house was in the seaside town of Southwold, not far south of the Wash, and north of Benjamin Britten's musical colony further down the coast at Aldeburgh, near the nuclear power station. I arrived early, parked my car and walked along the sea front and up into the dunes. The water was rough, stirred into breakers and sea horses by a cold wind blowing across the north sea. It was a bleak place at that time of year despite the sedate rows of wooden bathing huts and the calm little nineteenth-century houses on the front.

The smell of Adnam's brewery mixed with the saltiness of the wind, blowing as harshly as if it came straight from the Russian steppes to the east. The skies in that part of England are open and austere, harsh and luminous grey. To the south-west across marshland lay Walberswick and the great spire of the church, once a place of great importance, now slipping under the wind and the water into obscurity.

It was not a place, I should have thought, for a man interested in the sophistication of Poussin's paintings; it seemed too bleak, too penitential, and slightly stagy. I drove away from the sea front, parked near the flintstone church and walked through the town, passing the brewery's dray horse pulling a cartload of barrels. Sir Miles lived in a white house looking out to sea across a little green. There was a flag-pole on the green, with a small cannon on either side, and the grass was cut short and well, suggesting a tidiness and a cosiness at odds with the astringent East Anglian skies.

The house was pretty, early nineteenth-century and one of the leading houses of the town. Sir Miles let me in himself, and he was, I saw again, a very imposing man, tall, slightly stooping and handsome still. His blue eyes seemed to have faded and the blood to have left his face and lips, but he still had a powerful smile, drawn rather tightly across his teeth. Because his mouth was slightly crooked he gave an unfortunate impression of sneering.

'How good of you to come so far,' he said, as if I were conferring the favour. 'Do you know East Anglia well?'

'No, not well,' I replied. 'It seems a little austere.'

'Perhaps it is, a little,' he replied, 'but it suits my feelings.'

He took me into a pretty drawing room, filled with prints and architectural drawings, and asked me if he could get me anything.

'I could even offer you some Madeira and a little seed cake, as people did in my youth.'

But I refused. After the usual preamble, in which he gave a good impression of being charmingly vague, he asked me to tell him why I had come.

'I have a strange story to tell you. The more convinced I am that it's true, the more frightened I become.'

He looked as if he were going to interrupt me but I went on.

'You might ask why I don't go to the police; I am fairly sure I can't, or afraid I can't, because at several stages I've been warned off, and I think I would get nowhere. And no protection. In any case I don't think they'd believe anything so preposterous. But it seems to me I ought to tell someone about it, and I can't think of anyone better placed to judge it than you. You even know France well, or so I'm told.'

'What a preamble,' he said smiling.' Are you sure you won't have some Madeira, or something a little stronger. Tell me, who has warned you off what? I think you should begin there. Perhaps I ought to be warned off too, you know.'

Of course he was quite right to be careful, but I had the feeling he wasn't the sort of man to be easily intimidated by anyone.

'I was told by someone I believed to be in MI6 to drop my interest in an elderly Frenchman, the Comte de Villancourt.'

Sir Miles began to look mildly interested.

'That name is extremely familiar,' he said, 'but I can't for the life of me remember why.'

'It was at his château that a document was found about Georges de La Tour, about ten years ago.'

'Oh, yes, of course. I do regret the passing of my memory for academic detail. Not that it's quite my subject, but it was quite an important little discovery, now that I think of it.'

'I was visiting the château recently, and I was told that the Comte had died only a few days earlier.'

'Well, that seems ordinary enough – you said he was elderly.'

'Yes, he was. But I think he was murdered.'

'Did you tell the police that, at least?'

'No, I didn't. It seemed too implausible. He was in his mid-eighties, he'd had an accident in his wheelchair. But I was in a strange state myself. I had just had some very unpleasant experiences working on a documentary. I went to the château as a tourist, but with murder and betrayal on my mind.'

'Curiouser and curiouser. Do you usually have murder and betrayal on your mind?'

This question was put so quizzically, so delicately, that I was made to smile.

'More than I should, I suppose. I read a lot of crime fiction. But of course I don't know what other people have on their minds.'

'Forgive me for asking, but how could I possibly cast any light on this?'

'Well, partly because of your Intelligence experience and because of your knowledge of France, of French society presumably, and of French painting.'

He raised an eyebrow at me in a way that must have alarmed his students.

'I don't know whether it's common knowledge, but I was told by a family friend that you worked for MI5 during the war. She said everyone who was anyone was in Intelligence.'

The eyebrow went down and the smile returned.

'But also,' I went on, 'because of what emerged later.'

'I am still hopelessly perplexed,' he said.

'Our documentary was about the occupation of France in the forties – something about which you might have or could get privileged information, I assume.'

He shrugged, perhaps to suggest that I was wrong.

'Anyway, I happened to find out that the Comte had indeed some very nasty skeletons in the cupboard. Collaboration in Jewish deportations and also a Jewish son. Though he may not have known that. The son shot himself. That is why thoughts of murder came into my mind.'

'Those kind of thoughts are your bread and butter,' said Sir Miles.

'It was only later I began to think of blackmail.'

Sir Miles's crooked mouth moved into its sneering smile.

'Oddly enough, it was the mysterious Mr Meadows or Mr McAusland from the Secret Service, who told me the worst of the story, although he claimed he was warning me off. I admit he nearly succeeded. But later I discovered the La Tour documents were missing, that the Comte had been having a sale and that he'd died before the people from Huysmanns' even began on the inventory. Just in time.'

'Just in time for what?'

'Just in time for someone to remove the documents, before they went on the open market.'

'Are you seriously suggesting that someone murdered a harmless old man just for the sake of a few seventeenth-century domestic details, which have in any case been widely published for years?'

'Yes, I am.'

'But why not just steal the documents; why murder the old man as well?'

'That's why I mean about blackmail. Blackmail is only reliable with those who are *compos mentis*.'

I could see at that point that he was debating with himself whether I was sane or not; it is frightening to be on the receiving end of a look like that, and the fear that rose up then didn't leave me for a long time.

'And I suppose you still didn't see fit to inform the authorities?'

'No. I'd been told to lay off. And of course I felt extremely sceptical myself. But I'm beginning to be sure. What I believe is this. The Comte was blackmailed into having these documents planted into his house. By someone who knew all about what happened in 1942. And he was told to let someone discover them, but not to let the papers out of the house. He did all that. But then, a few years later, he went gaga. And he wanted to have a big sale. Whoever it was who'd planted the documents couldn't trust him to hang on to them or keep quiet about them, because he was so confused all the time.'

'But why did these documents have to be kept so quiet? They're in the public domain anyway.'

'Somebody didn't want them to be expertly examined.'

'But they must have been expertly examined already, long since.'

'Maybe. But by whom? And not necessarily. When they were discovered they were not thought particularly important.'

'And why would it matter so much if they were exposed to critical eyes?'

'Because they were fakes.'

'Even if they were, what then? Not particularly important, you say. Hardly worth killing for, surely?'

'Oh, yes, I think so. They became very important. Indirectly they must have been worth several million pounds. Without them, if they were shown to be fakes, the reputation of the Rensellaer *Magdalen* would be shot to pieces. Because, I think, the Rensellaer *Magdalen* is a fake too.'

'Ah,' he said. 'the fake La Tour trail. A thorny path, as you no doubt know. I congratulate you both on your inventiveness and on your powers of investigation. But I am afraid that so far I remain sceptical.'

In front of him, on a little occasional table, was a tray with a decanter and some glasses. He lifted the decanter and began to pour from it; I noticed that his hands were surprisingly smooth, with the veins still flat and the fingers tapered. He had probably never done any kind of physical work in his life.

'You will have a little Madeira now, won't you?' he asked. 'To help you along with your wonderful fable. It's most imaginative. It does you great credit. Particularly as you say you know very little of the world of painting and collecting. And although you clearly have some French, you seem not to have many connections in France. It's plausible too. But

197

plausibility and truth are not always the same, as even journalists know. In fact they usually pull in opposite directions. What you need, my dear young woman, is a little evidence.'

I saw that I had at last caught his interest.

'Oh, but I have,' I said. 'Exactly the same thing happened in Nancy, at the same time. And that really was murder.'

Sir Miles's hand stopped his glass, for a moment, before it reached his lips.

'I believe that somebody – and I think I know who – planted documents in the various archives in Lorraine, and arranged over a very long period for their discovery, by students or researchers. I think the man responsible is a professor of history, Claude Mesnil. Anyway, the documents were discovered. They referred to paintings by Georges de La Tour that had evidently been lost, and that was that. Nothing very remarkable there. It's exactly what has happened before with La Tour; as you know, for a long time he didn't exist at all except as forgotten details in provincial archives. But gradually he and his pictures began to re-emerge from oblivion. Why shouldn't crime imitate history? And so, several years later, these two pictures appeared – the New York *Job* and the *Deposition of Christ*.'

'Three fakes, now?' asked Sir Miles, smiling. 'You show rather scant respect for the judgement of art historians.'

'Disrespect is also my bread and butter, as well as nasty thoughts,' I said. All the same, my own belief in the story suddenly slipped, yet again.

He sat back, challenging me, I thought, to justify my theory. So I tried. It seemed to me to stand up, as I told it, all too well.

'You've left out the little detail of scientific testing – all those canvases, I'm quite certain, went through authentication tests.'

'I think I can explain how the pictures got past them. Although several people must have been involved, this crime is obviously the construct of one mind, a mastermind.'

'As the thrillers say,' he interrupted.

'Obviously a Frenchman, with very wide-reaching powers – into Lorraine, into academic life, into society, the world of dealers and connoisseurs, into the past, into the English establishment, into Comecon.'

'Into Comecon?' he said, so incredulously that his voice rose steeply.

'Yes, judging by the places where the pictures were found – supposedly in East Germany or Argentina. Where would you have fake pictures emerge from? A place that couldn't really be checked. But the East German authorities would have to be on your side wouldn't they? Someone would have to be doing the mastermind a favour; there would have to be someone who, if necessary, would admit to finding an old canvas or two in the attic, a forgotten Nazi art theft. Don't you agree?'

'Now we have everything,' he said. 'Forgive me, but I understand now your doubts about telling me this fable. But do go on. I am enjoying it hugely.'

His charm was so great that I almost felt like laughing with him, but equally I felt very irritated.

'Look at it back to front,' I said. 'There are only about forty La Tours in existence. Since the exhibition in the 1930s here in London, and the big one in Paris in the early 1970s, he's become enormously popular, extraordinarily valuable. A good La Tour today would be worth at least five million pounds. At least. Wouldn't you say?'

'Certainly very valuable and fairly rare, yes.'

'And all of them have fairly ropy histories.'

'Incomplete, certainly.'

'And connoisseurs don't necessarily agree, even now, on which are actually his work. Nor do the experts do all the tests, or read the results the same way. I'm told they don't even always accept scientific evidence when it goes against their aesthetic judgement. And what's more, dealers could present experts with serious temptations. Or threats.'

Sir Miles got up, rather awkwardly, and poured me some more Madeira.

'I think, you see, that the scientist at the Manhattan whose department authenticated them was threatened, coerced at various points into declaring the three pictures scientifically OK. He's Hungarian, and his family has stayed behind: that offers all kinds of possibilities, I should have thought. He seemed pretty uneasy to me, when I talked to him.'

'You've been to see him?'

I told him that my work had not been going well and that I'd managed to get to New York.

'Did you subject him to this perplexing tale?'

'No. We just talked about scientific analyses of paintings.'

'You seem to have had a lot of time to pursue these interests.'

'Failure, like everything else, has its fringe benefits,' I said.

Sir Miles stood up and moved nearer to the fire. It was burning low and he put another log on it, with the clumsiness of an elderly man.

'Again I congratulate you. This is a crime of a certain elegance, this elaborate plot you have invented. And your mastermind is an interesting personage. He is by definition someone with whom you have a very great affinity, since you have created him, given birth to him, so to speak. But I feel you've left something rather sketchy about his motives.'

'The money, obviously. Over twenty million dollars,' I said.

'Too simple,' he replied, looking down at me. 'You cannot allow him to spend more than twenty years inventing a history for these pictures, and laying their trail, commissioning, supervising, corrupting officials and so forth, with a positively inspired attention to detail, without some better motive than money.'

'How should I know his real motives?'

Sir Miles smiled at me, as though he were indulging me.

'Let me suggest some. He is a man troubled, I should say, by an excess of impatience, and by unbounded pride – by contempt for the ignorance and stupidity and blind optimism of our times. Yes, there is a hint of contempt in this edifice, a contempt so vainglorious that it derives secret pleasure from the unrecognized manipulation of other people's truths. A sort of close deity.'

'Why not?' I agreed, wondering whether he really disbelieved me.

'Yes, I think so. An aesthetic contempt. A contempt that you feel very strongly yourself, a contempt for the shabbiness and stupidity of Grub Street, a hatred perhaps of bad faith and self-deception. A retreat into the pleasures of one's own perception.'

'But my feelings have nothing to do with it,' I said.

He smiled the infuriating smile of someone who disagrees.

'Either he exists or he doesn't,' I said.

'How very quaint of you to assume it must be a man. Refreshingly old-fashioned. But I must say I agree. If I were inventing this story I would make him a man. I think he's rather remarkable.'

'So you think this is all quite impossible, preposterous? That I should forget about the missing documents?'

'They may not really be missing,' he said, quite gently. 'I'm afraid I think you are in an unenviable position. I'd like to offer you a piece of advice, if I may. You have, after all, paid me the compliment of coming all this way to see me. It seems to me you are in difficulties whichever way you turn. If you are wrong, and this story is nothing but sound and fury, and you persist in believing it, you will certainly undermine your own position as a journalist. There are some people who might even consider you certifiable, though that would not be my view; your theory has at least the merit of coherence.

'If you were right, which I hardly think, you would probably be in very great danger. I don't want to sound extreme, but unless you want to destroy your existence, one way or the other, I advise you to drop this obsession. I take it you haven't told anyone else?'

'No,' I said, 'unless you count Duncan Lloyd. I started to tell it to him and I thought he seemed a little agitated. I even wondered, just wondered, whether he knew something about it. But he assured me it was all nonsense and he practically threw me out.'

'Ah yes, poor Lloyd. So you actually went to see him? I don't think there's any danger of anyone taking him seriously. A sad case of misplaced integrity. You know the story, I suppose?'

'More or less,' I said.

'There's a moral in it for you,' he said with his lazy smile. 'But if it would make you any happier I could probably make a few discreet inquiries, arrange for some toiler in the academic vineyard to find where all those documents have got to. It would be a pity if they were really lost.'

'Could you do that,' I asked, 'without arousing any suspicions?'

He smiled rather patronizingly.

'Oh, yes, I think so. That kind of thing's not my pidgin really, but I'm sure it could be arranged.'

'Would you be able to, with your Secret Service connections?'

'That was a long time ago,' he interrupted. 'Over forty years, and only what everyone else was doing. Most of us were amateurs, and by now rather a lot of us are dead.'

'I just wondered whether, from those wartime contacts, you might be able to find out what it really was that Hubert de Villancourt did.'

'I doubt it, very much. And even if I could I think it should be forgotten. I wouldn't tell you, to be blunt. Let the dead bury their dead.'

'I've always wondered what that meant.'

'Besides, I don't see what it's got to do with your theory.'

'Nothing, perhaps. But it might make a good programme.'

'I'm not the person to ask,' he said, again quite kindly. 'Do you know, I think I used to know your mamma. I was very sorry to hear of her death. You must have been very young.'

'Yes, I was.' For some reason I did not encourage him to tell me about her.

'Tell me,' I said, 'what do you think of the paintings? The ones I've been talking about.'

'I think they're exquisite. A remarkable addition to the *oeuvre*. And if they are fakes, they are certainly good enough to fool the connoisseurs, even an elderly fanatic like me.'

Before I left, I asked him not to repeat my theory to anyone. He had convinced me that I would soon be considered as paranoid as Duncan Lloyd. He agreed, rather gravely, and said goodbye with what seemed to me like sympathy. Until I started driving away I didn't know how relieved I was to have told someone. I was trembling slightly and my sense of distance was disturbed so that I nearly knocked into one of the cars parked near the church close. I drove through the winding roads and turned on a classical music programme. Immediately I started crying. Crying at Mahler, I thought. I must be very near a wobbly. Relief is a curious sensation. I was glad that Sir Miles hadn't invited me to lunch. Despite everything he had said to reassure me, I still felt troubled, perhaps simply by having made a fool of myself.

28

The next day I went into Wireless House to my office, to see whether there was any mail. The room was empty. My desk was covered, too late, with books and articles by Tremaine that I had ordered from the reference library to prepare myself for our meeting. I nearly sent them back without looking at them. But in the end I glanced at what Peter had sent me. Some of it was recent: well-produced, glossy books on French painting and architecture, some popular, some erudite. He had a curious style, it seemed to me, oddly lacking in lucidity. The tone of assurance was justified, of course, but it seemed obtrusive; he was clearly a man who took his own gifts very seriously and it disfigured his writing.

I wondered whether he'd always had that tone, even as a young man, and I looked back at some of his earlier work. There were one or two photocopied articles about La Tour which had appeared in the *Burlington Magazine* and *Apollo*. I hadn't realized that Tremaine himself had actually written quite a lot about La Tour, before the painter became really fashionable. I should have read the catalogue raisonné with more attention. He'd written an important-sounding piece on the La Tour discovered in Lvov in the early 1970s. There were also some pieces he'd written in the 1930s for literary and political magazines when he must have been a very young man. They were quite different; they had that unmistakable socialist cast that was intellectually fashionable at the time. There was even something in praise of Stalinist art. He had come a long way from the radical chic of the pre-war intelligentsia to the charming, snobbish establishment figure that he was now.

Most of the pieces seemed fairly dull to me, homilies on progressive art, art under capitalism, art as propaganda, all muddled up with academic work on painters and sculptors I had never heard of. But there was one that interested me, because he was talking about Balzac. He had written an article about *Le Père Goriot*, just before the war, and it reminded me of our conversation in Southwold, about the French master criminal he thought I had invented.

'For Balzac,' Tremaine had written, all those years ago, 'a disapproval amounting to outrage against his own society paradoxically gave him an amoral detachment. Perhaps the most florid expression of this is achieved in the superhuman deceptions of Vautrin, his supremely powerful criminal-hero in *Le Père Goriot*, whose triumph is simultaneously to deceive and to rule his world, and whom Balzac cannot judge.' A curious coincidence, I thought, wishing I had read the novel.

There was one book left that I hadn't looked at. Peter had attached a note to it with a Corporation elastic band.

'Hope I'm not over-egging the pudding but am sending this very old edition as it was on the shelves – Tremaine's first book.'

It was modestly called *Some Aspects of French Painting*. Wondering when the young Tremaine first got himself into print, I opened it at the front pages. The date was 1940; the book was a first edition. I turned the page to see the dedication. You don't expect something out of a forgotten academic text to make your heart miss a beat, as they say, but that's what happened. The book was dedicated to Guy Burgess. In 1940. I seemed to have told my story to the wrong person.

That was my first assumption. Guilt by association, the crudest form of journalistic response, is one of the most useful. We hear so much of moles and spies and treason that it's perhaps too easy to suspect one person because of another. But anyone whose closest friend was Guy Burgess in 1940 cannot but have a lot of explaining to do. I checked in *Who's Who*. Tremaine had of course been at Trinity, and had become a don. He was a few years older than Burgess would have been. They must have been friends at Cambridge, both members of the Apostles probably. All the same, it might mean nothing, the youthful pro-Soviet sentiments, the bad company of his youth. I was not in a position myself to suspect a man, just for falling into bad company.

I thought again about our meeting, wondering what I had missed. With his charming tight smile and cold eyes, his urbanity, his fluency, his behaviour had been wholly convincing. I tried to replay the scene in my mind, but whole sections of it were fogged, or appeared in sound only, or out of synch with the picture, and so I heard him saying again, with his mouth moving to different words, standing by the fireplace in Southwold: *Not my pidgin*. That was what was wrong. And if I mentally laced up another can of memories I could see Claude Mesnil in his lecture room, surrounded by students, using exactly the same expression. When he was saying goodbye he spoke in excellent idiomatic English, but he had used that one phrase that was too self-conscious, too unusual for a foreigner. '*Not really my pidgin.*' They had betrayed each other with a turn of phrase.

Sexual jealousy teaches that awareness. It was almost as if one man actually smelt of the other, as if one bore the guilty mark of someone else's expression, a fingerprint left by one person on another's language, and it was as clear to me as if I'd been in love with one of them, that Claude Mesnil and Sir Miles Tremaine knew each other. They must have been seeing each other secretly. Otherwise, of course, Sir Miles would have acknowledged that he knew Mesnil.

Just as jealousy can sometimes induce a state of shock, so can fear. I'm not used to extreme physical fear, and I hate sweating. Hot drops trickled down my ribs inside my loose jersey, my mouth was dry and I felt faint. I also felt confused. My first thought was not for Duncan Lloyd. After a while I rang the London Library and persuaded a librarian to get out the Tremaine book in the most recent edition. I asked him for the date and dedication.

'I'm afraid it's not a very new edition. First published in 1940, this one came out in 1954. There's no dedication.'

There would have to be a very exceptional reason for striking a man's name out of a dedication of a first book. And a very particular reason for pretending not to know another. I had been right to think Sir Miles a particularly suitable person to tell my story to. He was all too suitable.

Slowly I began to think more calmly and it seemed to me

that he must surely believe I had successfully been warned off, that I had been successfully browbeaten by his charm, his knowledge and my own confessions of ignorance, or if not, then by fear. I was not very much reassured, but I thought there was probably a reasonable hope of being safe from Tremaine. I began composing abject letters to him, in which I apologized for wasting his time, with slightly unbalanced constructs, or in which I confessed to a period of mental strain which his response had made me see more objectively, and after a while the worst of my fears lifted.

Then at last I remembered I had admitted that I had told Lloyd part of my story. Actually it was Tremaine himself who had put this anxiety into my mind – 'I don't think there's any danger of anyone taking him seriously,' he had said. But of course there was.

I dialled Lloyd's number. It was busy. Some of the Corporation telephones have a last-call redial facility, and owing to some bureaucratic error, no doubt, one of my lines had one. I tapped in Lloyd's number and the code and waited for his line to be free. Meanwhile I started to wonder what to do myself. It was not a comforting thought to realize that the persuasive Mr McAusland might have had more than one reason for trying to deflect my interest. Everyone had been warning me off. In France it was not difficult to guess at Mesnil's influence with the police; it might even have been innocent. But there had been something extremely thin about McAusland's line of argument.

Still Lloyd's line was engaged. At last I rang the Corporation switchboard and told them I couldn't get through to his number.

'Why don't you use the redial facility, dear. For system use instructions call 146 internal.'

'I have already put it on last-call redial. That's my point. I'm worried there may be a fault in the system.'

'A fault in the system? No one's notified me. Why didn't you say?'

'I don't know whether there's a fault. But I'm worried. It's urgent.'

'For faults in the system you should really call system inquiries on 147.'

System inquiries were engaged and I put that number on internal redial and tried the British Telecom operator and told her that Lloyd's line was persistently engaged.

'Well, that's probably because they're using the phone,' she said.

'No, I'm certain that's impossible,' I said, with rising irritation and fear.

She rang back a few moments later.

'The party at 229 0081 has left the receiver off the hook. We have put out a signal, caller, but that's all we can do.'

At that point Maudie came round with the tea trolley.

'Hello, love,' she said. 'All alone? Aren't you a stranger? Weak lemon tea and no sugar, isn't it?'

Maudie had the limp perm which is still a badge of oppression: despite or perhaps for that reason she conveyed a normality, a cheerfulness and security for which companies should pay handsomely out of their public relations budgets.

'You look a bit peaky, dear,' she said, handing me a thin plastic beaker which burnt her hand and mine.

'It's true,' I replied. 'I don't feel well.'

'I should go home then,' she replied. 'No point staying here. You go on home, love. Wish I could do the same.'

She coughed wetly and turned to push her trolley through the doorway and along the interminable circular passages of that part of the Corporation.

As I drank the tea I began to think I should go home. My anxieties had eased, like an acute pain that has subsided into an ache. I could always call Lloyd from my flat. Before I went I wrote a note to Dan by internal mail telling him he'd been right; my imagination had been doing overtime and there was no story, and I'd be very grateful if he didn't mention it to anyone as it wouldn't do me any good. I told him I particularly didn't want to lose credibility with the art establishment as I wanted to work in the arts department when I came back from New York. Finally I said it might reflect badly on him if he gossiped about it. An appeal to friendship and a mild threat were perhaps not enough of a warning, but I thought he was too busy and too self-protective to talk.

On my way out of the building, I went down to Hank's cutting room.

'Hank, you remember what I was telling you about those La Tour paintings?'

'No, darling heart. What was it? Oh, sorry,' he said, seeing my expression. 'Naughty of me. I do remember. Some of it.'

Hank stared at me like a La Tour himself, with his unquiet eyes, hidden and remote.

'Hank, you must never mention any of it. Not one single word. You've never heard anything about any of it. It's really important.'

'Now, now, my dear, office politics are not as difficult as all that, surely?'

'It's not office politics, Hank. It's very important. Really. Promise me.'

I couldn't tell what he thought. Being a film editor is a strange job; half the time is spent in semi-darkness, with sounds and pictures travelling backwards, and the other half in dealing with other people's fits of temperament, listening to their posturings and demands about their films. It is not surprising, perhaps, that they retreat emotionally.

Hank considered me for a while, his face unusually bare of expression. Perhaps he was shifting me into the large category of difficult people.

'My firmly sculpted lips are sealed,' he said then, closing them and turning back to the pic synch.

I should have liked to stay there, sitting unnoticed among the piles of cans or behind the racks of film trims, listening to the familiar sounds of an editing room, drinking cups of coffee and imagining in the half-light that all my fears were just part of a bad film, as insubstantial as the images Hank kept snipping out of the reel on the Steenbeck. But I owed it to Duncan Lloyd to call him, and I did, as I'd said to Maudie, feel unwell.

I walked out of the tower block, through the scenery and props section and out of the main gate into a cold day that had the first smell of spring about it. The afternoon was overcast but there was a freshness in the air as I walked away from the Corporation. The Underground line was above ground in that part of London; the station looked as if it had been dropped by mistake into the flat waste of the cityscape. The little building was curiously isolated, near the parking lot leading down to the rows of half-deserted lines of the main railway, with empty sites all around.

At that time, about 3 o'clock, it was quiet. Few people used it except to get to the Corporation and there were only a few stragglers coming and going. I would have thought it was too early for the evening papers but the news-vendor was already setting up his stand and I could just see the first headlines on the board propped up against it, the letters still out of focus at that distance. As I walked down the wide pavement the wind came up, and old papers and sweet wrappings and cartons were blown against my legs, almost slowing me down. I had to go at least a hundred yards before the black lettering on the news-stand sharpened into legibility. 'Brutal West London Killing', said the sign.

Instantly my stomach fell. Almost equally quickly I told myself I was wrong. I ran towards the news-stand and snatched a paper without paying for it and without looking at the news-vendor. I was right. There was a picture of the canal where Lloyd lived; there was a caption I hardly took in except that it said something about the dead man's home. Fear is like pain; you think it can't get worse. But it does and, like pain, it blots out everything else.

'Police suspect that Lloyd, a known homosexual, may have been the victim of vicious sex attack.'

'Police would not comment on the suggestion that there were signs of a sex orgy at the flat.'

'The victim was the author of several books on art history and a lecturer on topics in painting.'

'Anything wrong?' the news-vendor asked me.

I realized that I had dropped my bag and was holding on to his kiosk for support. It took a large effort to smile and tell him that I hadn't realized that I was too unfit to run after a long lunch.

'All right for some,' he replied. '20p.'

I paid him and walked automatically to the platform for my train home. The long stretch of grey concrete was quite deserted and the train didn't arrive for several minutes. At first I had to sit down on the station bench, feeling faint, but I felt restless too and had to stand up and move around. I had no idea where to go.

I walked up and down the platform, restless with fear and with anger at myself, at my stupidity, and confused, too, by my remaining uncertainty. It still seemed impossible to believe Sir Miles was anything other than what he seemed. He was a charming, elderly man, head of one of the greatest intellectual foundations in Europe, friend and ally of the entire establishment. He was even the Queen's artistic adviser. But my judgement had always been bad. I was too easily flattered. No good in the penalty area, Dan would have said, if I'd ever let him.

I thought again and again about my conversation with Tremaine, seeing his remarks, his questions in different lights but never in a way to make me sure, one way or the other, whether he felt he'd succeeded in silencing me. Perhaps he was assuming the death of Lloyd would do that. Perhaps Lloyd's murder did not necessarily entail some sort of accident for me, like a fall into the Thames from one of the high walkways of the warehouse where I lived, or some other momentary terror.

The train arrived. It was empty, and that scared me too. After sitting in it for a couple of stops, I got out at Notting Hill, perhaps because I had once lived there. The platform was empty, which meant at least that no one was observing me. I stood there wondering what to do. I felt I could not go to my flat, or to the home of anyone I knew, or anywhere I usually went: perhaps Tremaine must have known for some time that I might come to too many conclusions. I moved off the empty platform and stood inside one of the arches marked Exit. Finally I walked up the steps and into the open air, just out of fear of being under ground.

I found myself walking to the telephone boxes at Notting Hill Gate; one of them, surprisingly, was working. There was still one very obvious thing to do, something I had been avoiding. It was true, what Dan had said, about the net of the establishment drawing tighter and tighter; I myself was drawn into it, willingly and unwillingly, and now my only thought was to close ranks with that part of it to which I had once belonged. I called the private number of my godfather, Henry Etherington. I had not seen him since before my marriage. It was a direct line to Admiralty Arch; my godfather was First Sea Lord.

He wasn't there. One of his staff answered, and brought his wife Claire to the telephone. When she heard my name she paused for only a second.

'How lovely to hear from you at last,' she said. 'It's been far too long. I hope this means you're going to come and see us.'

'I know,' I said. 'I'm very sorry. Please forgive me. I'll have to speak quickly, I'm in a call box. Could I please come round now? Immediately?'

'Is something wrong?' she asked.

'I can't tell you on the telephone. I need to talk to Henry.'

'But Henry's not here, and he may not even be back to change. I don't know when you can talk to him, I don't know when I shall see him myself.'

'I'm very sorry. I know what it must sound like, after all this time. But I must come now. Couldn't you possibly find Henry and tell him it's important? Really.'

'I'll try,' she said. 'You know, he'll be very glad to see you.'

I got a taxi outside the telephone box and asked to go to Admiralty Arch; in the midst of my anxiety it seemed also absurd to me to be rattling along to that address. The cab moved easily along the Bayswater Road and through the park, past Hyde Park Corner, along the side of Buckingham Palace and into the Mall. The driver pulled up just before the Arch and I went to a side entrance, and up some stairs, into my godfather's flat.

29

Claire met me, and offered me some tea. A Wren brought a tray in and we sat in the drawing room, directly above the London traffic, talking of nothing very much: Claire was kind enough not to try to get me to say why I'd come. After a while, perhaps half an hour, perhaps longer, there was a knock on the door.

'The Admiral's just arriving now, ma'am,' said a young man, looking in.

'Thank you,' said Claire. 'Please make sure that he's not disturbed.'

She got up and went towards the door to meet Henry, who kissed her as he came in. He turned to me.

'My very favourite black sheep,' he said.

'You will excuse me, won't you,' said Claire to us both. 'There are just one or two things I must deal with that won't wait.'

My godfather looked at me with exasperation and kindness.

'I'm very glad to see you at last. You didn't need to wait so long.'

'I assumed you'd find me a bit of an embarrassment.'

'I don't think you've ever really given me credit.'

'And you didn't like him, ever,' I interrupted.

'That's true,' he said.

'It was hard to forgive you for being right.'

'You know, you've always had the benefit of the doubt with me. I can't tell you how sorry I was.'

I wanted him to stop and he saw it.

'Anyway, this time you have come,' he said. 'What is the matter? Claire tells me it's very urgent; I'm assuming it really is.'

I told him the whole story, from beginning to end. It took a long time. Occasionally he asked questions or made me repeat something I'd said earlier. He had a remarkable way of paying attention. Sometimes he seemed to be studying his hands, sometimes he stared out of the window, sometimes his expression changed as he looked at me, as if quite other thoughts, unrelated thoughts, were going through his mind, but he was listening carefully. It is an unusual ability.

Told with its conclusion in mind from the beginning, the story began at last to seem really plausible, even when I mentioned the name of Sir Miles Tremaine. At that my god-father almost interrupted me, but he stopped himself and listened on in silence.

'I don't know exactly what happened to the caretaker at Nancy,' I said. 'I can only imagine. It seems obvious enough that someone was trying to take the fake documents away, to keep them out of the expert hands of the Mormons. It was probably overcautious, but the Mormon researchers would almost certainly have taken out the box they were in – it was full of christenings and announcements of death, all the things they're looking for – and they could well have noticed in passing that the La Tour documents were not quite as they should have been. Of course that was Claude Mesnil. It was Mesnil who was anxious about that, but I doubt if he actually killed the man himself. At any rate he had some sort of alibi – when I tried to contact him for our film his wife said he was away.'

Henry moved back in the sofa. He looked tired, but obviously not of what I was saying.

'I was slow to realize it was Mesnil. I liked him too much. But it's inescapable. He lied to me about the archives, pretending to know very little about them, but actually being a sort of local hero there. And from Mademoiselle Autran I realized that he was very conscious of the presence of the Mormons. He even tried to suggest to her that they were responsible for any confusion in the archives. He was perfectly placed, an expert in old manuscripts, someone who probably treated the archives at Lunéville and Nancy as an extension of his own library. Widely liked, widely trusted, a well-known historian.

'I think what happened is this: Mesnil was away for a time, as his wife thought. He travelled a lot, on academic jamborees I suppose. But he came back, perhaps hearing that Bob Kitzinger had arrived, and perhaps made a secret visit to remove a few documents. If they were missed people could easily think it was a temporary misplacement. After all, poor Monsieur Joly had been complaining how difficult it was to keep track of things. And Mesnil must have done it before – the previous time the Mormon researchers came. It should have been so easy, so unobtrusive. But I think the *gardien* must have seen him. Perhaps Mesnil had someone with him, perhaps he killed him then. Perhaps he quickly arranged for someone to kill him – it would have been easy. Joly lived on the premises and there was a strike. I think it's quite possible that Mesnil actually had a key to the archives. Perhaps Joly would normally have let him in at times when the building was closed, as a favour. Anyway something must have gone wrong. Joly knew and he would have grumbled. And then it would have emerged which documents were missing. And so on. It was too much of a risk. It wouldn't have been difficult to get him killed at short notice, would it?'

My godfather spoke at last. 'It depends what circles you move in,' he said, without smiling. 'Have you got a motive for Claude Mesnil? It doesn't sound as though he'd become rich.'

'That's true, although I think he is definitely sybaritic. At the time he seemed rather sad and rather restless, but I thought that was something quite different.'

'His age,' said Henry. 'A difficult age for a man.'

'And for a woman, too. I think he is a little like Sir Miles. I think he's contemptuous of the world around him, unnaturally detached in the same way. As for his politics, I have no idea, really.'

At last I came to an end.

'Well,' I said, 'what do you think?'

'Who else have you told about this?'

'So you do believe me?'

He gave me an odd look. I couldn't tell whether it was sympathy or pity, or irritation, even.

'Whether or not,' he said, 'we'd better get it sorted out. I need to know who else you've told.'

I explained to him what I'd done about the people I'd told, about Hank and Dan. I said that I thought Andrew McAusland would surely assume, seeing no story, that he'd been successful. Henry said nothing. Perhaps he knew him, perhaps he didn't.

'Do you know Tremaine?' I asked.

'I've met him,' he replied.

'Do you think I was right not to go to the police?'

'I think in the circumstances, and given your state of mind, you were right to come to me. You could have come before, you know, at any time.'

'I do know . . .

'There really is a rift between our generations, isn't there? It's not just something the media made up. And, you know, I think it comes from your side.'

'Perhaps,' I said.

He stood up and walked to one of the windows, and looked out into the darkness out down the Mall and towards the Palace. At the same moment there was a knock on the door and one of the stewards walked in.

'Draw the curtains, sir?' he said, doing so. 'Will there be anything else, sir?'

'I should think we could both use a drink,' Henry said to me. 'What would you like?'

When the steward had gone to fetch our drinks Henry began to speak again about what I had told him. I was afraid that the steward would reappear and I looked at the door.

'You don't need to worry about him. They are all completely discreet. They have to be.'

'Henry, you talk as though you'd never read the Sunday papers. There's no such thing as security.'

'Journalists are paid to take a sensational view of life. We on the other hand are paid to ensure that we do have security. Among other things.' He smiled, but he looked tired and irritated.

Then the steward did come in with my vodka and tonic and Henry's whisky on a silver tray.

Henry was silent for a while; I couldn't tell from his

expression what he was thinking; despite his powerful air of frankness, he was well able to disguise his thoughts.

'I'm going to look into what you've told me,' he said at last. 'I'd like you to stay here with us for a while. Certainly tonight and tomorrow, perhaps a little longer. Very quietly. And I'd rather you didn't go outside. We won't send to your flat: I'm sure that Claire will be able to find you some things to wear.'

'I shan't know myself, I shall be so elegant,' I said.

He smiled, but both of us, it seemed to me, were in our different ways equally anxious and weary.

I stayed there for three nights and nearly three days, a very comfortable prisoner, feeling like a female impersonator in my well-cut, borrowed clothes. Claire had a lot of official and semi-official engagements so I was often alone. I wandered round the immaculate flat. I had never seen anything so clean and tidy; life cannot really be so ship-shape.

One afternoon I had company in the shape of a young officer. Henry must have detailed him to while away my time, and he talked very steadfastly to me. Knowing how strict Henry was about public servants and public money, I wondered how he justified this sober frivolity. And then it dawned on me.

'I'm afraid you must really be off duty; all this is rather above and beyond, isn't it?'

'Oh, not at all,' he said, blushing. I can't remember when I last saw a hack blush. 'It's a pleasure. It's so interesting to meet a journalist – one can't help being fascinated by the media. Not always our best friends.'

'No,' I said. It's a curious thing about young officers. They look you directly in the eye, they speak very openly but they often look ill at ease, embarrassed, wrong-footed by their very straightness.

I hardly saw Henry all that time, except at breakfast when we were discreetly waited on, and we ourselves talked discreetly about very little. Finally on the third day, in the afternoon, he came up to the flat and talked to me alone in the drawing room. He looked tired still and there was something reluctant about his expression. He didn't sit down, but stood above me, looking down.

'I'm very sorry about what I'm going to have to say to you. What I have to tell you is simply this. You are to say nothing about this to anybody. Absolutely nothing. You are to write a brief letter to Sir Miles Tremaine, thanking him for his indulgence and apologizing for your flight of fancy. Say, perhaps, that you've been overworking, under strain. Nothing very substantial, but showing you've lost all interest. I shall want to see the letter first. And after that, no further comment to anyone.'

I stared at him.

'But was it true?' I almost shouted. 'Was I right? How can you talk to me like this?'

'I can only repeat,' he said sadly and very firmly, 'the subject is closed.'

'If you were appealing to my cowardice alone, you'd certainly succeed. I have been terrified. I still am, even here. But a man has just been murdered, in fact very likely two or three. What am I supposed to think?'

'You were right to come to me. I must ask you to trust me. I know how hard that is. And I know that it must go against every journalistic response, to trust someone in my position on a subject like this.'

'To spike my own story. I've been asked before,' I said.

'I understand. All the same, that's all I can do. You must judge for yourself. Believe me, it's of great importance that you do as I ask.'

'Why, why, why?' I asked, becoming angry again, but again my rage fell away at seeing his face; it was the look of a man biting the bullet, a man not permitting himself even to hint at what he knows, whatever the temptation.

'Will I be watched?' I asked.

'Possibly, but you needn't worry.'

'Can't you explain at all?'

'It is best not to tell you anything. I ask you to believe me.'

'I do. I do believe you,' I said finally, and I did at the time, although in retrospect, we might both have judged differently.

> *You cannot hope to bribe or twist,*
> *Thank God, the British journalist.*
> *But seeing what the man will do*
> *Without, there's no occasion to.*

I wrote the letter to Sir Miles Tremaine, I sent a telex to Marie-Blanche saying our film had been completely abandoned, and I went back to New York almost immediately; I stayed there not just for the *Weasel* run but for another six months, attached to an arts programme. When I came back to Wireless House at Christmas, no one mentioned any of it to me, not even what had happened to the original wartime documentary. The Current Affairs department was full of new faces. Not only my story, but I myself had been completely forgotten. Even my personnel officer had been changed.

The only person who brought it up, briefly, was Dan Cohen, when I ran into him in the sixteenth-floor canteen. He was very full of himself and his Wagner film. He told me he'd just won another award.

'How about you? How about the slaughtered French and the fake paintings? You should have got in touch. You promised you would.'

'No, I didn't,' I said, putting my arm round him. 'I stayed in New York. You only wanted me to get in touch if I got a story, so you could step in and get the credit. Remember?'

He grinned.

'There wasn't a story,' I said. 'Nothing at all, nothing that would stand up. Looking back on it,' I said to him, as we sat down to canteen lunch together, 'I seem to have made it all up.'


Over a year later, in response to a question in the House of Commons, Sir Miles Tremaine was exposed by the Prime Minister as a Russian agent, stripped of his knighthood. He resigned from the Owermoigne Institute and from his Fellowship at Trinity College, Cambridge.

Claude Mesnil was last seen in East Berlin.

The three La Tour paintings remained in the same galleries in the United States.